The U

Once Dinah thought herself as indifferent to men as they were uninterested in her. That was before she met thrillingly handsome, dazzlingly charming, eloquently adoring Godfrey Bellingham.

Now it seemed quite natural to go unchaperoned with Godfrey into the morning room. Dinah was oblivious to everything save her inner excitement as Godfrey pulled her gently into his arms. No thought of propriety or resistance entered her head, and her first kiss would surely have been an exciting event had she been granted the time to savor it. But she was barely past the initial shock of a man's lips when an annoyingly familiar voice caused her to leap back.

"It grieves me to cast stumbling blocks on the path of true love, but this really won't do."

The owner of that soft, silky voice, Charles Talbot, lounged against the doorframe. If this infuriatingly arrogant gentleman dared to stand between Dinah and the fulfillment of her heart's desire—how on earth was she to get him out of the way?

THE AWAKENING HEART

by

Dorothy Mack

A SIGNET BOOK

SIGNET
Published by the Penguin Group
Penguin Books USA Inc., 375 Hudson Street,
New York, New York 10014, U.S.A.
Penguin Books Ltd, 27 Wrights Lane,
London W8 5TZ, England
Penguin Books Australia Ltd, Ringwood,
Victoria, Australia
Penguin Books Canada Ltd, 10 Alcorn Avenue,
Toronto, Ontario, Canada M4V 3B2
Penguin Books (N.Z.) Ltd, 182–190 Wairau Road,
Auckland 10, New Zealand

Penguin Books Ltd, Registered Offices:
Harmondsworth, Middlesex, England

First published by Signet,
an imprint of New American Library,
a division of Penguin Books USA Inc.

First Printing, November, 1993
10 9 8 7 6 5 4 3 2 1

1

A slanting sunbeam ventured into the empty room, gaining a toehold against the dimness. Gradually the little puddle of radiance grew, revitalizing muted gray and greens in the patterned carpet and lending a sheen to the wooden floor beyond its limits. Though the corners of the fair-sized room remained shadowy, vague humps became recognizable objects of furniture as their outlines sharpened into chairs, tables, a cabinet with glass doors faintly gleaming in the sunlight.

A distant murmur outside the room disturbed the peaceful scene only slightly at first; then the opening door signaled a burst of human activity. First to enter was a tall, soberly clad woman of indeterminate age, gaunt of frame and sour of aspect, who flung back the door and stood against it, directing two stalwart young footmen carrying someone between them in an improvised chair formed by gripping their crossed hands together. Their passenger was an immensely stout old lady, which no doubt accounted for their perspiring red faces and bent knees.

"Take care that you do not tip Lady Markham!" the woman with her back pressed to the door cautioned in sharp tones when one of the footmen stumbled a little coming over the threshold. He quickly regained his balance, but not before the passenger gave a gasp of alarm and tightened her grip on the back of his coat, her nails digging into his shoulder.

"Your usual chair, ma'am?" The other footman spoke up loudly to cover his partner's wince of discomfort.

"No," Lady Markham replied in a voice whose strength did not accord with her general air of debility. "Put me in the chair near the drum table. I have a fancy for some sunshine after so many dull gray days in succession."

At these words the hovering woman cast her burden of shawls, reticule, workbag, can, and other impedimenta onto a settee and darted over to the chair toward which the procession was heading. She swept up pillows covered with handsome needlepoint designs just as the footmen tenderly lowered their precious cargo into the green velvet wing chair. While one of them fetched an ottoman, also covered in needlepoint, to place under Lady Markham's feet, the other footman straightened and surreptitiously eased his coat away from his tender shoulder.

Seeing him standing idle, her ladyship said, "Bring me the hand bell before you leave, Dugald, and see to it that you remain at your post in the hall while I am in here. Yesterday I had to ring for ten minutes before you finally answered the bell."

"Yes, ma'am." The young servant's eyelid twitched but he preserved a respectful mien as he brought the bell to his mistress.

"Put it on the table," she commanded. "No, wait. This drum table is inconveniently high for my workbag. Take it away and bring that small table by my usual chair over here instead. Move the footstool closer," she added, addressing the second footman, who had started to get to his feet.

When these several orders had been carried out to her presumed satisfaction, Lady Markham waved a dismissing hand at the footmen, who retired gratefully, leaving their employer free to turn her attention to her female attendant. "Well, what are you waiting for, Telford? Are you planning to stand there clutching those pillows to your chest all day?"

This rhetorical piece of sarcasm evoked no change of expression on the abigail's long, bony face as she proceeded to arrange the pillows behind her mistress's back. "There was no point in trying to make you comfortable until you had settled into your chair, my lady," she replied woodenly before turning her steps back to the settee.

"*Comfortable!* I wish I might remember when last I felt comfortable," Lady Markham declared on an explosive breath. "You wouldn't toss that word around so casually if *you* were the one suffering from rheumatics!"

"At least the winter is nearly over," the maid replied, disposing a cashmere shawl about the old woman's shoulders. "A few sunny days like this one will see you much improved in health and spirits."

"That shows how much you know about it," the determined sufferer retorted, rebuffing this attempt to raise her spirits. "Don't forget my cane," she reminded as her tirewoman retrieved a large workbag and a reticule from the settee and placed one on the table and the other in her mistress's lap.

"When have I ever forgotten your cane?" Telford asked, impervious to snubs after thirty-odd years in service to Lady Markham.

Her ladyship ignored this question as she extracted a pair of spectacles from her netted reticule and placed them on her nose. She watched the abigail stand the malacca cane against the table within easy reach. "I'll have coffee and bisquits precisely at eleven."

"As usual," Telford murmured, casting an assessing eye around the room. She moved the hand bell closer to the edge of the table but away from the workbag and adusted the window blinds to keep the sun out of Lady Markham's eyes. "Will there be anything else?"

"No, just leave me in peace to get on with my work." Lady Markham was already rummaging in the tapestry bag for her current piece of fancywork as Telford's narrow figure retreated from the room in a rustle of stiff skirts.

Silence settled over the pleasant room as the old woman threaded her needle and applied herself to her embroidery. Some few minutes later, becoming conscious of the sun striking the corner of her left eye, Lady Markham reached for the bell and rang it vigorously.

Within seconds Dugald appeared in the doorway.

"The sun is in my eyes; lower the blind." Lady Markham turned her head to follow the footman's motions and, in doing so, noticed for the first time a large sketching book leaning against the left side of her chair.

"Is that better, ma'am?" The footman spoke from beside the window.

"What? Oh, yes. Hand me this sketchpad on the floor before you leave."

When the door had closed behind the footman, Lady Markham repositioned her spectacles on her nose and opened the sketchpad. Horizontal grooves on her forehead deepened and vertical lines indented themselves at the corners of her mouth as she turned several pages. Shock, disbelief, and outrage chased across her rounded countenance as she continued to turn over the sheets until one particular page caused her to emit a strangled sound and drop the pad on her knees. She groped in her reticule with shaking fingers, drew out her vinaigrette, and had recourse to its pungent fumes. After a few seconds to steady her nerves, she grabbed the hand bell and rang it with all the enfeebled force at her command.

"Yes, ma'am?" said the footman, putting his head into the room.

"Find my niece immediately and send her to me," commanded Lady Markham in failing accents before sinking back among the pillows.

Miss Dinah Elcott, wrapped in a large white apron, hummed softly to herself as she rolled out pastry dough on a marble-topped table under the cook's critical eye.

"Don't bounce it, Miss Dinah; keep a steady pressure on the rolling pin and make your strokes long and even. It saves energy."

The humming ceased. "Sorry, Mrs. Hodges. Like this?"

"That's better. Keep rolling until it's about half that thickness. After that we'll put more butter on top and fold and roll it again."

"I never realized it was such a time-consuming process."

"That's the only way to end up with flaky layers. There's no shortcuts to good pastry," Mrs. Hodges said categorically.

Splashing and squealing sounds from the scullery proclaimed that the kitchen maids were washing up the breakfast dishes. Atop the enclosed Bodley cooker against one wall a huge pot of soup simmered, wafting savory scents into the warm air of the kitchen. At the fireplace a houseboy basted a leg of mutton that was revolving on a mechanical spit. A large wooden table in the center of the room held piles of carrots, onions, and potatoes just brought in from the root cellar.

The cook had gone over to stir the soup and Dinah had resumed her tuneless humming when Dugald burst into the kitchen.

"There you are, miss! I've been all over the house looking

for you. Her ladyship wishes to see you in the back drawing room directly. She looked a bit . . . put out," he added as the young woman's hands continued to wield the rolling pin for another moment or two while she evaluated this piece of information.

"Thank you, Dugald; I'll be along as soon as I make myself presentable," Dinah said gravely, displaying no inclination to rush to obey her aunt's command.

The footman bowed himself out of the kitchen under the girl's calm gaze.

"You'd best be off, Miss Dinah," Mrs. Hodges advised. "Her ladyship's temper is a bit short these days, what with all the cold, damp weather we've had lately aggravating her rheumatism worse than usual."

Dinah whipped off the apron enveloping her slight figure and shook out her flattened skirts a bit. "Do I have flour all over my face?" she inquired, tucking a stray lock of hair into the bun at the nape of her neck without undue haste.

"Just a smidgeon on your chin, dearie. There, you've caught it," the cook said with a cheerful smile as the girl rubbed her chin with the apron. "I'll finish up this pastry if you can't come straight back. There now, shoo."

"Thank you for the cookery lesson, Mrs. Hodges," Dinah said from the doorway before she disappeared.

As the young woman made her way up to the back drawing room her brain was busy trying to account for the unusual summons, but a cursory examination of her conscience failed to uncover any recent sins of omission or commission serious enough to impinge upon the hours sacred to her aunt's greatest passion and pastime, the artistic needlework upon which she justly prided herself. Dinah was therefore woefully unprepared for the storm that broke over her unsuspecting head the instant she stepped over the threshold.

"You wished to see me, Aunt?"

"Were I in the habit of consulting my wishes rather than my duty, miss, I would certainly not elect to have dealings with anyone so devoid of all sense of what is due her breeding, so lacking in delicacy of thought or perception, so willfully blind to what is expected of someone in her position as to engage in behavior that, if it became generally known, would unfailingly sink her so far beneath reproach as to leave an indelible stain on her family name among persons of gentility."

Dinah had blinked once or twice during Lady Markham's tirade, surprised but not noticeably disturbed by the spate of invective, if her calm demeanor was a true indication of her emotions. She still had no idea what had triggered the denunciation, but her ignorance on this point was enlightened as she came farther into the room and got a closer look at the object her aunt was clutching in her lap. Understanding flooded over her and she checked momentarily, then continued to approach the enraged occupant of the wing chair, now fighting for breath as she regarded the serene countenance of her niece with patent distaste while taking a reviving whiff of her vinaigrette.

"Wicked, wicked girl, have you no proper shame even now? Is this how I am repaid for devoting ten years of my life to my brother's child to the irreversible detriment of my health in this horridly damp country?"

"I am sorry if my drawings offended your sensibilities in some way, Aunt Lavinia. I did not realize I had left my sketchbook in this room." Dinah held out her hand for her property, but Lady Markham's grip on the pad tightened and she continued to stare balefully at her charge.

"Is that all you have to say? If you believe a casual apology may take care of the matter, then I take leave to inform you that you are far and far out in your reckoning. If it were merely a case of offending my *sensibilities* I would be well pleased to let it rest there, but the very existence of this . . . this excessively vulgar conglomeration is proof of a deficiency in your character despite all my efforts to inculcate the basic refinements essential to a lady of quality." Lady Markham made a scornful gesture with her hand indicating the pad on her knees. "The mere fact that you could even consider associating with such low company points up my abject failure after ten years of sacrifice for your sake."

"Do you not think you may be refining too much on a relatively unimportant incident, Aunt Lavinia? It isn't as though I planned to run away with the gypsies or reject all the precepts you have been at pains to teach me."

Dinah's mild attempt to excuse her behavior was instantly condemned as rank impertinence by her irate relative.

"I'm sorry," she said penitently. "I don't mean to upset you. If you could think of my brief association with the gypsies who were camping on the edge of the moor last autumn in the light of a marvelous opportunity to increase my skill at drawing the human form from life, perhaps you would not be so disapproving. You cannot really fear that I plan to emulate their rough manners, but I was grateful to them for their willingness to tolerate my company and the good-natured way they agreed to pose for me for a nominal fee. It truly was an invaluable experience. My ability to accurately render the human body improved tenfold."

Lady Markham's fingers had been drumming on the sketchpad during her niece's reasoned explanation, and now she flared, "It is one thing to execute clever little pencil portraits of one's friends as gifts but quite another to be the perpetrator of *this* abomination!" She thrust the open pad toward Dinah with every indication of revulsion. "If decent people knew you were in the habit of drawing naked men your reputation would be ruined!"

Dinah accepted the pad with relief at having her best work safely back in her possession. "He wasn't naked, Aunt. He'd merely removed his shirt while he lifted the greasy wheel of his caravan. I was trying to concentrate on the muscular structure of his back and shoulders. What is indecent about that? The human form has been the legitimate subject of artists throughout the ages."

"Not executed by gently bred females, it hasn't!" Lady Markham swallowed her spleen and strove for a reasonable tone. "Far be it from me to denigrate the importance of art in a lady's background. A thorough appreciation of the fine and decorative arts and of music is an essential part of every girl's education, and a certain degree of skill in these areas is highly advantageous if she is to consider herself at all accomplished. I believe, without desiring to appear immodest, that I may claim a fair amount of achievement in all the finer types of needlework—"

"Oh, much more than mere achievement, Aunt Lavinia," Dinah interrupted, reverently fingering the exquisite white work cover adorning the small table. "You have created works of art with your needle!"

Lady Markham's regal nod acknowledged this sincere tribute before she resumed her theme. "In the years since your mother died and your father entrusted your upbringing and the task of overseeing your education to me, I have actively encouraged you to pursue your studies in these areas, and while your performance on the pianoforte is not exceptional, at least you need never be ashamed to take your turn to entertain the company. Nor need you hesitate to exhibit your own needlework for the critical eyes of the most talented practitioners of the art, despite the regrettably limited amount of time you have devoted to this activity. I have deliberately left your flower paintings, which *are* exceptional, to the last. You have a definite flair in this direction and your facility with pencil and watercolors will no doubt give pleasure to your friends and family in the future. But that is the extent of it. Get right out of your head, I beg of you, any idea that you may with propriety pursue those areas of art that are exclusively the province of men."

"I do not see why I may not," Dinah argued, undeterred. "The Royal Academy has accepted a few female students and actually invited Mrs. Damer to exhibit a few years ago, besides electing Angelica Kauffmann and Mary Moser as Founder Members in the last century. It must be perfectly acceptable for someone like me to seek tuition in an artist's studio. I am longing to paint in oils, but I am woefully ignorant of the techniques to be mastered or even of how to mix the colors, and it is not something one can fully learn from books."

"Your father would never countenance such a thing. It would be considered very odd behavior indeed in a well-brought up girl, and it would quite destroy your chances of contracting an eligible alliance if you were perceived to be so singular in interests. Do not be misled by the fact that you are your father's sole heir into thinking you have only to make your bow to society in order to have eligible gentlemen vying for your hand, because it is not so simple as that."

"Then it is fortunate that I don't wish to contract an alliance, eligible or otherwise," Dinah said distinctly. "Marriage has no appeal for me. I intend to become an artist. I am very sorry if I seem disobliging after all your unswerving efforts to turn me into a conventional female, but do not tease yourself that the failure is yours, Aunt. Not everyone is born to be stuffed into the same mold. You will allow there is room in the world for some variation. Not all women are meant to marry, just as there are men who are not suited to the married state. I am persuaded Papa is one of these."

"Nonsense, your father was devoted to your mother," snapped Lady Markham.

Dinah shook her head. "I was not yet ten when Mama died, but I could see that Papa did not share her interest in domestic concerns. Her conversation bored him and her timidity irritated him. It seemed she could do nothing to please him, though she spent her life trying. Their natures were sadly incompatible, poor things. They'd have been much happier had they never met."

"Let me tell you, miss, it is not at all becoming in you to criticize your father; in fact, there is nothing more reprehensible in a child!"

Faint surprise flitted across Dinah's features. "I did not intend any criticism; I felt sorry for them both. At least Mama had me to love and care for. Poor Papa might have derived some satisfaction had I been a son, though it may be that he is simply not a paternal sort of person. Certainly he does not find me of any intrinsic interest. His pleasures must come more from reading and traveling than tending to his property, or he would spend more than a few weeks a year here in Devonshire."

"I do not propose to enter into a discussion of your father's character with you, it would be most improper, but you will soon discover a strong paternal streak if you mean to approach him with this idiotish notion of becoming an artist. Now we see what comes of alienating one's closest relatives. I begged him to ask your Aunt Eliza to bring you out last year, and what must he do but quarrel with her instead. This year she does not even plan to hire a house in town for the Season. Here you are, turned twenty years old, with your head stuffed full of artistic rubbish and radical theories, and no more notion of how to get along in society than a schoolroom child. It won't do, and so I shall tell Leonard when he arrives next week!"

Lady Markham's manner had grown increasingly more agitated during the course of this jerky speech; her breathing rate had increased and her cheeks had taken on a purplish tinge. She appeared to have forgotten the existence of her niece, who was about to ring for Telford when the butler arrived bearing coffee and an assortment of small cakes. Dinah prepared her aunt's coffee with quiet efficiency and sat beside her in silence until the choleric spell had faded into a lively pleasure in placating her palate. Eating was one of the few enjoyments left to Lady Markham since the increasingly debilitating rheumatism had rendered her virtually housebound. By the time she had consumed all but one of the cakes and drunk the pot dry she had ceased to mutter to herself and had regained a measure of calm, though she bent a number of speculative glances on the serene visage of the motionless girl staring dreamily out the window from a rush-backed straight chair. A stranger might have wondered at the lack of interaction between the two, but intimates of the household would have found nothing out of the ordinary in this situation. Unless specifically invited to speak, Miss Dinah Elcott generally preserved an unruffled silence in the presence of her elders, the contents of her imagination remaining a mystery they had rarely elected to probe over the years of her adolescence.

The long-established pattern altered in that respect, however, the following week, when Sir Leonard Elcott arrived to pay one of his infrequent visits to his ancestral estate. He scarcely had time to refresh himself when his butler informed him that his sister sought an audience at his earliest convenience. Eventually, intelligence filtered to Dinah that her guardians had been closeted together for the best part of two hours, information that heightened a sense of impending change that had arisen from her aunt's odd behavior toward her since the discovery of the offending sketchpad full of what the invalid persisted in describing as "vulgar drawings." She was certainly curious but neither alarmed nor thrilled by any anticipation since her elders were not in the habit of consulting her preferences when making decisions that concerned her. Therefore it imposed no great strain upon her nerves to contain any eagerness she might be expected to harbor to learn the nature and extent of any imminent changes in her life.

Her father not having sent for her earlier, Dinah's first opportunity to welcome him home did not come until shortly before dinner, when she joined him and her aunt in the small drawing room.

"Welcome home, Papa," she said, coming forward to give and receive a dutiful kiss. "You are looking very fit, more rested than on your last visit."

Two pairs of gray eyes of striking similarity in shape, color, and clarity assessed their respective owners with the same unselfconscious directness. Dinah saw a man in his early sixties, of medium height and thin, wiry build, with sparse gray hair and unremarkable features in a countenance that narrowed sharply from a high, broad brow to a long, thin chin. Her father gave no indication of the results of his keen scrutiny except to say he was glad to find her in her customary good health.

The evening passed as numerous others had over the years, with Sir Leonard describing some of the places he had lately visited and Lady Markham filling him in on any significant events that had taken place in the neighborhood during his absence. As usual, Dinah's participation was neither sought nor offered.

The earlier prickle of anticipation waned in Dinah only to be revived the next morning when her father summoned her to his study. Again the footman tracked her down in the kitchen where she was having a lesson in sauce making from Mrs. Hodges.

One of Sir Leonard's mobile eyebrows lifted as he took in his daughter's faded and stained cotton dress, but he did not comment on her costume, merely waving her to a chair in front of the table desk before he reseated himself behind it. His measuring glance rested on Dinah's face for a long moment.

"It's a pity you didn't inherit your mother's looks," Sir Leonard said dispassionately.

"Yes," Dinah agreed, equally unruffled. "Mama always said I favored you in appearance."

"Well, it can't be helped. We have to work with what we're given."

"Yes."

Silence reigned unbroken for a few moments while father and daughter pursued their own thoughts; then Sir Leonard seemed to recollect himself. "Your aunt is rather concerned about your future," he began. If the pause that ensued was meant to be an invitation it went unaccepted by the young woman who waited placidly for elucidation, her steady gaze fixed on her parent.

"Your aunt feels, with some justification, I'll not deny, that I have been remiss in my duty to provide for your future. I should have arranged for your Aunt Eliza to bring you out in London last year or even two years ago, but you seemed perfectly contented here, and had I thought about it, I would have said you were perhaps still a bit young at that time. Your aunt tells me you are already turned twenty," he added, looking rather disbelievingly at his only child.

"Yes." Dinah nodded, adding, "Last week."

A fleeting shadow that might have been regret appeared on Sir Leonard's brow as he continued. "Well, there is nothing to be gained by dwelling on what might have been, but if you feel I have been neglectful of your interests, I apologize."

"I don't, Papa."

Sir Leonard acknowledged his daughter's brief, calm denial with a tiny nod. "You relieve my mind. Let us proceed to the reason I requested this meeting. It is clearly incumbent upon me to rectify past omissions, but your aunt informs me that the uncertain state of your Uncle Hiram's health at present will prevent your Aunt Eliza from taking a house in London for the Season this year."

"That's all right, Papa. I have no wish to make my bow to society. That sort of life holds no appeal for me."

Sir Leonard looked at his daughter with quickened interest. When she did not elaborate on what must be regarded as apostasy in a young female, he said consideringly, "I do not say that your sentiments are faulty in any way—I myself find the sort of posturing and relentless exhibitionism that passes for society during the Season intellectually stifling and tedious in the extreme—but it is my understanding that this . . . parade is an inescapable part of the process of arranging a suitable match for the daughters of the aristocracy, especially when there are limited possibilities in the local environment, as is definitely the case in this corner of Devonshire."

"I have no interest in marriage either, Papa," Dinah said.

Sir Leonard's left eyebrow rose above the line of its fellow at this calm dismissal of a female's natural state. "Again, I do not say that you are wrong in your preference for a single life, only that one's choices should be based on information and experience as well as inclination if they are not to prove a source of future regret. What reasons have you to abjure the state of matrimony?"

"I wish to be an artist." With this daring statement Dinah displayed emotion for the first time in the interview. Her clear gray eyes shimmered with inner excitement and her body tautened with the effort of remaining still as she spoke with a touch of bravado.

"I . . . see." Sir Leonard's many faults as a parent, only recently admitted to his conscious consideration, did not preclude an intellectual tolerance for a wide-ranging sphere of idiosyncracies in his fellow humans. He did not therefore ridicule his daughter's surprising ambition on the grounds of unsuitability, nor did he raise the practical question of attainability, asking merely, "Is this ambition of long standing or recent formation?"

"I have enjoyed sketching and painting since I was very young, Papa, but it is only in the last few years that I have realized that I possess a natural ability above the common and—conversely—how very much I do not know and cannot learn all on my own. It is so frustrating to keep bumping into the limits of one's ability when attempting to express one's vision!"

Sir Leonard's expression had grown increasingly pensive as he listened to the passion he had never before glimpsed in his hitherto phlegmatic daughter. "Do you have any examples of your work that I may examine?"

"I'll get my portfolio," Dinah cried, fairly jumping out of her chair.

A half hour later Sir Leonard slipped the last watercolor sketch into the large folder his daughter had tremblingly thrust into his hands. Unlike his sister, he had expressed no shock or outrage at the series of drawings of gypsies or those of his servants going about their respective household tasks. He had studied them and the delicate botanical paintings and still lifes with an air of deep concentration, impervious to the palpable tension in the waiting girl, who offered no explanations or apologies for the products of her labors, a restraint that did her no disservice in her father's eyes.

He glanced briefly into that still, waiting face and then down at his hands, frowning a little. He pulled out a handkerchief and proceeded to remove some traces of pastels from his fingers before saying abruptly, "I concur that you do indeed possess an uncommon talent, my child." As a glad light replaced the anxiety in her eyes, Sir Leonard raised a cautionary hand. "I am not prepared to delve into the knottier question of your becoming a professional artist at this juncture. I stand by what I said earlier about the importance of making informed choices. I cannot in good conscience permit you to eschew the normal life of a young woman of your station without ever having experienced it. Therefore, I have begun a letter to Natasha Talbot, the daughter of my old friend Lord Phillips, requesting her hospitality and chaperonage on your behalf for a few weeks this spring."

"But . . . I am a stranger to Lord Phillips's daughter, Papa. She might well feel it is an imposition to have me foisted onto her in such a way!" Dinah protested.

"I ran into Natasha quite by accident two weeks ago when I was passing through London. She is now the wife of Cameron Talbot, a promising young man in the Foreign Office. My impression was that she has inherited her father's fine brain and her mother's kindness and common sense. I am persuaded you will find her quite compatible, and since the Talbots have the entrée everywhere, she is ideally placed to oversee your entrance into polite society."

"But, Papa, I would much rather not enter that sort of society. I have no looks or conversation. Poor Mrs. Talbot will find me a sad bore—worse, a millstone around her neck!" cried Dinah in a near frenzy of dread.

"Dinah, I do not admire cowardice in any form," replied her cold-eyed parent. "A well-bred ease among all sorts of people is a desirable asset that will serve you well all through your life and is worthy of being cultivated, the more so since it apparently does not come naturally to one of your introverted temperament. I was very favorably impressed by Mrs. Talbot and can think of no one more able to guide you through your initial steps in society."

The look of misery that settled over his daughter's wan features at his insistence melted Sir Leonard's sternness to the degree that he added in a softened voice, "I will offer you this compact, my child. If you will allow yourself to be guided by Mrs. Talbot and make an honest effort to participate in the typical social doings of the capital, I will give my permission for you to dedicate a reasonable amount of time to the pursuit of artistic training, as long as these activities do not become an inconvenience to Mrs. Talbot. Will you agree to this?"

A spark of life crept back into Dinah's cloudy eyes. She swallowed back her instinctive objections to the demands her father was making on her and accepted the only chance she was likely to receive to gain her own unconventional objective. Slowly she nodded her head.

"Very well, then. I'll complete my letter to Mrs. Talbot without further delay," said Sir Leonard, satisfied that he had secured his daughter's cooperation, however reluctant she had been to grant it.

Accepting this as the dismissal it was, Dinah left the room quietly, her thoughts a mixture of doubts, fears, and tenuous anticipation, the balance of which shifted continuously over the next sennight while her elders busied themselves in making plans for her immediate future.

2

A comfortable quiet enveloped the small yellow-and-while-painted breakfast parlor at the back of the Portman Square town house, broken only by the homely sounds of toast crunching, cups clicking against saucers, and the rustling of paper as the room's two occupants looked through their post while consuming their morning meal. Sunshine bathed the near side of the round table, picking out red lights in Mr. Cameron Talbot's rich brown hair and glinting diamond sparks from the crystal goblet of orange juice he raised to his lips and emptied in one long pull. He set down the glass and extended one long-fingered hand holding an envelope across the table to his companion.

"Here, darling, this is addressed to you, not me. It's franked by Harry Flint."

"A letter from Susan—at last!" his wife squealed, eagerly grabbing the missive and tearing it open.

Mr. Talbot's green eyes lingered appreciatively on his wife's expressive face, admiring the extravagant length of her thick black lashes and the glowing color in her satin-skinned cheeks and the soft lips she pursed as she perused her letter. To think that he had once considered blonde hair and pale coloring the epitome of feminine beauty! He smiled at his former blindness to the glory of olive-tinted skin, brown velvet eyes, and near-black hair as combined in Natasha's enchanting person.

She looked up and caught his expression, her face breaking into a radiant smile before she indicated the sheet of paper in her hand. "Susan writes that she is increasing again, which is good news, of course, but she is feeling even less well this time than with Michael, so she and Harry have decided to remain in Wiltshire this spring. She says they might spend a few weeks in Brighton in June if all goes well."

"Please convey my felicitations with yours when you reply," her husband said with a smile that faded as he noted the little sigh with which Natasha laid aside her letter. "You will sorely miss Susan's companionship during the Season, my love, will you not, especially with Peter and Serena still traveling in the east and Aunt Hester fixed in Paris with the Pangbournes this spring."

"Yes, but I am thrilled for Aunt Hester all the same. It has been the dream of her life to see Paris. You will remember how she reveled in being in Vienna and Brussels two years ago."

Cam pulled a wry face. "I fear my memories of our stay in Brussels and Vienna will always be overshadowed by regret at the brutal way I treated you at that time. I doubt I noticed, or cared, whether Aunt Hester was enjoying the experience; my concerns were entirely selfish. I was hell-bent on tearing you out of my life. I still can't recall those days to mind without breaking out in a cold sweat when I think of how close I came to getting my just desserts, to condemning myself to a lifetime without you."

"Hush, my darling. You have always been too harsh on yourself with respect to our estrangement. You were badly hurt by what you honestly believed was my treachery. I understood that, even during the bleakest period when I nearly gave up hope that our marriage could be salvaged. We didn't know each other very well when we married, and we were separated before we had time to develop the loyalty and trust we now enjoy."

"There would have been ample time had I had the wit to discern the gold from the dross when it came to women. I knew less than nothing about the female of the species three years ago, and the little I thought I knew was proved wrong," Cam admitted with a rueful grimace. "I never was one of those fellows like my cousin Charles, who is completely at home in feminine company."

Natasha directed a sweet and saucy smile at her husband. "Speaking as the woman in possession, my love, I do not find this an entirely disquieting circumstance. I am quite prepared to come to your rescue whenever predatory females persist in casting out lures to the handsomest man in London." Her teasing smile widened as the uneasiness she associated with any reference to his extraordinary good looks settled over her husband's countenance. Cam had never appreciated or been comfortable with the reaction his face and person elicited from the majority of her sex, especially from those members in whom the traditional constraints of maidenly modesty were lacking. In his wife's eyes this was one of his most endearing traits, further enhanced by the unfailing courtesy with which he repelled the advances of the bolder females.

A knowing glint replaced embarrassment in his eyes as Mr. Talbot said firmly, "That is quite enough from you, young lady. It is far too early in the day to submit to being the butt of childish humor."

"That puts me in my place," Natasha agreed pertly before returning her attention to the stack of envelopes at her place.

Reabsorbed in the details of their post, neither spoke for several minutes until Natasha said, "Oh, dear!"

"Bad news?"

"No . . . that is, I hope not . . . I mean . . . " Natasha glanced from her patiently waiting husband to the single sheet of paper she held between her hands and began again. "Do you remember a fortnight or so past when I introduced you to an old friend of my father's at the Castlereaghs' reception?"

"I think so—Elcott, was it? A clever sort of fellow with a cool manner?"

"Yes, that's right. Sir Leonard Elcott was almost a neighbor in Devon. He used to drop in to see my father whenever he returned from one of his trips. He was seldom at his estate for more than a few weeks consecutively, but the two had formed a close friendship during their school days that endured through the years. Until that accidental meeting in town I had not seen Sir Leonard since my father's death five years ago." She fell silent.

"I apprehend the letter is from Elcott?" Cam prompted.

"Yes. He wishes me—us—to invite his daughter here for a few weeks during the Season and sponsor her at Almack's."

"Did I say cool? The fellow has the nerve of a pirate. On the strength of one meeting in five years he presumes to commandeer your hospitality and time to his daughter's benefit for a period of eight or ten weeks?"

"Ye . . . yes." Her eyes met his briefly and returned to the paper in her hands.

Silence descended again.

"Natasha?" Cam's momentary indignation passed and he examined his wife's lovely face, which was a study in indecision at present. "Do you wish to invite Miss Elcott here, darling? Do you know the girl?"

"No, not properly. I met her on several occasions when our mothers were alive, but that was ages ago. Dinah's mother died before she was ten, and her father's widowed sister moved into Wemberly to care for her niece. She and my grandmother detested each other, so the households soon ceased being on visiting terms. Dinah is just turned twenty, nearly four years my junior."

"As I see it you need feel yourself under no neighborly compunction to oblige Sir Leonard to the extent of taking in his daughter. Why cannot the aunt sponsor her come-out?"

"She has long been a martyr to rheumatism and cannot climb stairs or even walk without the aid of a cane. There is another aunt who might have brought her out in the past year or so, but evidently she will not be situated in London this spring. It seems Sir Leonard has just recently been brought to an awareness that something should be done to arrange his daughter's future."

Cam smiled at the dryness in his wife's tone, but he knew his Natasha. "The letter has aroused your sympathy on the girl's behalf."

"She has always had that in the abstract. My grandmother was vociferous in her condemnation of the situation at Wemberly. She held that Sir Leonard should never have married in the first place. In her opinion he was too . . . coldly inhuman to make a satisfactory husband or father. He was above forty when he was bowled over by Dinah's mother, who was a beautiful girl in her first Season when they met. According to Grandmother, she was too young and soft and not nearly intelligent enough to hold the interest of a complex man like Sir Leonard, so it was not surprising that the marriage did not prosper. Instead of the son he wanted, Dinah was their only child. Her mother doted on her, but Lady Markham, who came to live with them after Lady Elcott died, is another cold-natured person like her brother. Except for her mother, that poor girl has never known much family affection, nor to my knowledge has she enjoyed much society beyond her home. Hers has been a rather barren existence so far."

"Would you like to invite the girl to stay with us, Tasha?"

"Would you object to it, darling? After all, her presence in our home will affect you too and will to some extent curtail the amount of time we shall have together."

"I would only object if you found having her here tedious, my love. If she is cold-natured like your cousin Lucretia it will be a misery for you to have her constantly underfoot. On the other hand, if she proves to be congenial, a new friendship will go some way toward making up for the lack of Susan's or Aunt Hester's company. It is definitely a gamble."

"Sir Leonard says she is a rather unusual girl," Natasha said dubiously.

"So were you," her husband declared with a chuckle.

Natasha made a little face at him but did not take the bait. "It seems Dinah is not at all eager to make her come-out but has taken it into her head that she wishes to become an artist. Her father made a bargain with her to permit some artistic training while she is in London doing the social rounds."

"Good Lord!"

"It sounds as if she might prove more interesting than the run-of-the-mill bud," Natasha said, with a twinkle at her husband's heartfelt expression of dismay.

"It sounds to me, my love, as if she failed to inherit her mother's beauty."

"How did you know that, Cam?" asked his wife, impressed with his perspicacity. "Sir Leonard writes that Dinah has no pretensions to good looks and he does not expect me to undertake to find her a husband, just to help her to acquire some town bronze as it were."

"Good of him!"

"On the contrary," Natasha retorted, "it is all of a piece with his callous attitude toward his daughter. That poor child. It fairly makes my blood boil!"

"Aha! My admiration for Elcott's intellectual percipience

grows by the moment. Having taken your measure at one brief meeting, he knew exactly how to set about enlisting your sympathy on behalf of his poor neglected child. He has thereby succeeded in acquiring a champion for his daughter who will exert all her considerable powers to prove him wrong in his assessment of the girl by making a splendid match for her. Machiavellian strategy!"

"Now you are simply being foolish beyond permission." The effect of Natasha's dignified refutal was somewhat marred by a suspicious quiver at the corners of her mouth.

"Is the girl well-dowered?" Cam asked, dropping his teasing manner.

"Exceedingly, I should imagine. Wemberly is a large, prosperous estate, and it is not entailed."

"Then if I were you, my love, I think I should take care not to mention this circumstance to Charles. He has been hanging out for a rich wife for years. I doubt Sir Leonard would thank you for dangling his daughter before the avaricious eyes of the town's gazetted fortune hunters."

"I think you do Charles less than justice, Cam, when you imply that he is a fortune hunter," Natasha said quietly.

"I am not implying anything my cousin hasn't said on more than one occasion."

"Oh yes, in that facetious manner he affects. Charles is always at his most outrageous when you are present. He has never outgrown the unworthy desire to provoke your disapproval by pretending to be a hardened care-for-nought, but his actions belie his verbal claims in this area at least. To my knowledge he has not offered for a single one of the heiresses who have appeared on the scene during the length of our acquaintance."

"If that is so, and I agree you would be in a better position to know than I, I would postulate either that none of the aforementioned heiresses gave him any encouragement to press his suit, or none of them came up to his exacting standards in other areas apart from fortune."

"Miss Bell fairly threw herself at his head last autumn," Natasha pointed out with a little smile that did not reach her eyes.

Cam shuddered artistically. "That is no argument, love. The

girl was an antidote, and Charles's eye for beauty in all forms is well established."

"In which case Dinah Elcott should be safe from his attentions, since we are assured of her lack of beauty by one who might be supposed to be prejudiced in her favor. Do you dislike the idea of taking on the responsibility for a wealthy young girl, darling? If you do, I shall refuse Sir Leonard's request."

"No, no, sweetheart. I am simply trying to ensure that you know exactly what your generous heart is getting you into. We shall have to give a party for the girl."

"I'll enjoy that," Natasha assured him. "It's a pity the house isn't large enough for a proper ball, but I'll contrive something."

"Ah, I see the beginnings of a hostesslike gleam in those beautiful eyes. It's time I was on my way, but I think I'll steal a few minutes to look in on Justin before I leave. Coming?"

Natasha hastily used her napkin and took the hand her husband held out, all thoughts of future entertaining evaporating in the immediate delight of a visit to the nursery.

Natasha made no plans for the day Dinah Elcott was expected, not wishing the girl to arrive in Portman Square to find her hostess absent. A poor sort of welcome that would be for a young girl being tossed among strangers in a somewhat cavalier fashion. The polite, chilling reserve with which her cousins had once accepted her unwanted presence in their home was still vivid in Natasha's memory after three years. The situations were not dissimilar, though Sir Leonard had not had to resort to bribery to secure her acceptance of his daughter as her brother Peter had done when, faced with the prospect of being sent off to the American war immediately after the end of the Peninsula fighting, he had made arrangements for his mother's cousin to bring out his sister in company with her own daughter. Natasha had no difficulty in imagining what must be Miss Elcott's feelings at present. With no one but an abigail for company, the poor girl would have had the long carriage ride in which to ponder and worry about her reception by the strangers her father had arbitrarily decreed would become her closest companions for what must seem an inordinately long period of time.

From the instant of deciding to accede to Sir Leonard's request, Natasha had resolved to make his daughter feel wanted and welcome in her home. She had caused the best spare bedchamber to be thoroughly turned out, substituting crisp white lace window and bed curtains for the heavy fabrics that muted the light in order that a girl from the country might not find a town house too dark for her liking. She had ordered a profusion of the brightest flowers available to fill two large Chinese vases, creating dramatic splashes of color in the room. Her best inspiration had come while poring over Sir Leonard's letter seeking clues to his daughter's taste or personality. Regrettably, there were none. Apart from his bland statement that the girl had no beauty to distinguish her, her father's old friend had not been forthcoming. His letter contained no physical description of his daughter, nor any comments on her character or personality. The only scrap of information was contained in the fact that Dinah's father had evidently secured her agreement to engage in the social activities associated with the London Season by agreeing to underwrite some unspecified artistic tuition. With this in mind, Natasha had conceived the happy notion of clearing out the small box room at the back of the house on the second floor and creating an artist's workroom with the addition of an easel, two mismatched chairs, and a couple of scarred tables.

After satisfying herself that all advance preparations for receiving her guest had been carried out, Natasha dismissed Justin's nurse and spent a couple of hours playing with her son. At twenty-one months, Justin Talbot was an intrepid, curious, and determined toddler with his mother's dark hair, his father's green eyes, and his own potent brand of charm that reduced his attendants—principally his mother—to a state of fawning admiration. To Natasha, the perfect little being she and Cam had created was a source of unending wonder. She begrudged his nurse each new word or accomplishment that devoted lady had the great good fortune to witness first. Fortunately for the smooth running of the household, Mrs. Evans, a middle-aged widow, was a sensible woman who, unlike so many of her jealous breed, did not attempt to fob off the claims of young parents to a hand in the care of their infants. She was perfectly willing to efface herself when Natasha descended on the nursery, confident of her ability to prevent any lasting harm to the ultimate civilizing of her charge that might be wrought by the overindulgence of a doting mother. Actually, she mentally bestowed a qualified approval on young Mrs. Talbot, accepting that any errors she made in her approach to dealing with a strong-willed toddler sprang from inexperience rather than a basic lack of common sense. Relations between nursery and employers remained amicable, thanks to Mrs. Evans's large-minded tolerance for the excessive indulgence of new parents.

Today Natasha stayed to supervise Justin's lunch, a decidedly messy affair since he was determined to manage everything without assistance, and she left the nursery only when her darling had succumbed to exhaustion after a hectic morning of play. His mother eyed her own bed with unadmitted longing while she changed her rumpled and food-stained gown, but she revived after a solitary and peaceful luncheon and repaired to the front sitting room to attend to her correspondence while awaiting the arrival of her guest.

Charles Talbot found her thus occupied an hour later. Natasha had left instructions denying herself to callers that day, but Dawson, the Talbots' butler, exercizing that odd subterranean sense essential to real success in his field, had no hesitation in making an exception in the case of his employer's cousin.

"Dawson says you are not receiving today, Natasha," the gentleman remarked by way of a greeting, after announcing himself with a brisk rap on the partially open door to the small saloon. "I trust I am not *de trop*?"

"Would you care if you were?" Natasha's brown eyes were full of amusement, but the bright blue ones gazing limpidly back maintained a pose of wounded innocence.

"But of course! I should be devastated to appear gauche. You wrong me by implication, dear girl."

Head tilted, elbow on desk, the goose-quill pen she'd been using resting against her lips, the "dear girl" contemplated her good friend as he sauntered down the room toward the desk under the window where she was situated. A quick glance would dismiss any similarity between the cousins. Their coloring was dissimilar, Cam having unusually pale skin in combination with dark red-brown hair, while Charles had warmer skin tones that tanned easily. That same summer sun set gold streaks in his light brown hair each year. Cam's features recalled the perfection of Greek heroic sculpture, while Charles remained merely a good-looking man with no distinguishing characteristics in the arrangement of the pleasant elements that made up his particular physiognomy.

Only two years separated them in age, but his military experiences and the weight of responsibility had stamped Cam's face with a maturity that was missing in the younger man. Though Charles would shortly celebrate his thirtieth birthday, nothing, not even a cynical bent to his nature, had as yet left a mark on a visage that contained no clues to his character. The family resemblance that existed was more to be found in their physiques and a similar cut to their jawlines. Cam was taller, but Charles, though of no more than average height, shared the same perfect balance of bone and muscle that translated to a lithe grace in all his movements. This quality was evident in the easy motion with which he approached and seated himself in the chair nearest the limewood desk.

"Do I detect a shade of criticism in your basilisk stare today, my dear one?" Charles inquired anxiously. "Can it be that I have offended—unwittingly, I need not add—in some way not immediately apparent? Is it this coat? It *cannot* be my cravat, which I flatter myself you will agree is a rather pleasing variation—and my own invention, I modestly add—of the Oriental style. My cousin, of course, would stigmatize it as 'sheer dandyism,' but I would not so insult you as to suggest that less than three years of marriage to someone so lacking in what, for want of a better term, I shall have to call flair, could have irreparably damaged your discriminating eye. Therefore it *must* be the coat. I told Weston I feared this particular shade was a touch too near bottle-green to be acceptable, but he pooh-poohed my reservations, assuring me it would become all the crack in a month. Now we see what comes of permitting a mere tradesman, when all is said, to override one's instinctive feelings upon such a delicate matter. You are absolutely justified in turning up your delightful nose, and so I shall tell him tomorrow when I send back the coat. Let him foist his execrable taste onto some slavish follower of his autocratic dictates!"

"*Charles!*" Natasha begged, amused exasperation sitting lightly on her face. "Do stop talking such arrant nonsense. You are perfectly well aware that there is nothing amiss with your coat or your cravat, though mind you, I think Cam is quite right to prefer a less constricting arrangement."

"Do you? Such loyalty is truly admirable," Charles murmured. "You relieve my mind, at least in a sartorial sense, but yet I still detect a hint of reserve in your manner. I have annoyed you in some fashion. Tell me how so that I may abase myself or perform whatever trials you may deem necessary to return to your good graces."

"If you must know, I *was* a bit annoyed at your unkindness to Lady Claremont the other day when we were discussing the debate over the sedition bill."

Charles's mobile eyebrows escalated. "How was I unkind? I merely made the civil observation that if the government tried to act upon Lady C.'s spartan advice to pursue each and every person present during a mob scene it would soon find itself in the position of needing to mobilize another army, most of whose members would consist of the very persons she desires to see prosecuted. The old trout is willfully blind to the causes of the unrest that is becoming more widespread in the mining areas and the manufacturing towns all across the country."

"Yours wasn't a civil but a sarcastic observation," Natasha retorted. "Lady Claremont is elderly and she is uncomfortable with the changes taking place in the country. With the example of the revolution in France in her memory, she is understandably frightened by the specter of mob violence."

"And so her solution to the present unrest is government violence. That doesn't seem to frighten her in the least, though it leaves me trembling. Lord knows I don't see myself as a champion of the great unwashed, but I have no patience with those relics who refuse to acknowledge that legitimate grievances and real suffering have sparked off the riots."

"My point, Charles, is that Lady Claremont was not an M.P. declaiming in Parliament but a morning caller in my home,"

Natasha said, "and as such, was entitled to courteous treatment from all within."

The blue eyes cooled and shifted. "I stand rebuked. All shall be sweetness and light within these walls in future, no matter the provocation. I trust you have no rooted objection to a state of supreme dullness?"

"No, and no fear of it either if you plan to be among those present," Natasha said with a warm smile that succeeded in its intent to conciliate. "I would be particularly grateful to secure your assistance in the immediate future in making my guest feel at home."

"Guest?"

"Yes. A young woman who lives near my old home in Devon will be staying with us for a while. She arrives today, which is why I am not at home to callers."

"This is the first mention I've heard of an imminent visit. A sudden impulse on someone's part?"

"Not at all."

"I take it the young woman in question is an old friend?"

Natasha hesitated. "Not precisely. Our families have known each other for many years. I promised Dinah's father I would take her about with me this spring."

Charles's alert gaze grew penetrating in the wake of this elaborately casual statement. "Are you saying you allowed yourself to be talked into sponsoring an unknown girl's bow to society?"

"No such thing." Natasha tried to infuse conviction into her voice. "Dinah is not unknown to me, and I am delighted to have her here."

"How well acquainted are you?"

About to declare under his irksome catechism that she had known her expected guest all her life, Natasha caught the sound of carriage horses coming to a halt outside in the square and was compelled by the prospect of instant contradiction to admit, "We have not met since we were children."

There was a moment of churning silence, then Charles said softly, "My dear large-hearted, small-brained Natasha, are you familiar with the expression 'to buy a pig in a poke'?"

"Nonsense, Charles. I have absolutely no doubts that Dinah

will prove a charming and amiable girl. I am going to love having her here."

"Brave words, dear girl, and I trust you won't find it necessary to ingest them in the near future."

Blue eyes with laughing devils in them withstood a brown-eyed glare as Dawson appeared in the doorway.

"Miss Dinah Elcott," he announced.

3

As Natasha rushed forward to welcome her guest, Charles Talbot got to his feet, his brain furiously active behind the bland facade he presented to an unwary world. He had no difficulty in smothering his initial amusement at what must be Natasha's chagrin at having her optimistic predictions so quickly confounded because some implications for himself soon reared their ugly heads. Natasha was committed to being at the beck and call of this unprepossessing visitor for the forseeable future and would surely test the bonds of their friendship by dragging him into her plans for the girl's entertainment.

Unprepossessing was a mild term, Mr. Talbot reflected, making a lightning assessment of Miss Elcott as, initial greetings over, she suffered herself to be led toward him by her hostess. Physically, the girl seemed not to possess a single positive attribute. Like her hostess she was quite small, but where Natasha's delicate frame was sheathed in unmistakably feminine curves, Miss Elcott's form, as near as he could tell, given the disguising effects of a shapeless pelisse, appeared to contain no curves whatsoever. Beside Natasha's vivid coloring, the girl was so neutral as to fade into the background. What could be seen of her hair, scraped back beneath a dated brown bonnet and confined in a bun at her neck, was neither blond nor brown but some indeterminate shade in between. Eyes, lips, skin, were all colorless. Her individual features, though free from any actual deformity of shape, yet achieved nothing in the way of beauty or distinction in their assemblage.

In the next moments Mr. Talbot ascertained that Miss Elcott was also completely lacking in the saving grace of charm. In response to Natasha's warm welcome she had uttered a formal platitude in a wooden voice and instantly subsided. It was not shyness, he concluded after sustaining a direct look from the visitor's light gray eyes, which were full of awareness and, possibly, intelligence, though it was too early to tell.

"Dinah, may I present Mr. Charles Talbot? We are to have the pleasure of Miss Elcott's company this spring, Charles," Natasha explained, her voice a shade too bright to be normal.

As Charles bowed and said what the occasion demanded, the minutest change occurred in Miss Elcott's impassive features, a change that, given the information in her next words, he interpreted as puzzlement.

"Was my father mistaken then in thinking your given name was Cameron, Mr. Talbot?"

"My *husband*'s name is Cameron, Dinah. He and Charles are cousins," Natasha said before he could speak.

"I see." Having signified her comprehension, Miss Elcott fell silent once more.

"For my sins," Charles murmured, again detecting a little increase of awareness in the pale, still face of Natasha's visitor. Peculiarity noted and cataloged, he thought with amusement before Natasha hurriedly suggested he might help Dinah remove her wraps while she cleared the table in front of the sofa for the refreshments she ordered. He complied, his smile and manner all eagerness to be of service to a fellow human being, something he intended as an object lesson for the tiresome creature whose silence arose not from an excusable timidity but from an indifference to her duty to cooperate in easing the awkwardness of first meetings. Sadly, his estimate of her figure was confirmed when he took the pelisse to lay over a chair. There were more angles than curves to Miss Elcott.

Charles's poor impression of Miss Elcott's social conscience also received ample confirmation during the strained interval that followed. She sat sedately, feet flat and together, back straight, and sipped at her tea, leaving the burden of conversation to others unless directly questioned. Her one voluntary contribution concerned the maid who had accompanied her from Devonshire. For her own part, she declined to accept sympathy for supposed discomforts when it was offered by Natasha, merely stating that she had enjoyed observing the passing scene, but she requested her hostess's intervention on behalf of the elderly attendant, claiming that Mrs. Meggs was hovering on the brink of migraine from the jostlings and fatigues of the journey. Natasha immediately rang for the housekeeper and enlisted that lady's assistance in aid of the ailing Mrs. Meggs, for which consideration Miss Elcott gravely thanked both in a few simple words. Charles awarded the gauche girl grudging marks for basic humanity while retaining the privilege of criticizing her lack of effort in smoothing her hostess's path.

"Is this your first visit to London, Miss Elcott?" he asked, partly to give Natasha a rest from her labors but mainly to coerce the wretched girl's participation.

"Yes," she replied.

When his look of invitation produced no amplification he went on smoothly, "I assume you are looking forward to becoming acquainted with the capital and making your bow to society?"

"Do you?" The silence that greeted this *bêtise* finally pierced Miss Elcott's eerie composure to the extent that she added, "Naturally, I shall be pleased to see the sights and famous buildings of London, but I fear I have no aptitude for society."

Charles *would* have restrained the ardent agreement hovering on his tongue, but Natasha evidently did not care to put his magnanimity to the test, intervening at this point. "It is perfectly understandable that you should feel unsure of your ability to fit in with strangers, Dinah," she assured her guest with a sympathetic smile. "I well recall how . . . alien I felt during my first weeks in London three years ago. Like you, I was staying with people who were unknown to me, though they were relatives, and for a time I was convinced there must be something fundamentally different about me that set me apart from the people I met. That feeling of isolation does wear off in time, I promise you. You will meet kindred souls with whom you may share common bonds of intellect or taste. In any case, we will not plunge into a social round until you have become comfortable in this house and in the city atmosphere."

Charles noted that Miss Elcott never removed her disconcertingly direct gaze from her hostess's face during this reas-

suring speech. It would be too much to suggest that all inner
resistance crumbled, but he sensed a thawing of her icy reserve
in the presence of Natasha's warmth and genuine concern.

"Thank you, Mrs. Tal—"

"It was a long time ago, I know, but once we were Natasha
and Dinah, and so we must be again."

"Of course, Natasha, thank you."

She did not quite return Natasha's friendly smile, this odd
girl, but she did at least look gratified, Charles decided with a
sense of relief for Natasha's sake. He bit into an inviting-look-
ing small cake, but Miss Elcott's next words caused him to
choke on the morsel.

"I'm afraid I won't be fit to meet your friends until I acquire
a new wardrobe," the girl said with a hint of apology. "My
aunt has been in the habit of ordering my clothes made up by
her own dressmaker, but my father said I must on no account
be seen in anything I own at present. He said I must throw myself on your charity to guide me in acquiring the proper
wardrobe. He gave me a draft on his bank for four thousand
pounds when I left. I am aware that this is a great imposition,
but—"

Charles's fit of coughing curtailed the rest of Miss Elcott's
little speech. Natasha, her face alight with laughter, jumped to
her feet and pounded him on the back. She avoided his eyes as
she firmly assured her apologetic guest, "My dear Dinah, I
promise you it is not an imposition but a rare treat to assist in
the spending of four thousand pounds."

Miss Elcott seemed relieved. "Papa said if I incur additional
expenses to send the bills directly to him."

Charles Talbot, his breathing restored, said with great affa-
bility, "How delightful it must be to have a doting parent. My
felicitations, Miss Elcott."

Large eyes the color of a fogbank regarded him coolly. "I
would not know about that, Mr. Talbot. My father is naturally
concerned with seeing me suitably established. He hopes that
fine feathers will go some way toward disguising the fact that I
have no looks."

Charles's eyes narrowed as he returned Miss Elcott's im-
placable gaze, ignoring Natasha's dutiful protests. This terrible
girl had deliberately backed him into a corner, denying him ac-

cess to any socially acceptable reply that could even be loosely aligned with the truth. He mentally glided over the small matter of his own remark having been the opening salvo in the skirmish. This presumptuous provincial must be taught that she could not with impunity challenge her elders. "But my dear Miss Elcott," he observed gently, "surely you know that all heiresses are beautiful? I would go so far as to predict that you will be swamped with offers as soon as you appear on the social scene."

Charles ignored Natasha's shocked intake of breath, never taking his eyes from his opponent's. No indication of anger, chagrin, or any other emotion disturbed the quiet planes of Miss Elcott's unremarkable countenance as she considered this pronouncement before saying, "I hope that you may be wrong, Mr. Talbot, because I have no interest in marrying. I intend to be an artist."

"Ah, an Original! Miss Elcott, you have just ensured your popularity among the more discriminating members of the *ton*, to whom the annual parade of nubile young women with nothing to recommend them save a temporal prettiness and an amiable nature has become a source of unending ennui. You will change all that." That angry gleam in Natasha's eyes told him he'd gone too far, and Charles rose to his feet. "Natasha, my dear, my delight in such stimulating company must be my excuse for outstaying my welcome and depriving you ladies of this opportunity to become acquainted. Your servant, Miss Elcott. My best wishes for a happy sojourn among the *ton*."

He bent over his hostess's reluctant hand with a languid grace and recalled his earlier prediction to her ears alone. "May I suggest salt and pepper to aid in the ingestion of the items mentioned earlier?" Then, raising his voice, "Do not bother to ring for Dawson, I'll see myself out." Bestowing a benevolent smile on the two women, Charles got himself out of the room with magnificent aplomb.

Natasha turned to her guest as the door closed. "I must apologize for Charles's outrageous manners and promise you you will not meet their like among the rest of our friends. Charles rather cultivates an outspoken style, but he does not mean anything unkind by it. It is just that he cannot forgo an opportunity to exercise his wit or cleverness. It can be disconcerting to those who don't know him well."

"I fear I may have provoked him," Dinah said ruefully. "I have been so little in company that I have never learned to guard my tongue. I'm afraid I may prove an embarrassment to you."

"Nothing of the sort," Natasha declared warmly, experiencing a strong desire to box Charles's ears. "As far as Charles is concerned, you have most likely earned his respect by standing up to him. I must say in his defense that he is a good friend to those persons he respects. As for the rest of society, you will soon find yourself going along very comfortably."

Natasha did not mistake Dinah's polite silence for agreement, but she thought it advisable to turn her guest's thoughts to a less alarming topic. Consequently she embarked on a rambling monologue on the architectural attractions of the city while they polished off the refreshments. Dinah's face remained composed and revealed none of her inner concerns, but Natasha's training as a dancer had heightened her sensitivity to bodily reactions, and eventually she had the satisfaction of seeing a lessening of a tension she had detected in the other's shoulders and jawline. Not until then did she cease talking like a guidebook and propose a tour of the house.

The serene simplicity and charm of the bedroom that was to be hers elicited a spontaneous expression of admiration from Miss Elcott, who delicately fingered a bright coral rose in one of the Chinese vases as she assured her hostess she would be happy and comfortable in such a lovely setting. Not until Natasha opened the door to the former box room with a dramatic flourish and invited Dinah to step inside was she privileged to observe her guest's first real smile of the afternoon. It was scarcely more than a tentative effort and trembled on her lips for only an instant before Dinah fastened large eyes made luminous by incipient tears on her hostess's smiling face.

"This room is for me?"

Natasha nodded. "All artists need a place to work in peace and solitude. It isn't a large room, but I hope it will serve you as a studio while you are here. If there is anything else you will require in the way of furnishings, you have only to ask."

"You are so very kind to have me here at all; it is such an

imposition, but this—" The bemused girl flung apart her hands, which had been clasped together, and embraced the whole room in an expansive gesture as words failed her. Two tears welled up and spilled over and she dashed them away with her hand. Knowing Dinah had deposited her reticule in her bedchamber earlier, Natasha obligingly produced a handkerchief from a pocket in her gown and passed it to her guest. She laughed, pleased at the response to her surprise, but declined to accept instant sainthood on the strength of it.

"There is nothing out of the ordinary in turning over an empty room to good use. Your father has told me of your artistic ambitions, and I am delighted to be able to assist in your efforts in this small way. As for imposing on me, no such thing! None of my particular friends are here in London at present and I had expected this Season would be no more than a dutiful round of boring affairs. I am going to enjoy having you here prodigiously."

Dinah's candid gaze searched the older girl's smiling face as she said with an attempt at jauntiness that did not quite succeed, "I . . . I assume Mr. Talbot was merely joking when he spoke of men paying suit to me because of my father's wealth?"

Reading the anxiety in her eyes, Natasha again felt a passing urge to do violence to her old friend, but she did not try to evade the issue. "It is a sad fact of life that impecunious men will court a girl for her expectations, my dear, and you did rather proclaim yourself an heiress earlier when you mentioned your father's gift for your wardrobe."

Color surged in the stricken girl's cheeks. "I . . . I did not realize . . . Is four thousand pounds a great deal of money?"

Natasha stared openmouthed, then said with a gurgle of laughter, "Many a genteel family exists on half that income per annum."

"I am so appallingly ignorant!" Dinah cried. "I am not fit to enter polite society. I will put you to the blush every time I open my mouth. I knew I ought not to have agreed to come to London, but Papa was so determined that I should."

"Calm yourself, my dear," Natasha urged in a soothing voice as she took Dinah's cold hands between hers and squeezed them briefly. "This ignorance of worldly matters that terrifies you is the natural result of a restricted upbringing and is soon overcome by exposure to a wider society. I have no slightest fear that you will bring disgrace down upon our heads. You have an innate reticence that makes listening more natural to you than speaking, and this will serve you well in your initial encounters with strangers. Trust me, you will soon laugh at these qualms."

Closing the door of the studio behind them, Natasha conducted her silent but disbelieving guest up to the top story of the town house, promising mysteriously, "And now I shall unveil my greatest treasure, and I give you fair warning that I anticipate reams of admiration."

Natasha derived a good deal of secret amusement in watching the beginning stages of her guest's acquaintance with her small son. It struck her that Dinah and Justin regarded each other with identical expressions of clinical interest, devoid of emotional accompaniment. The toddler, who had been gleefully demolishing a tower of blocks as his nurse erected it, presented his visitor with one of the blocks, announcing simply, "Red bock."

"Yes," Dinah replied, "a red block. Thank you, Justin."

Before the words were out of her mouth, the gift had been taken back by the giver, who dropped it on the pile and selected another. "Green bock," he said, presenting it solemnly.

"No, this is a blue block."

"Green bock," Justin insisted, jutting out his lower lip and fixing the recipient with a defiant eye.

Dinah shook her head. "Blue block," she repeated, staring calmly back. The other two women held their breath while the peace in the nursery trembled in the balance. Neither antagonist blinked for a palpable second as they weighed each other's determination; then Justin smiled seraphically, bowing to higher authority. "Boo bock," he agreed, taking it away again. Natasha and Mrs. Evans released their captured breath while the toddler inspected the pile of blocks and returned to Dinah presently with another, which he offered with an air of triumph.

"Green bock."

"Yes, Justin, green block." Dinah smiled at the child, who

proceeded to take it back into his possession again before continuing with their identifying game in mutual harmony.

Recounting the incident to her husband later while they dressed for dinner, Natasha said wonderingly, "It was like watching two swordsmen take each other's measure before a duel."

"But it wasn't a duel, darling," Cam objected, "merely a matter of fact. The block was blue, not green. Justin is still a bit shaky with his colors."

"But it was not as simple as it seemed on the surface. That little imp was trying to exercise power over Dinah. She didn't permit it, and he accepted the limitation with good grace. Without even knowing it, she gained his respect with her honesty. When I asked her afterward if she'd had much experience with young children, she said Justin was the first little one she'd ever come within speaking distance of. Imagine! My heart aches for that girl, Cam. It's as if she's been raised in a dark room, waited on by unseen hands, she's had so little close human contact. She nearly wept when I showed her the studio. I have a feeling her wishes or feelings have never been a real concern to anyone since her mother died."

"She doesn't seem to have suffered greatly from the lack," Cam pointed out in a practical spirit. "You said she stood up to Charles at his most overbearing. It sounds as though she has plenty of sense and is not devoid of spirit. She'll find her feet with your help."

"I could have cheerfully strangled Charles at the time for his lack of consideration, but the actual result was that Dinah and I got beyond the surface platitudes faster than might have been expected in an effort to understand each other. That never happened when I stayed with Cousin Edwina and Lucretia, who kept me at a distance with a formal civility that was intended to be off-putting."

"It is Miss Elcott's good fortune that you are cut from quite another bolt of goods, my love," said Cam, planting a butterfly kiss on his wife's nose. "Now, if you will allow me to fasten that necklet with which you have been wrestling these last ten minutes, it is time I made the acquaintance of our guest."

Cam found Dinah Elcott to be much as described by his wife. He saw nothing repellent in her plainness and approved of the quiet, sensible demeanor she displayed. There was about her nothing of that arch or flirtatious eagerness to engage his attention that never failed to awaken a corresponding mental resistance in him. She did not fidget or call attention to herself, but neither did she shrink away from social contact with the morbid timidity some young girls displayed that made a man feel like a bully. Though the last man in the world to pretend to special knowledge or interest in feminine fashions, Cam was confident that something could be done to enhance Miss Elcott's appearance. Her complexion, though too pale, was beautifully clear, and her eyes were lovely and full of intelligence. Natasha would know how to rig her out to better advantage.

"I apprehend that you met my cousin Charles today, Miss Elcott," Cam remarked after the initial pleasantries had been completed. "How did he strike you?" He was curious to discover whether a retroactive concern for good manners would cause her to dissemble her impressions.

Miss Elcott did not disappoint his expectations. Raising clear gray eyes to his she said as though still surprised, "He looks so innocuous."

Cam grinned. "He does, doesn't he? But I see you are not deceived by appearances. It's always unwise to underestimate people. Charles has the tongue of an adder and the unerring instincts of a tiger for discovering his victim's weakest point. He has his uses, though. Half the women in this city consult him before they attempt to redo their drawing rooms." Noting Miss Elcott's dilating pupils, Cam nodded. "Oh, yes, my cousin is considered an artistic arbiter of good taste, even more so now that Brummell has fled to France to escape his creditors. Have you any artist in mind with whom you might wish to study?"

Dinah blinked at the sudden change of topic but replied with a decisive shake of her head. "No, I wish I knew of someone, but on this point my father was not able to advise me."

"You could do worse than consult my cousin on this matter. Charles has always been *au courant* with respect to the artistic news in town. He was used to dabble in paints as a boy but found he had not the skill to equal his vision. I believe this unpalatable discovery soured his nature. If he cannot do a thing better than anyone else, Charles prefers to avoid the activity altogether."

"Rather a pusillanimous attitude," Dinah said with an air of impartial judgment that caused Cam to pull in the corners of his mouth to keep from losing his countenance.

"Quite."

Having neatly disposed of Cousin Charles, the two turned satisfied faces toward Natasha, who had been holding a discussion with Dawson on some problem in the kitchen. She in turn was delighted to see that her husband had been able to set their guest at her ease, and she beamed upon both.

An exhausted Dinah tumbled into bed later that night in a state of mild elation the like of which she had previously experienced only during the weeks when the gypsies had camped near her home. It was going to be all right, this interlude of city dwelling. She was still not looking forward to the social part of the experience—it was disconcerting to picture the awkward conversation with Charles Talbot duplicated scores of times—but Natasha had promised her that this would change. Natasha had recognized her sense of apartness from city people; she'd had to overcome the same sort of thing herself, though it seemed inconceivable to Dinah that her hostess, with her warmth and kindness, not to mention her vivid beauty, could ever have been unappreciated by any person possessing an ounce of discrimination or common humanity.

She must write to Papa first thing tomorrow, Dinah resolved, settling deeper between the sweet-smelling sheets. Although she had said nothing of an unfilial nature to him before she left home—what was the use, after all, when he had made up his mind to do something?—she had harbored far from charitable sentiments toward him for proposing to thrust her upon strangers. Her concerns had been mainly selfish; she had cringed at the idea of herself as a barely tolerated intruder, but she had also spared a *soupçon* of sympathy for the unfortunate people whose lives would be altered and disrupted by her presence in their home. After less than eight hours in the attractive Portman Square house she was ready to concede that her father's had been an inspired choice. Who but Natasha Talbot would have accepted with every evidence of pleasure a plain gawk of a female with an odd kick in her gallop and a total want of even the most rudimentary social skills? Moreover, this obviously happy young woman with a handsome and charming husband and a fascinating infant had convincingly expressed a delight at the prospect of having the questionable companionship of this odd female for an extended period of time. Quite incomprehensible but so quixotically generous. Thrilled though she was to have a real studio placed at her disposal, Dinah's deepest gratitude was reserved for this generous acceptance of a stranger into the center of a happy and complete family group.

Much as she wished to remember and analyze her first experiences as a member of the Talbot ménage, Dinah's thought processes were becoming submerged in a wave of drowsiness as she was forming a resolution not to disappoint her new friend. She would, she promised herself, even refrain from any action that might evoke Mr. Charles Talbot's antagonism—something that obviously distressed Natasha—no matter the cost to her patience. It shouldn't be too difficult, she decided, puzzled by the uncharacteristic assertiveness of her own response to Mr. Talbot's sarcasm today. It wasn't like her to seek confrontation with anyone, and she was unable to account for the effect this caustic person had on her. Whatever the reason for her own unbecoming return of the antagonism she sensed in him, she must not permit such aggressive behavior again, at least not when Natasha was present to be wounded by it. On this worthy but conditional resolve, Dinah drifted into a dreamless sleep.

4

An uneasy conscience brought Charles Talbot to his cousin's doorstep at an unusually early hour on the morning following Miss Elcott's arrival in town. By the time he'd reached the corner yesterday, his transitory satisfaction at routing an untried girl in conversational skirmishing had been reduced to the petty pique it must have been. What had possessed him, he'd wondered, to treat the wretched chit as fit to clash verbal swords with him? A girl barely out of the schoolroom and just up from the country was unworthy game. He'd pondered his unbecoming slip, passing the entire episode under critical review in an attempt to discern the motive, but could come up with nothing better than the lame excuse of some challenging quality in Miss Elcott's calm, clear eyes that had sparked his ire. If he'd wounded the girl's sensibilities or feminine pride, naturally he would have to apologize, but further probing of his memory produced no evidence of even superficial damage. Either Miss Elcott was more skilled at hiding her feelings than any female he'd ever come up against, or she had no sensibilities to wound.

Though he'd been unable to summon any significant contrition on Miss Elcott's behalf, his conscience smote him for the distress he'd caused Natasha. She'd been shocked at his boorishness to her guest and had felt all the affront the girl herself failed to register. He disliked being at odds with Natasha. She was at the top of a very short list of persons whose good opinion he valued. Hence his presence in Portman Square at an hour when he was generally drinking his first cup of coffee while discussing his choice of clothing for the day with his valet. Charles's lips twitched as he recalled Grigson's expression of restrained displeasure at being roused nearly two hours earlier than usual. He'd not been so rigidly "sirred" since the unfortunate occasion when he'd abandoned his customary tact in refusing to add a puce coat to his wardrobe on his man's advice.

Just as Charles raised his hand to the brass knocker the door opened and he found himself staring into his cousin's cool green eyes from the disadvantageous position of a lower step, which added to the discrepancy in their respective heights.

"Ah, good morning, Charles. Have you come for breakfast?"

"Kind of you to suggest it, coz, but I've already eaten," Charles drawled, rallying in the face of his cousin's ill-concealed amusement.

"If you are here to make it up with Natasha, may I suggest you adopt a posture of abject humility? She's not best pleased with your treatment of our guest."

Charles hid his chagrin at his cousin's knowledge, letting his eyes rove over the other's raiment. "One good piece of advice deserves another," he said affably. "If you'd like to send your man over to my lodgings, I am persuaded Grigson would be more than happy to demonstrate the proper technique for ironing shirt points."

Cam laughed outright. "And chance losing a pleasant, willing servant whose ideas on the relative importance of being in the high kick of fashion exactly march with my own? I'm not so foolish. I'll continue to leave that field to men who have the time and inclination for such pursuits, thank you, Charles."

"And the aptitude?"

"Oh, definitely," Cam agreed with mock seriousness, too well acquainted with his cousin to be misled by deceptively innocent blue eyes, but refusing to take offense at the studied insult. Having finished donning his tan gloves during the brief exchange of courtesies, he settled his hat more firmly and wished Charles a smiling good day as he started down the steps.

His state of mind unimproved by the unexpected meeting with his cousin, Mr. Charles Talbot set himself to the task of concealing this from Dawson, who had escorted his master to the entrance and as a consequence had been an unintentional eavesdropper on their conversation through the open door.

The Talbots' butler, a markedly tall individual whose extreme thinness cloaked a robust health, had been engaged on their wedding day and had long since proved himself efficient and loyal. He was devoted to the young family's interests, but also had a soft spot for Charles Talbot dating back to an episode early in his employment when Charles had assisted him during an attack of food poisoning. His dark, rather forbidding features softened now as he informed the early caller that Mrs. Talbot was in the nursery but would doubtless join him presently in the small saloon.

As he followed Dawson upstairs and entered the front reception room Charles was not quite so sanguine as the butler that Natasha would drop what she was doing to give him the opportunity to purge his conscience. She could not fail to guess the purpose of this unseasonable call. In similar circumstances many women would not scruple to let a man cool his heels for an hour if they deigned to receive him at all so after the offense. One of the things that set Natasha apart from the majority of her sex, however, was a total lack of feminine affectations designed to captivate or ensnare unwary males. Even before her marriage her dealings with both sexes had been characterized by an impartial honesty and genuine friendliness that drew people to her.

Natasha did not disappoint him, appearing in the doorway a scant five minutes after Dawson had shown him into the room, but Charles was not encouraged by her unsmiling composure as she came toward the center of the room where he stood.

"Well, Charles?"

She did not ask him to sit down, he noticed, and promptly abandoned any thought of appealing to her sense of humor. "I came to apologize for my behavior yesterday. It was not the conduct of a gentleman, I know."

She looked searchingly at his serious face. "Why did you do it, Charles? And should you not be directing this apology to Miss Elcott?"

"I will, of course, if you think it proper, but I had the impression my conduct offended you much more than it did Miss Elcott. As for your first question, I have asked myself that since I left yesterday, but I am not sure I've reached a satisfactory answer. There is something about her that invites criticism." He held up a hand as Natasha opened her mouth to protest. "It isn't my intention to be rude, but to try to explain my behavior. There is something essentially . . . unfeminine in the way the girl stares at someone as if trying to decide whether to undertake the bother of a reply, and then replies in monosyllables, leaving the burden of conversation to others. It isn't shyness," he said, anticipating her objection. "There is no blushing or shrinking or stammering. Her manner has more the appearance of an uncivil refusal to participate that is bound to set up people's backs. I am not the only one from whom it will provoke a sharp return. Not that I am trying to excuse my own rudeness, which was calculated and inexcusable, given her immaturity—I am merely attempting to explain, not very coherently, I fear, that it was in response to this strange kind of challenge in Miss Elcott's manner."

"Something you *perceived* as a challenge, you mean, Charles, and you are correct, it still doesn't excuse your rudeness. It is merely that Dinah is an unconventional girl because of her upbringing. Her mother died when she was quite young, and she was turned over to a widowed aunt with no children of her own and scant sympathy for the young. Her father, who is scarcely ever at home, and the aunt are both in their sixties. Not only did she lack the company of siblings, but because the aunt is of a reclusive habit, Dinah has had almost no social contacts with persons of her own generation or station. She has all to learn about social intercourse."

Charles had listened with intense concentration to Natasha's biographical sketch of her guest. "You have undertaken a chore that will rank with the labors of Hercules if you think to bring this backward girl into fashion. It might be possible if she had a modicum of beauty to recommend her, but—"

"I have no such ambitions and neither does Dinah, who has no interest in a social career. I merely wish her to enjoy her stay in London and to share in some of the pleasures available to a girl of her age."

"Whether she considers them pleasurable or not," Charles put in slyly, detecting a hint of Messianic fervor in his friend's tones.

The swift, all-encompassing smile full of mischief and delight that was Natasha's greatest attraction dawned and she retorted, "We won't know what things will be most enjoyable to Dinah until we widen her experience, and that is where you can be of great service to me, Charles. Cam is so tied to the Foreign Office at present that he won't have much free time to act as our escort."

"While indolent, useless, pleasure-loving Cousin Charles may be presumed to be always available for escort duty, is that it?" he demanded, quizzing her unmercifully.

"While dear, kind, obliging, artistically knowledgeable Cousin Charles, who wishes to atone for previous uncivil behavior, would be the perfect escort," Natasha retorted calmly.

"I take your point," Charles replied with a mocking bow. "Very well, consider me at your service, guidebook in hand, to conduct Miss Elcott on a tour of London's tourist attractions. Would you like to begin today?"

Natasha hesitated. "Dinah's father prefers that we should bring her appearance up to date before exposing her to social situations, so perhaps we had best set about that task first."

"Certainly, but you will not care to spend the entire day in dressmakers' establishments—Miss Elcott won't thank you for that."

"What do you mean, Charles? You heard Dinah say that her father expects her to acquire a complete wardrobe before going about town."

"Before being *seen* about town, which is not the same thing. I am willing to bet a monkey against the chance of running across any of your acquaintance in the Abbey or St. Paul's or admiring the Bank of England."

"That is true, of course, but Dinah may still prefer to begin our shopping first."

"Somehow, I doubt that shopping is a burning priority to a girl who meekly allows her aged aunt to order all her clothes sight unseen," Charles said dryly.

"Mr. Talbot is quite correct, Natasha. I would be delighted to put off our shopping until I have seen something of London . . . unless, that is, you would prefer not to chance my being seen at present?"

Two heads spun around to face the girl walking into the room carrying a wrapped parcel. Charles scowled at this fresh example of tactlessness but could not detect any shade of sarcasm in Miss Elcott's earnest words. He ran his eye over the mud-colored gown that hung loosely from bony shoulders, noting in passing that the scraped-back hair was even less becoming to her features without the softening effect of a hat brim. He reflected sourly that even with these disadvantages, Miss Elcott was more fit to be seen than heard at present.

Natasha hastened to deny any implication that she was ashamed to present her protégée to her friends before the proposed refurbishing. Her remonstrations brought Miss Elcott to a belated recognition of the effect of her words, and she had the grace to apologize. "I am so sorry, Natasha, I didn't mean that the way it came out. I only meant that I wish to fall in with your plans."

Natasha smiled at the crestfallen girl. "That's all right, Dinah. My only concern is that you not think I would treat your father's injunction lightly."

"Oh, I do not regard Papa's recommendations as commands," Dinah assured her hostess.

"Come, this is promising," said Charles, unable to resist the opening. "A girl who is prepared to disregard a parent's dictates cannot fail to charm a large segment of the male population, especially the choice spirits among the younger set."

There was a little silence while Natasha bit back an exasperated exclamation and Miss Elcott considered his words at face value before addressing a bland-faced Charles. "I can see I must always preserve the appearance of filial obedience in my conversation. Thank you, Mr. Talbot, you remind me that I have much to learn about how to get along in company."

"What is the package you are carrying, Dinah?" Natasha asked, thinking a change of topic could only benefit the situation.

Dinah handed the parcel to her hostess, saying, "It is something I have been making for you, that is, not making, precisely, but decorating. I had not unpacked everything last night and remembered it only at breakfast, so I went back to my room for it when you headed up to the nursery. Mrs. Evans told me you were here. I wasn't aware that Mr. Talbot had called until I came into the room."

"You behold in me a penitent come at this unseemly hour to apologize for any offense my conversation might have pro-

duced yesterday, Miss Elcott, and to offer my services as
guide to London's sights."

"There is no need for apology, Mr. Talbot. I found your
conversation . . . instructive."

Natasha, who had been tearing off the wrappings on the
square parcel, missed this latest skirmish. "Oh, Dinah, this is
absolutely exquisite!" she breathed, lifting a small trinket box
from its nest of paper, and turning it slowly to reveal on each
surface of the ivory-painted box an oval-shaped wreath of gold
leaves containing a minutely detailed floral painting, each one
different.

Charles raised his quizzing glass to his eye and bent forward
to examine the side nearest him, which depicted delicate vio-
lets venturing bravely from a sheltering nest of tender leaves.
"You painted this free hand."

It wasn't really a question, but Dinah looked affronted. "Of
course."

"This is beautiful work, Dinah," Natasha said, running rev-
erent fingertips over the lovingly executed rendering of the
humble daisy that graced the box's lid. "I am so pleased that
you chose to depict the local field flowers that I recall from
my childhood. I am thrilled to possess such a lovely object and
shall display it in this room for a time so others might admire
it also. Thank you so very much, Dinah."

Glancing up from his absorption in an exquisite portrait of
foxgloves, Charles made the interesting discovery that the
most reliable clue to the seemingly emotionless Miss Elcott's
state of mind was her eyes. Her demeanor was as coolly composed as ever, but her large eyes had taken on an opalescent
glow in response to Natasha's pleasure in her gift. It was a relief to know the girl was capable of some ordinary human re-
sponses, he thought as he expressed his appreciative but more
restrained approval of Miss Elcott's work. In all fairness, he
must also revise his earlier estimate of the girl's looks. She did
have one redeeming feature. It took some getting used to the
relentless and naked intelligence with which those eyes ap-
praised the world, but there was no denying that the eyes
themselves were beautiful in design and clarity, and he confessed himself amazed by the range of color that was encom-
passed in the bald description "gray."

* * *

Some five hours later the Talbot town carriage drawn by a pair of perfectly matched chestnuts wended its way back toward Portman Square. A comfortable silence enveloped the three persons within, all of whom were busy with private thoughts.

Natasha, surreptitiously flexing her toes within their fashionable half boots of Moroccan leather, resolved to search her wardrobe for more flexible footgear before embarking on another sightseeing expedition with the indefatigable Dinah. She was looking forward to changing out of the torturous items she now wore and popping up to the nursery to play with Justin before he had his supper. Her lips curved as her glance rested on her guest, who was staring out of the window, determined to miss nothing of visual interest on their route. She could not recall when last she'd seen anyone so unabashedly thrilled to visit places rich in the nation's history.

Charles had called for them after an early lunch and they had driven first to the Tower at Dinah's request. She had taken a rather ghoulish pleasure in tales of past tragedies enacted within the walled acres and shuddered deliciously at sight of the Traitors' Gate under St. Thomas's Tower which spanned the moat. Her eyes had gleamed at the colorful warders' uniforms of scarlet cloth with their abundance of gold-lace trim, but she had taken only a tepid interest in the imperial crown and the golden orb and scepter and the other coronation trappings kept in the Jewel Office. By promising her a trip to Exeter 'Change, where there was a finer menagerie, Charles had finally persuaded her to forgo a personal inspection of the wild animals kept in the Tower in favor of a visit to Westminster Abbey. Dinah had exclaimed against the entrance to this magnificent shrine being by way of the mean dwellings along Tothill Street, but she eagerly led the way up the two hundred and eighty-three steps in one of the west towers to enthuse over the glorious view of London that made the ordeal worthwhile. It was this unanticipated climb that was mainly responsible for the sorry state of her feet, thought Natasha, wishing herself at home so she could remove the wretched boots and massage her protesting members.

Charles's eyes were also on Dinah's rapt face, but his

thoughts were firmly fixed in the present. During the course of
the afternoon he'd found himself becoming intrigued by the
capacity of this odd girl to concentrate on the physical aspects
of a scene without taking in the human element. Though listening intently to any commentary from himself or the self-appointed guide who attached himself to their party in the
Abbey, she had been no more prone to comment this afternoon
than she had been in Natasha's saloon. Trailing in her wake
through every accessible corner of the vast building for more
than two hours, he'd seen her eyes glow with pleasure as she'd
stared up at the incomparable stone vaulting of King Henry
VII's chapel until aching neck muscles forcibly intervened.
She had stood mesmerized before the bronze gates to this
chapel whose design elements were comprised of the Tudor
badges. She lost awareness of her companions as persons and
looked startled when they recalled themselves to her consciousness by some remark that chanced to pierce her near-
total absorption in the beauty and history surrounding her. It
gradually dawned on Charles that Miss Elcott seemed to have
little sense of herself as a physical entity. In her enjoyment of
the artistic beauty around her she was totally unself-conscious,
caring nothing for the impressions her person or personality
might make on others.

Endowed—or cursed—by his Creator with a lively appreciation for the ridiculous, Charles would be prepared to sit back
and enjoy the effect on the more stiff-necked members of the
ton of Miss Elcott's unbridled candor were it not for the proba-
bility of unpleasant repercussions in store for Natasha. Out of
the corner of his eye he noted her contented gaze on Dinah,
well pleased with the success of the afternoon as measured by
her guest's enjoyment. An unsuspecting lamb to the slaughter,
that was Natasha. The affectionate loyalty to her friends that
was one of her most appealing qualities was going to prove a
liability in the present situation. The unconscious Miss Elcott
would need a firmer hand on the reins if they were to steer her
through the obstacle course of the Season without the kind of
incidents that provided fuel for clacking tongues.

It began to dawn on Charles that his own looked like being
the only firm hand in view. He could dismiss his cousin from
serious consideration. Cam would lend the girl his protection,

right enough, but despite his attraction for the fair sex, he was
no practiced hand with the ladies when it came to avoiding
conversational pitfalls, being much more comfortable in masculine society. Natasha would see to Miss Elcott's wardrobe,
of course, but the beautiful eyes notwithstanding, a new
wardrobe was not going to turn this peculiar creature into a
passably attractive girl.

His assessing gaze traveled between the two young women,
both isolated in private ruminations. Natasha had arrived at the
style most complimentary to her exotic coloring, sticking for
the most part to white or deep, vibrant colors and unfussy designs that skimmed her small-boned figure, accentuating her
graceful carriage and perfect proportions, but she had never
taken much interest in fashion as such. To her, shopping was
an unavoidable chore to be undertaken with all practical dis-
patch rather than an enjoyable pastime in itself. She did not
give much thought to her own looks and might not be the best
choice as adviser to an inexperienced girl. As for Miss Elcott,
though she was clearly appreciative of beauty in the abstract,
Charles would take his oath that she had no ideas or preferences when it came to a question of making the most of her
own person.

"Miss Elcott," he said to test his theory, "what is your favorite color?"

The gray eyes reluctantly quitted the passing scene and
turned to him in some confusion. "Sir?"

"I asked what your favorite color is."

"Oh." After a second's concentration, Dinah said, "All of
them."

"I meant," Charles explained patiently, "what colors do you
think best become you? What shades do you favor for your
new wardrobe?"

"I haven't the faintest idea," she said blankly, preparing to
resume her window-gazing.

"Even worse than I thought," Charles said as if to himself,
but now he had caught Natasha's attention.

"Why, Charles? Do you not agree it is advisable to maintain
an open mind until we see what is being offered this spring?"

"No, I do not. It isn't a question of a philosophical debate
where an open mind is an asset, but of selecting the best frame

to make the most of Miss Elcott's attributes, regardless of what is considered fashionable at present."

"Since I haven't any attributes," Dinah interjected in reasonable tones, "why not simply choose what is fashionable in preference to what is not?"

"That is not true, Dinah!" Natasha cried, aghast. "You—"

"It's perfectly true that you aren't pretty," Charles agreed, ruthlessly overriding Natasha's protest. "Your forehead is too high and too broad, your nose is too short, your mouth too wide and your chin too narrow, but these faults can be rendered less obvious by the right hairstyle. Also, you are not entirely without attributes." Encouraged by Dinah's unwinking interest, he listed them: "There is no fault to be found with your eyes in any respect, though their pale color will somewhat limit your choice of wardrobe colors. Your skin is beautifully clear and smooth, but your natural pallor will definitely rule out white and all strong colors from consideration. I have not been privileged to see you smile as yet, but I suspect your teeth might be another asset. Ah, yes," he added as Dinah bared her teeth in a grimace with no sign of self-consciousness. "It is always a source of satisfaction to have one's impressions confirmed."

Neither Charles nor Dinah noticed Natasha's speechless consternation at the unalloyed frankness of this analysis. Charles had the immediate satisfaction of knowing his words had fallen on fertile soil when Dinah asked him how a hairstyle could be expected to obscure the faults of nature.

"By creating the illusion that your face is closer to a perfect oval instead of the inverted triangle that it actually is. Natasha's face is heart-shaped rather than oval, but the widow's peak gives her a dramatic frame for her features, and her brow is not so high as yours, so that the width at the temple becomes an asset. Your hair is fairly thick and straight, isn't that so?"

Dinah nodded, impressed by the accuracy of his judgments.

"Does either of you have a pencil?" Charles pulled a small notebook out of an inner pocket as Dinah produced a stub of a pencil from her reticule. "Thank you." He sketched rapidly under Dinah's critical eye, first outlining a heart, an oval, and an inverted triangle, which he proceeded to embellish while an expectant hush held the fascinated ladies in check.

It was Natasha who spoke when Charles ripped the page out of his notebook and turned it toward them. "Oh, but Charles," she said, disappointment coloring her voice, "the long fringe to her eyebrows could be cut perhaps, but no one wears straight hair hanging almost to collar level. It would be most strikingly singular. Could she not still put the rest up on top of her head behind the fringe?"

"Cut this way," Dinah said, still studying the drawing, "there would be no need of nightly curl papers or pins. Nor would it take hours to dry as it does now."

"Do you *like* the idea, Dinah? You would be the only girl wearing her hair down, you know," Natasha warned, still doubtful.

"Does that worry you, Miss Elcott?"

"Not at all." Dinah's eyes interrogated Charles. "Cam told me that people consult you when decorating their houses, Mr. Talbot. I can see from the sketch that you have a good grasp of form. What do you recommend for colors and styles for me?"

"Soft, rather deep colors," Charles replied promptly. "Pale pastels will render you insipid, not to say invisible, and most bright colors will overwhelm you. Grayed blues and greens, rosy pinks, and mauve should be flattering to you, as well as champagne and perhaps a deep yellow or soft brown shade. As for styles, you cannot do better than to take Natasha as your model. She has learned that an unbroken fall of color imparts an illusion of added height, which small women seem to think desirable."

"Aunt Lavinia advised me to wear a bust improver or bosom friend, but I cannot quite like the idea of such subterfuges."

Charles preserved his countenance with aplomb while Natasha succumbed to a sudden fit of coughing. He said, "I tend to agree with you that such tactics smack of deceit, and to what point, when they will be discovered in the end anyway?"

Innocent eyes queried his. "Discovered?"

"One presumes on the wedding night, if not before."

"*Charles!*"

"Well, I do not intend to marry," Dinah, no whit discomposed, said over Natasha's exclamation, "but I am persuaded you are correct about such practices smacking of deceit."

"Dinah," Natasha said desperately, "I think we had best leave discussions of fashion for the modistes' rooms. Most gentlemen find such matters tedious."

"But my dear Natasha, surely you know it is a matter of pride to me to avoid being lumped with 'most gentlemen.' So commonplace."

"I think it is our good fortune that Mr. Talbot is willing to advise me with regard to fashion, do not you, Natasha? It will make our task much easier if we have only to select one or two designs and have gowns made up in several colors. That will leave more time for sightseeing."

This practical suggestion did not meet with quite the enthusiasm that its author might have anticipated. Natasha bit her lip and sent an indignant look toward a laughing Charles before saying gently, "I'm afraid assembling a wardrobe for a London Season is a rather time-consuming process at best, Dinah. Unfortunately, it is not just a matter of buying a few dresses for daytime and some for evening,"

"No, the well-dressed young lady making her bow to society also requires carriage dresses in which to be driven around town by the young sparks," Charles said, taking up the tale, "as well as dresses for walking and receiving callers. In addition to promenade dress, there is morning dress, garden dress, full evening dress, theater dress, opera dress, riding dress, and, of course, full court regalia. Have I left anything out?" he asked, turning from Dinah's dismayed face, showing emotion at last, to Natasha, whose gravity was being sorely tried. She turned a shoulder on him and addressed herself to the worry in her young friend's face.

"Pay no heed to Charles, Dinah, he is in a teasing humor. The clothing for a girl in her first Season is much less elaborate than that of women whose main concern it is to be always in the forefront of fashion, and your father has not indicated any desire to have you presented at court, so all that attendant fuss may be avoided. You won't have to practice curtsying in hoops."

"Natasha has neglected to mention that hats and outer wraps are as important as gowns, Miss Elcott. Though the vogue for the Kutusoff mantle and matching hat has rather gone past, you will naturally wish to acquire a Coburg bonnet, and no wardrobe would be complete without a poke bonnet or two. I predict that the Armenian toque will become the rage this Season, but you are too young to wear a turban, so in that respect you will have to gnash your teeth in helpless envy."

"Charles, will you please stop talking fustian! Don't let him fluster you, Dinah. It would be foolish to attach too much importance to the subject of fashion."

"Now, I would have said it would be impossible to attach too much importance to the subject of fashion," Charles demurred.

Dinah, looking from one to the other of her companions, experienced a little pang of loneliness at being once again outside the charmed circle, but this chill was dispelled somewhat in the next moment when Mr. Talbot apologized for his teasing and offered with careless good humor to escort Miss Elcott to see the menagerie at Exeter 'Change the following afternoon as a reward for enduring a morning of shopping and visiting dressmakers.

5

It would be tampering with the truth to intimate that Charles Talbot nearly failed to recognize the plain, colorless Miss Elcott in the impeccably turned out young lady who rose to greet him in Natasha's saloon the next afternoon, but he did stop short and grope for his quizzing glass, the better to study the combined effect of a shining, straight fall of honey-brown hair around the slender neck and a simple but beautiful dress in a muted shade between rose and pink. It crossed his mind to wonder if she had after all resorted to the subterfuge discussed the previous day but decided the improvement in her figure could be accounted for by the cleverly cut and meticulously fitted gown and a more erect posture. She was still more wiry than curvy, and the epithet "pretty" did not spring to mind on beholding Miss Elcott, but there was an arresting gamine quality to her small-boned face that projected a distinctive charm.

Charles let his gold-rimmed quizzing glass drop the length of its black ribbon and executed a pronounced bow. "My congratulations, ladies, on the rapid transformation. You look like a waif, but an elegant waif," he said to Dinah, "and elegance is more to be desired than mere commonplace prettiness. A little animation would enhance the image, but I shan't quarrel with such a delightful metamorphosis."

"I fear that liveliness is foreign to my nature, Mr. Pygmalion. You will have to be content with a flawed Galatea," Dinah said, taking back her hand, her manner retaining its customary matter-of-fact composure.

A bubbling Natasha was the more obviously elated of the two ladies at the dramatic improvement in her guest's appearance. "Is Dinah's hair not beautiful, Charles, so soft and silky, with subtle variations in color? My maid cut it for her last night, using your sketch as a guide. She had to cut it a bit shorter than the sketch in her efforts to even off the sides, but it will grow longer in a few weeks."

"No, leave it like this, just below chin length; the line of the throat is good, so why cover it?"

"Yet another attribute," Dinah murmured, naively pleased.

"We'll have to take care to limit the compliments lest Miss Elcott become so puffed up in her own conceit that she'll be impossible to live with," Charles said to Natasha in a playful and audible aside that he regretted immediately as a shadow settled over Dinah's features.

"I don't think that is very likely," she said in a soft, lifeless voice.

Natasha made a bright comment on their shopping trip that Charles, engaged in speculating about Dinah's family life, did not really take in. In the interest of helping Natasha to restore the earlier tone of mild jubilation, he asked, "Are you ladies ready for our excursion to view the wild animals?"

"Dinah is looking forward to it, Charles, but you will have to hold me excused today. Mrs. Edgerton wishes to come by to discuss some details about the party she is planning for her daughter next month."

"Perhaps you would prefer to put off the outing until Natasha can go too, Mr. Talbot?" Dinah suggested, proving there was nothing lacking in her powers of observation.

"Not at all, Miss Elcott," Charles countered swiftly, annoyed that his powers of concealment had proved less acute. "My hesitation was due to a regret that I had not known of this earlier so I might have brought my curricle. I walked here in the expectation we should be using my cousin's town coach again," he added, addressing Natasha.

"Naturally you are welcome to the carriage, Charles, but it would be no trouble to send a footman to the mews to order your curricle, unless you are pressed for time this afternoon?"

"My time is entirely at Miss Elcott's disposal this afternoon," he replied at his most urbane. "Would you like to take an open carriage, Miss Elcott? You will be able to see much more of your surroundings, and the weather is quite fine for March."

Upon Dinah's pleased agreement, this plan was carried out. Charles and Natasha indulged in their usual easy discourse in the interim, while Dinah maintained her usual silence until prodded. In less than thirty minutes Dawson brought word that Mr. Talbot's curricle had arrived. Charles helped Dinah into a modish pelisse in a deeper shade of rose than her dress, taking leave of Natasha while the younger girl placed a charming wide-brimmed bonnet on her head and tied its satin ribbons under her chin without benefit of a mirror.

"What is that?" he asked as she tucked a large pad under her arm and pronounced herself ready.

"I thought I might sketch a few of the animals, that is, of course, if you do not object, sir?"

"Of course not, Miss Elcott. Being conspicuous in a good cause holds no terror for me," Charles replied airily, and whisked her out the door while she was attempting to clarify this deliberate obscurity in her mind.

Dinah was favorably impressed with the handsome curricle with its light brown leather seat and yellow-painted wheel spokes, artlessly explaining that she had never before ridden in a sporting carriage. She eyed the small tiger holding the restive chestnut pair with frank interest but forbore to comment, to Charles's relief. In addition to cherishing an inflated opinion of the dignity of his calling and the impressiveness of his person clad in brown and yellow livery, Jem was, at best, highly intolerant of feminine foibles. He made no secret of his dislike of driving females, claiming they made the horses nervous with their squeaks and squawks. Apart from this irremediable hostility, which the tiger was at few pains to disguise, Charles had no criticism of his henchman, who was highly attuned to the horses' moods and needs.

In the event, Jem had little to complain of that afternoon. He jumped on the back after Charles assisted his passenger into the vehicle, and they set off smartly in the direction of Oxford Street. The horses were fresh and Charles, fully occupied in getting them together for the first few minutes, was vaguely grateful not to be compelled to attend to any frivolous chatter. In due course he angled his head, the better to inspect his companion's face beneath the wide-brimmed hat, and was able to satisfy himself that Miss Elcott's silence was not due to any alarms about her safety at his hands. She sat completely relaxed, gripping her sketchpad and avidly gazing upon the passing scene, her eyes darting from roadway to sidewalks to the buildings lining the way. Something, the cool little breeze, her eager interest in her surroundings, or mayhap a kind reflection from the rosy pelisse, had put some faint color in her cheeks today, and Charles was conscious that she actually did him credit at present. Having already gained a fair idea of her lack of—or perhaps disdain for—social skills, he was resigned to having the onus of maintaining a polite conversation entirely on his shoulders. His eyes lingered on the attractive pelisse.

"What feat of legerdemain did you and Natasha accomplish this morning that you are already costumed in the height of fashion, Miss Elcott?"

"It was sheer blind luck," Dinah replied, not removing her gaze from the antics of a trio of boys bowling hoops along the flagway to the annoyance of pedestrians. "Mrs. Simmons, Natasha's favorite dressmaker, had this outfit all but completed for another customer who had ordered it made up two months ago for the spring. Since then she has discovered she is increasing and has already gained too much weight to fit in the clothes. Mrs. Simmons put two of her seamstresses to work finishing the garments while we shopped for a hat and shoes."

"May I be permitted to tell you how charmingly you look in it?"

"Thank you."

The lengthy pause that ensued convinced Charles that compliments were a dead end as far as stimulating conversation went, and he sought another avenue to get Miss Elcott to pay for her outing by entertaining him. "What has impressed you most about London so far, Miss Elcott?"

"The noise, I think." This time she did look at her companion and was impelled by the lifting of his brow to elaborate on her observation. "Sometime I am going to stay awake all night to find out if the noises ever die down completely. The sounds of carriage wheels and horses' hooves striking on the cobblestones seem never to cease. Heavily laden wagons rumble and creak along the streets; church bells ring out from several directions; all kinds of street vendors hawk their wares at the top of their lungs throughout the day; the signs outside the shops squeak against their chains; the walking sticks of the men make sharp clicks on the flagstones or cobbles; dogs bark and cats yowl from alleys—" She broke off and qualified her list. "Of course, we have some of these noises in the country too, but here they go on all at the same time, creating a unique city cacophony."

"Are you longing, then, for the peacefulness of the country?"

"Oh, no. I expect in time I shall become so used to the noise that I won't even notice it, so I am trying to drink it all in now. I wish to remember what it seemed like in the beginning."

She lapsed into her trancelike state again and Charles smiled indulgently, encouraged to find the phlegmatic Miss Elcott capable of drinking in sensations even if her face revealed little of her emotional reaction to them. He confined his own conversation to an occasional identifying remark as they proceeded down Charing Cross toward the Strand. The cruel contrast between the wide streets and handsome squares of Mayfair and the mean noisome lanes leading off Charing Cross Road was too blatant to go unremarked. Dinah's eyes were wide with dismay at the brief glimpses of decaying buildings crowded together and spilling over with ragged humanity.

"There are pockets of squalor in all cities, but since the end of the war, conditions have worsened. There has long been an exodus of the unemployed poor from the country in search of a better life in the cities. The closing of mills that produced war goods has markedly exacerbated the problem," Charles explained in response to her horrified questions. "There aren't enough jobs to go around and it isn't a problem that will be solved in the near future."

"Do you say there are other sections of the city as impoverished as this area?" Dinah asked in faltering tones.

"You are very shocked, Miss Elcott. It should have occurred to me that such squalor would be unfamiliar to someone who has always lived in a rural district. I apologize for bringing you this way today."

"It is just that I am so appallingly ignorant!" Dinah said almost fiercely.

"Such knowledge is generally kept from gently bred girls, at least on a personal level."

"In the country gently bred females render assistance to the poor."

Charles compelled her glance, his customary drawling style of speech sharpening as he warned, "Do not take it into your head to play Lady Bountiful in the rookeries of London, Miss Elcott. You could not relieve an infinitesimal share of the poverty in this city by scattering largess, and you would be putting yourself in personal danger. Crime is rampant in such districts and violence is commonplace."

"I am ignorant but not stupid, Mr. Talbot," she retorted. "I apprehend that only an institutional approach could effect any considerable amelioration of widespread distress, and I am aware I shall be here for only a few short weeks."

Talk languished at that point as Dinah fell silent and Charles attended to his driving while they entered the narrow end of the Strand and proceeded in an easterly direction.

Exeter Exchange was a large building sporting a huge pair of Corinthian pilasters on the entrance facade. The menagerie was located on the first floor above a row of shops and was divided into three apartments, each costing a shilling to enter. Charles bought combination tickets admitting them to all three chambers and prepared to enjoy his companion's reactions to the exotic animals on display.

Miss Elcott did not disappoint his expectations. As in the Tower and the Abbey, the unusual girl feasted on the new experience as one starved all her life. He counted himself fortunate that hers was not a voluble nature, for Charles, though he had crafted a reputation as a sardonic wit and occasional flouter of conventional manners, did not care to figure in public as an ignorant gapeseed, even among a bunch of cits. Miss Elcott, neither knowing nor—quite probably—caring that only rustics showed themselves transported by the marvelous, permitted herself to stare to her heart's content at Mr. Polito's celebrated collection of jungle cats and exotic birds. She laughed at the antics of the monkeys in their cages surrounding the tawny lioness, and her eyes grew round at the gigantic girth of the Bengal elephant, Chunee. They grew huger yet and she clasped her hands together, hugging the pad to her chest when

Chunee possessed himself of Charles's walking stick and then obligingly returned it on command.

"You look like a five-year-old on Christmas," Charles commented smilingly.

"To someone like you it must seem childish to be so openly impressed with nature's wonders." The words were uninflected, but Charles spotted a spark of resentment in luminous gray eyes.

"Not at all. I came here with Byron a few years ago and watched him enjoy himself like any schoolboy. He was quite taken with Chunee's dignity and presence—said he wished he was his butler."

"Byron? Do you mean Lord Byron, the scandalous poet?" Her mouth as well as her eyes rounded this time and there was a decided squeak to her voice.

"The very same."

"I am acquainted with someone who actually knows Lord Byron."

Charles laughed at her awed satisfaction. "Are you another sighing female enraptured by the fellow's verses?"

"I've never read any of his poetry. Aunt Lavinia would not permit it, and the only novel I've ever read was one from the Minerva Press that one of my governesses left behind."

"Well, you are out from under Aunt Lavinia's thumb now, and with all London's lending libraries and booksellers at your fingertips, you may speedily remedy the gaps in your education," Charles said in a rallying voice to cover the pity aroused in his breast by this additional glimpse into Dinah Elcott's barren existence in Devonshire. "What kind of literature did your aunt sanction, by the way?"

"Sermons mostly and improving tracts and some poetry."

"Shakespeare?"

"Some of his plays, but I found all his works in Papa's library and read them in secret."

"Between the Bible and Shakespeare you cannot have emerged entirely ignorant of human nature. Would it be a fair assumption to say that by and large your filial obedience derived less from a dutiful nature than a lack of opportunity to disobey?"

She subjected this theorem to dispassionate consideration

and replied in the affirmative, concluding gloomily, "I fear I must possess very few natural virtues, despite the improving tracts."

"Don't put yourself in a tweak about it," Charles advised. "Whether or not they can be brought to admit it, most people would find saints utterly boring company."

"Natasha isn't boring, and I think she must be very nearly a saint! She is so kind-hearted and generous and loving, but she seems to have a wondrous capacity for enjoyment too."

"Natasha is a rarity, little one, one of nature's masterpieces. Have you gazed your fill in this place? Would you like to leave before the smell, which I have heroically endeavored to ignore, overcomes us?"

"Would you mind very much if I remained for a while to sketch some of these animals?" Dinah asked diffidently. "Perhaps you have an errand or two you wish to accomplish? You could return for me later."

"My dear Miss Elcott, your wits must have gone wandering if you believe a gentleman can go merrily off about personal business, leaving a lady stranded in a public hall, without incurring the deserved censure of society, not to mention betraying her guardian's trust. I'll give you twenty minutes to sketch, not a second more."

Any natural resentment Dinah might have felt at this cold setdown was submerged in the desire to accomplish what she could in the grace period allowed. She left his side without replying and was soon absorbed in making rapid sketches of the various denizens of the menagerie. She did not glance once in her escort's direction until his hand on her arm signaling that time was up caused her to start in surprise. She blinked at him owlishly for a second before returning to the present, but made no objection when he indicated that they should be leaving.

Charles could not recall another instance when his ostensible companion had been so utterly unaware of his existence before and decided it was a rather lowering experience. For his part, he had been surprised to discover his attention had scarcely stirred from the girl drawing with a pointed concentration that would not disgrace a dedicated scientist. He had wandered about the rooms in her wake, the better to observe her from all sides. By now he could have imitated her grip on the pencil when she made a decisive downward stroke, and he knew, as she perhaps did not, that she took one side of her bottom lip between her teeth when she was correcting a line.

Dinah would have closed her sketchpad and ended the artistic interval without further delay, but Charles, who had kept his distance out of respect for her concentration, was exceedingly curious to see the results of it and asked bluntly, "May I see your work?" holding out a hand for the pad. She relinquished it without demur, though he sensed her dislike of giving her work over to his evaluation.

There were several pages of rapidly executed sketches, some no more than a few lines suggesting the animal's movements, while others developed the muscular involvement more thoroughly and suggested the textures of fur or feathers or skin. One, a drawing of a sleeping tiger, was detailed enough to be called a portrait.

"You are a competent draftsman and have the skill to get down the essentials of a pose with accuracy in a short time, an accomplishment of which few amateur artists can boast."

"Thank you, sir," Dinah said, indulging in no maidenly disclaimers, "but I still find action drawing a challenging task. I am looking forward to enrolling in a life class while I am here this spring—perhaps at the Royal Academy."

They were descending the staircase at this juncture and Charles stopped abruptly, spearing her eyes with a disbelieving look. "Do not be absurd," he said flatly. "You cannot enroll in a life-drawing class. The Academy does not accept females."

"But of course they do!"

"Not in life classes, I assure you, Miss Elcott."

"You're blocking the passage," complained a hefty, red-faced citizen with his hand on the arm of a rouged and powdered redhead who stared brazenly at Charles.

Charles pulled an unresisting Dinah nearer to the wall, allowing the others to get by. Intent on digesting her escort's unwelcome pronouncement, she had not even glanced at the complainers. Her narrowed eyes searched his face, which had closed up against her. At last she said distinctly, "Then I must find another studio that will accept me as a pupil."

He took her elbow and led her down the stairs. "My dear

Miss Elcott, if, as seems likely, we are going to quarrel every time we meet, I really cannot continue to call you Miss Elcott. With your permission, it had better be Dinah." He laughed at her uninterested shrug. "I shall attempt to explain in words of one syllable that a young lady of quality does not enroll in art classes patronized by the general public. It simply is not done."

They had reached the pavement by now. As Charles looked about him for his tiger, who would have been tooling the curricle around the area to keep the horses from getting cold, Dinah marshaled her arguments, finally saying, "My father would have told me if it were a breach of good taste for a woman like me to become an artist."

"A . . . girl like you may be regarded as an artist among her friends; it is not beyond the realm of possibility that she may have her work accepted for exhibition by the Royal Academy. She does not, however, enroll in life classes."

"My father promised me I might study art while I am in London; it was the sole reason I agreed to make my come-out," she said with a stubborn jut to her pointed chin.

"There is nothing to stop you from engaging the services of a drawing master. I'll even undertake to find one for you."

"That won't do. I need models to pose for me so I may better learn how to paint the human body. You must acknowledge that this is absolutely basic to my preparation."

"What you are contemplating would make you an object of gossip. High sticklers would even cut your acquaintance and this would reflect on Natasha, which anyone with a scrap of gratitude would acknowledge to be a poor return for her hospitality."

"Why must anyone know? I should not speak of it in company," Dinah declared, looking both mulish and desperate.

"Here is Jem with the curricle. We will not continue this argument in front of a servant, if you please."

Dinah shut her mouth like a trap and allowed him to help her into the curricle. The drive back to Portman Square was saved from complete silence by a judiciously spaced series of pleasant observations on Charles's part that happily did not call for comments from his passenger. A stranger might construe Dinah's silence as mere sulking, but after only a few days' acquaintance, Charles had learned enough about this girl to acquit her of such childish retaliation. It was unhappiness, not a desire to punish him, that kept her silent. On the other hand, he was not so simple-minded as to believe that she had accepted defeat. Despite what seemed to have been a lifetime of having her preferences ignored or forbidden, Miss Dinah Elcott had not emerged as a meek, pliable creature. She might have no true conception of herself as a personality, having accepted her elders' estimation of her qualities up to the present, but she knew what she wanted and cared nothing that public opinion frowned on her choice. She would be evolving possibilities with that quick intellect, looking for ways to circumvent this latest stumbling block to treading her chosen path. She had annoyed him thoroughly, but he conceded a grudging admiration for her tenacity. Though she would not be inclined to believe his sincerity, he would like to see her achieve her desire. It was refreshing to meet someone, especially a female, with a strong idea of what she wished to do with her life.

Knowing how much she resented what she must see as his interference and not wishing to unduly prolong her purgatory, Charles left Dinah at the front door of his cousin's house. She uttered the polite formulas of thanks in a toneless voice, her face once more empty of all expression. In contrast, he favored her with his most guileless smile and graceful bow in taking his leave. His duty done, he went away with a feeling of relief to find some cheerful masculine company.

If Dinah's somewhat vague comments on her outing left Natasha more curious than pleased, she was too tactful to cross-question her guest. She praised the animal sketches and straightaway volunteered to speak to Charles about locating a school or studio where Dinah might pursue her artistic studies. Dinah, reluctant to wound her hostess by seeming to criticize her cousin, managed a weak smile and kept her own counsel.

Natasha was unable to fullfil her intention in the next few days because Charles did not call at Portman Square. The two women, embroiled in the time-consuming process of assembling a complete wardrobe, could not be said to have missed his company. They spent hours each day traversing the shop-lined streets that ran between Piccadilly and Oxford in search of the necessary accessories to complement the gowns and outerwear being currently made up in Mrs. Simpson's workshop. Though basically uninterested in personal adornment, Dinah was not proof against the sheer multiplicity of decorative items for sale, ranging from elaborate hair ornaments of feathers, ribbons, artificial flowers, or sequined lace, to bejeweled shoe buckles made of paste. She went about in a constant state of wonder during those early days of discovery. Natasha, intent on matching cloth swatches in choosing gloves or ribbons, would ask Dinah's opinion only to find herself talking to the air or to a perfect stranger, Dinah having been lured away from her side by some eye-catching display of merchandise. The younger girl was generally so ready to defer to her hostess in the selection of clothing that Natasha alternated between worrying that she was becoming too bossy and despairing at Dinah's lack of real interest in her appearance. The only item they bought in those first days over which she exhibited eager enthusiasm was an ivory fan whose sticks had been delicately painted to represent a scene from a Greek myth. It was staggeringly expensive, but since Dinah had no need to economize, Natasha swallowed her instinctive protest, happy to see the girl exhibit genuine delight in some purchase.

Dinah's unquestioning acceptance of the large sum of money given her by Sir Leonard had partially prepared Natasha for the subsequent discovery that her young protégée had precious little conception of the value of money or the economic aspects of daily living. Never having had the spending of any funds prior to her visit to the capital, she could not estimate the cost of even the most basic necessities, or recognize when a merchant was attempting to overcharge for his wares. After their first shopping trip, Natasha decided it was crucial to educate her charge before turning her loose in London. She was grateful that she had inherited her mother's practical nature and her paternal grandmother's financial acumen. This shrewd lady had encouraged her granddaughter to invest her inheritance and keep abreast of the financial doings in the City. Both ladies would have been highly indignant that neither Dinah's father nor her aunt had thought it incumbent upon themselves to teach the girl the basic practicalities of life. Natasha could not have reconciled it with her conscience to leave the girl in the sort of ignorance that prolonged the dependency natural to childhood into a state of arrested development that was all too common among young women and, in her view, much to be deplored. Fortunately, Dinah possessed a retentive memory and accepted what Natasha told her with an eager gratitude that did not permit any awkwardness to develop between them.

Dinah settled easily into the Talbot household. It took a day or two of observation to discern a pattern to their lives. Natasha rose early enough to breakfast with Cam before he went off to the Foreign Office most days. She then visited the nursery for an hour or so and conferred with her staff before dressing for their shopping trips. The women lunched together and separated for a while if there were no plans for the afternoon. If they were alone for tea, Mrs. Evans brought Justin down to the saloon. When Cam had no evening apointment the three dined together.

It had been obvious to Dinah from the first that the couple derived great pleasure from each other's company. Conscious of being unnecessary to their happiness, no matter how kindly welcomed, she had taken to delaying her appearance in the breakfast parlor until about the time of Cam's departure in order to give her hosts some private time at the beginning of the day. A little thought devoted to the problem of effacing herself occasionally after dinner produced nothing more inspired than an offer to play the pianoforte or a pretense of having letters to write. It was a genuine delight to learn that she could partially repay Natasha's kindness by playing the music for the ballet practice that, along with sessions of stretching exercises, made up part of her hostess's weekly routine.

By the end of her first week in London, Dinah was happier than she would ever have believed on the fateful day her father had announced his decision to send her off to live among strangers. Though vaguely aware that, apart from a brief introduction to a flint-eyed matron of Natasha's acquaintance whom they had encountered on New Bond Street one morning, she had not so far been exposed to anything resembling "society," Dinah had all but forgotten her recent misgivings about making even a modest come-out. She was reveling in the sights, smells, and sounds of London and thriving in the atmosphere of warmth and contentment to be found in the Talbots' house in Portman Square. For the moment, even the problem of finding a studio or school in which to pursue her art studies had receded to some dim recess of her mind, pushed there by the novel pleasures of her present routine and her quiet contentment in Natasha's company.

6

Silky black lashes lifted, revealing bright green eyes in which speculation dwelled. Set in a satin-skinned face of cherubic cast, those eyes were decidedly unangelic as they shifted from the plate of tea cakes on the table, enticingly at eye level, to the young woman on the sofa, busily sketching away, her attention narrowly focused on her moving fingers. One dimpled little fist extended toward the plate.

"Justin," Dinah warned, "Mama said no more cakes."

The chubby hand retreated.

"That's a good boy," Dinah murmured, smiling at the toddler, who did not appear to be gratified by her praise, if the pouting position of his rosy lips was a true indication of his feelings. She went back to her sketching, watched unwaveringly by the child for a moment before he darted out a hand, seized a cake, and crammed it into his mouth.

Dinah looked up in time to witness the last stage of this lightning-swift operation. "Justin, you little demon, you are incorrigible!"

Green eyes glittered in triumph, but the little mouth was too full to attempt a defense.

Dinah laid aside her tools and swooped on the still-munching infant. "You are a very naughty boy," she declared, spoiling the effect of her stern words by lifting the miscreant over her head before enfolding him, squealing with delight, in a whirling embrace.

"Yes indeed, it is obvious that you'll make a fine disciplinarian," said a drawling voice from the doorway.

The girl in the center of the saloon whirled to a halt and two pairs of equally assessing eyes marked Charles Talbot's sauntering approach. A sudden insight had Charles idly reflecting that he would not care to tell lies in the presence of either observer.

At sight of the visitor, Justin had begun squirming to be put down. Now he broke away from an obediently bending Dinah to lurch toward Charles. This prudent gentleman put a hand on top of the toddler's head to hold him off while he put up his quizzing glass to study the sticky little fingers with an expression of distaste. He glanced fleetingly at the young woman.

"I never cease to marvel at the perverse and unerring instinct shared by infants and cats that leads them to select those persons who will least appreciate the honor upon whom to lavish their suspect affections."

"Chars, Chars, throw me. Throw me, pease," Justin demanded, his arms upraised in a peremptory gesture.

Dinah, who had bristled visibly at Charles's words, was disconcerted to have him thrust a stack of books into her hands so that he could scoop up the insistent child, whom he proceeded to toss high in the air. Her gasp of fright was lost in Justin's squeals as he was deftly caught and set on his feet once more.

"Again, Chars, again," Justin implored, but his cousin was unmoved by this supplication.

"The allotment is one toss, brat, as you very well know, so you may cease your shrill importuning. Go play with your ball; I wish to talk to Dinah."

To Dinah's astonishment the determined toddler subsided without further protest and bent over to retrieve a red ball that had rolled under the tea table.

"How on earth did you get him to mind you so easily?" she asked, much impressed.

Charles looked up from resettling his shirt cuffs at the proper distance from his coat sleeves. "There's no trick to it," he said dismissively. "He knows I mean what I say. Shall we sit?"

"Yes, of course." She seated herself down on the nearest chair.

"Where is Natasha?" Charles asked, taking the chair beside her.

"She was needed in the kitchen."

When nothing followed this short reply, Charles's left eyebrow arched above its fellow. "Still annoyed with me?" he asked in silky tones.

"I am not annoyed with you," Dinah replied, giving him a cool look.

"Then why haven't you offered me any tea?"

"It's cold by now, but I'll ring for more if you wish some." Dinah made a movement to rise and her eyes dropped to the books in her hands. She held them out to him. "Here are your books."

He waved her back into her chair. "I don't care for any tea, thank you, and the books are a gift for you."

"For me?" She glanced down in some confusion and picked up the top book. *"Childe Harold's Pilgrimage."*

"Yes, these are all Byron's published works to fill up one of those gaps in your education that we were discussing the other day."

"How very kind of you, Charles. I . . . I am overwhelmed." She looked it, more at a loss than he had ever seen her.

"Is . . . is it permitted for me to accept such a magnificent gift?" she asked haltingly.

Had no one ever bothered to teach her the things all females seemed to know? It was almost as if she'd been born last week when she arrived in town. "Impersonal gifts like books, music, and flowers are perfectly unexceptionable; indeed, I venture to predict you will shortly be inundated with such tokens by would-be swains." Charles spoke in an offhand manner to assuage her embarrassment, but he was less displeased than he pretended to have the distraction of Justin's ball landing flush in his lap at that moment. He was sternly impressing upon the unrepentant toddler the inadvisability of throwing balls in his mother's drawing room when the mother in question came into the room, with Mrs. Evans a step behind.

Natasha took charge of the situation, bustling her protesting offspring and the offending ball into the arms of his nurse after a quick kiss to soften the deserved scolding.

"Lately he cannot bear to be parted from that wretched ball, and sooner or later the temptation to hurl it overcomes his control and all my dire warnings," she said with a grin as she flopped into a chair. "Dawson told me you were here, Charles. I've ordered sherry for you and another pot of tea. I need it after a hectic session negotiating peace between the cook and her minions."

"It's never more than a temporary cessation of hostilities at best. Why do you put up with that woman's histrionics?" Charles asked.

"Because she has an inspired touch with sauces and Cam likes her way with his favorite beef dishes."

"I wonder how much longer my cousin would continue to relish her beef if he were the one who had to deal with her tantrums."

"The question doesn't arise," Natasha said serenely. "He has me to oversee his domestic concerns. It seems ages since we saw you last, Charles."

Dinah looked from Natasha's smiling face to Charles's quizzical one, wondering if there was a hint of challenge in her hostess's mild comment.

"How gratifying to know one's absence is remarked," he drawled. "Actually, I have been busy on your behalf these past few days, or, more precisely, on Dinah's behalf." He paused dramatically to assure himself that both women were hanging on his words. "I've been all over town seeking a competent artist with an adequate studio who would be willing to accept Dinah as a pupil for a few weeks." Reading the anxious question in wide gray eyes, he said, "Martin Crossman, who has had pictures accepted by the Royal Academy the last three years, has agreed to work with you two mornings each week if he feels you show promise. He will provide a model, who will *not*, however, disrobe completely. You will have to be satisfied with this, Dinah, or risk possible unpleasant speculation that might involve Natasha and Cam."

"Oh, I will!" Dinah cried with shining eyes, her hands clasped together in front of her breast. "I was beginning to despair that my hopes of furthering my training this spring would come to anything. At the very least, Mr. Crossman will be able to teach me about mixing oils and painting techniques with oils. Thank you, Charles. This is wonderful of you. I am greatly in your debt."

"One more point." He held up his hand, cutting off Dinah's fervent thanks as he addressed Natasha. "I am persuaded Dinah should have someone with her during these sessions for propriety's sake, but it certainly need not be yourself. Just some respectable woman to accompany her to the studio."

"Hmmn," Natasha said with a thoughtful frown that gave way to a chortle of pure mischief. "I have the perfect solution. Mrs. Evans may accompany Dinah to Mr. Crossman's studio and I shall have Justin all to myself for a few hours while they are away."

"A sacrifice indeed. I hope you are properly grateful, Dinah," Charles said, his expression solemn, "at the lengths to which Natasha is prepared to go to accommodate your passion to become an artist."

"Charles, you horrid wretch! I'll have you know it is not a *sacrifice* to spend time with my child!"

Charles looked back at two indignant faces, his own at its most innocent. "This strange affinity females have for the infantry is a phenomenon that defies all logic," he replied, shaking his head in pretended perplexity. "In their early, un-civilized state, children possess no qualities that might recommend them to persons of even the most elementary level of discrimination."

"I shall remind you of this conversation when you have a child of your own one day," Natasha promised. "And now, Charles, if you will turn your attention to another problem. Dinah does not know how to dance."

"Hire a dancing master," he said promptly.

"I mean to, of course, but it would be a wonderful boost to her confidence if you were to practice with her on occasion after she has mastered the steps. She would be less inclined to be nervous when she attends her first dance."

"It would naturally give me a great deal of pleasure to oblige you both, but I fear I shall be rather engrossed with some personal affairs in the immediate future. Fortunately, my cousin is right at hand to perform this little service." Turning to Dinah with a brilliant smile, he added, "All of Wellington's officers are exemplary performers in the terpsichorean art. You will find Cam's performance vastly superior to my poor efforts."

"I'm sure I shall," Dinah said with a studied innocence that caused Natasha to pull in her lower lip as she observed Charles's narrowed glance.

"I hope you will not be too busy to accompany us to the opera one night this coming week, Charles?" she said hurriedly. "The first of Dinah's new gowns will be ready in a day or two, and it has been weeks since Cam and I have been anywhere."

Charles accepted this invitation with a graceful little speech and took his departure after arranging to conduct Dinah and Mrs. Evans to Martin Crossman's studio the following morning.

The next few days were the most wonderful of Dinah's life. The following day found her all ready, bonnet carelessly tied and portfolio in gloved hand, when Charles's knock penetrated the hall. Natasha's sympathy for her guest's anxious anticipation as Dinah merely toyed with her food at breakfast had led her to go directly from there to the nursery to chivvy Mrs. Evans forthwith into her outer clothing. She had smiled and signified her agreement with all the nurse's last-minute instructions and shooed that good woman downstairs to attend the impatient artist, with the result that Charles had no sooner put one foot over the threshold when he was joined by the two ladies and promptly steered toward the awaiting carriage.

At first glance, Mr. Crossman was rather a disappointment, being short of stature, thin to the point of attenuation, stooped and physically negligible. A fringe of graying rust-colored hair sparsely ringed his bald dome, his lashless brown eyes were enlarged behind a pair of spectacles that he habitually shoved back up to the bridge of his sharp nose with the middle finger of one paint-smeared hand, and his chin receded into a scrawny neck made memorable by a large Adam's apple. His voice was soft and cultured and his manner when he acknowledged Charles's introductions was absent-minded in the extreme.

"Oh, dear me, yes, I do recall that you were to bring the young lady here today, Mr. Talbot, but I fear I became engrossed in a problem and let it slip my mind. My apologies, ladies, for not being in better state to receive you." He had set down his palette at their entrance and was now wiping his fingers with an incredibly filthy rag as he bowed to them in turn. Mrs. Evans nodded and smiled politely, her eyes returning to the rag, but Dinah put out her hand, which was taken in a surprisingly strong clasp while his mild, magnified eyes ran over her face briefly.

As Mr. Crossman looked about him vaguely for a chair for Mrs. Evans, gratefully accepting that lady's practical offer to remove the pile of books and canvases from a wooden arm chair in a corner of the studio, Dinah seized the opportunity to make her own survey of the untidy room. Excitement welled up in her anew as she made the reassuring discovery that Mr. Crossman's paintings possessed all the strength and vitality his person lacked. That the studio itself was commodious and well lighted she appreciated on a lower level of consciousness. It was the paintings and drawings, finished or fragmental, that were hung or stacked against the walls that made an impact on her. Her eyes skimmed the few landscapes to linger on paintings replete with colorful, dynamic figures fairly breathing life. She had stepped forward to study the brushwork of a painting depicting a military skirmish between cavalry troops when the artist's diffident voice sounded in her ear.

"If I might look through your portfolio, Miss—er?"

"Elcott," Dinah said, flushing a little as she handed over her work for professional judgment.

Her heart was hammering against her rib cage and she felt light-headed, a most unpleasant combination that it was taking all her willpower to combat as she stood in tight-faced silence while Mr. Crossman examined the contents of the portfolio with agonizing deliberation. Charles was taking advantage of proximity to look over the artist's shoulder, but when he glanced at Dinah about midway through the material his eyes widened with concern at her stark pallor. There being no chair within reach, he flung an arm around her waist and hauled her up against his body, holding her firmly upright until he felt that she had conquered her faintness. She made no sound at all, and he did not look at her again, discreetly removing his arm when Mr. Crossman slipped the last drawing back into the portfolio and cleared his throat.

"Well, Miss—er, I can see that you have a delicate and meticulous style of drawing for the botanical studies and a fairly economical technique in sketching from life, but I believe I might help you to achieve greater confidence and accu racy in your rendering of the human body by setting you to work drawing my models under varying time constraints. Is that what you would like?"

Dinah was assuring him that nothing would make her happier when a knock on the door signaled the arrival of Mr. Crossman's current model. This was a tall, comely young woman built along heroic lines, who looked so unnerved at the sight of Mr. Talbot that he hastened to explain that he would be leaving momentarily, lest she fly away herself as she seemed poised to do. After settling with the artist the hour the Talbot carriage should return for Dinah and Mrs. Evans, Charles departed in the happy certainty that his presence was neither required nor desired by those he left behind. Dinah, he had no hesitation in predicting, would already have forgotten his existence before the door closed behind him.

By the end of the second session in Mr. Crossman's studio, Dinah felt the discipline of having a set amount of time to capture each pose had gone a long way toward curing her tendency to get bogged down in detail and miss some of the vital lines of movement in the body. Her confidence in her abilities was soaring and she was reveling in the experience of working with a live model and alongside a talented artist and teacher. Whenever she had an hour to spare, she retired to paint in oils on her own in the room Natasha had equipped for her use.

Life had suddenly become almost too marvelous to describe in her brief, hurried letters to her father and her aunt in Devon. The quest for a modish wardrobe in which to meet the cream of society was nearly completed in its essentials. The dancing lessons with Monsieur Bruneau had begun, and if these exercises were more laborious and demanding and less intrinsically pleasurable than painting, this opinion was something Dinah kept to herself. Not for the world would she have Natasha think her ungrateful for all the care and attention her generous nature heaped on one who was little more than an importunate stranger.

The delivery from the workroom of Natasha's dressmaker of a lovely aquamarine silk evening dress, its simple lines embellished by nothing more than a triple flounce of its own fabric at the hem and a narrow velvet ribbon of a slightly darker shade tied around the high waist, signaled the advent of the

second stage of Dinah's come-out. Natasha had accepted very
few invitations during the first fortnight of Dinah's stay, disliking to leave her guest home alone despite Dinah's insistence
that she was perfectly content with Lord Byron's works for
company. There was a tacit understanding between them that
the Season would begin with the anticipated evening at the
opera.

Natasha dressed early that evening and went to Dinah's
room to supervise Sally, the young housemaid newly raised to
the position of dresser to Miss Elcott, who was as unaccustomed to commanding such services as the maid was to supplying them. Happily, Dinah's unconventional hairstyle
required no more than the application of a brush to keep its
silky simplicity intact. After a short conference with Sally,
Natasha demonstrated how to apply a hint of rouge to enliven
Dinah's pale complexion. Fortunately, her lashes were several
shades darker than her hair and long enough to flatter the light
eyes they framed. Her brows were irremediably straight, but
some judicious plucking had made them less heavy-looking.
Natasha was satisfied that they had done all within the
province of art and the limits of modesty to enhance her docile
friend's appearance.

Dinah's father had sent her to London with all her mother's
jewelry, stressing that she should seek Natasha's advice on
what was suitable for a girl in her first Season. Natasha had inherited her Russian grandmother's fabulous collection of jewels, and the two young women had spent an enjoyable evening
examining every item they owned. Though alive to the intrinsic beauty of the glowing stones and admiring the exquisite
craftsmanship of many of the settings, Dinah was not much interested in jewelry as personal adornment. It was no sacrifice,
therefore, to have to eschew her mother's sapphire set and all
the intricate hair ornaments, which would have been considered too old for her even had she dressed her hair on top of her
head in the prevailing fashion. As it was, her simple straight
style did not lend itself to any kind of ornamentation and had
the added advantage, in Dinah's view, of rendering earrings
unnecessary since they could not be seen unless she shook her
head violently. She spurned her mother's rings, donned the
single strand of pearls Natasha had selected for her, and al-

lowed the delighted Sally to clasp a pretty gold bracelet about
one slender wrist, declaring in cheerful accents that between
them her helpers had come as close to making a silk purse out
of a sow's ear as was humanly possible. This remark, delivered with a perfectly straight face, caused Natasha a moment's
unrest, but she did not wish to add to her guest's nervous
qualms by seeming to criticize her conversation, especially
when it was generally as painful as pulling teeth to drag any
conversation from Dinah in company.

Cameron Talbot and his cousin, both exhibiting a sober
magnificence in black and white evening dress, awaited the
ladies in the entrance hall as they descended the staircase.
Natasha was slightly ahead, sparkling in unrelieved white,
which set off her rich coloring and provided a simple background for the ornate ruby necklace and earrings that had
made a number of women from Vienna to London gnash their
teeth in envy. Her white gown was also an excellent foil for
Dinah's lovely aquamarine costume.

"Very nice indeed," Cam said, smiling at both women.
"Well worth waiting for." He moved forward to take his wife's
cloak, draping it over her shoulders.

Charles, about to perform the same service for Dinah, said
accusingly, "You are wearing rouge."

She blinked at him. "Natasha said no one would notice."

"Natasha was mistaken, but I suppose it does give some life
to your face," he conceded.

"My cousin is noted for his address," Cam assured Dinah
gravely.

She almost smiled. "I have come to expect the truth from
Charles."

"Even the unpalatable truth?"

"Especially the unpalatable truth," she said, adopting his
gravity.

Natasha chuckled and Charles grumbled, "You are in danger of getting above yourself, my girl. Do not clutch your
cloak about you in that awkward manner; you'll have it a mass
of wrinkles before we even arrive."

As Dinah obediently relaxed her grip and smoothed her
hand down the slightly crushed folds of the silk cloak that
matched her gown, Cam's eyes sought his wife's in amused

disbelief at his supercilious cousin's assumption of even this negligible degree of concern for the actions of another human being. Of course, Charles detested anything he regarded as aesthetic abuse, and the shimmering aqua silk was quite lovely. Unsightly creases in it would no doubt offend his artistic sensibilities.

The drive to the King's Theatre in the Haymarket was enlivened by Natasha's bright chatter as she filled Charles in on their activities since last they'd met and expressed her anticipated delight in the evening's entertainment. "It has been simply ages since we've been to the opera; in fact, Cam and I have been in grave danger of becoming totally sedentary of late."

"The mind absolutely balks at conjuring up a vision of a totally or even partially sedentary Natasha," Charles said in musing tones.

Dinah and Cam laughed, but Natasha wrinkled her pert nose at him and went on undeterred. "You'll love the opera, Dinah. The spectacle alone is worth coming for, even without Mozart's music."

Some of Natasha's simmering excitement seeped into Dinah, whose senses were on tiptoe by the time they merged with the crowd of humanity entering the theater. Never in her life had she seen so many people in one place, nor such richly dressed people. Though white predominated, the ladies' gowns displayed every color in the spectrum, nestling like woodland flowers among the gentlemen's darker garb. Their jewels winked and flashed in the lights from hundreds of candles. A number of elaborate headdresses, some of them towering confections topped off by ostrich plumes, drew Dinah's fascinated gaze as their party made its way to the Talbots' box in the second tier.

Dinah's companions talked quietly among themselves as they settled into their chairs, leaving her free to look her fill around the handsome theater with its painted-cloud ceiling and carved lion and unicorn emblem over the stage area. An indulgent communal delicacy acknowledged that she was lost to them until the divertissement came on after the first act and people began to stir from their places.

Natasha laid a gentle hand on her guest's arm and Dinah

started, her glowing eyes still full of enchantment for another moment. "Are you enjoying the performance?"

"Oh, yes . . . I never dreamed . . ." Dinah stopped, bereft of words that could attempt to convey the sense of magic she was experiencing. She spread her hands in a helpless gesture.

"*Le Nozze di Figaro* is considered Mozart's finest work, but *Don Giovanni* is now in rehearsal. We'll come again when that goes on," Natasha promised.

A knock on the door of their box brought the first of many visitors desirous of paying their compliments to Natasha that evening and curious to learn the identity of the stranger. These gentlemen, varying from youths seeking a smile and a kind word from the lovely Mrs. Talbot, to colleagues of her husband whose motives were not too different underneath the trappings of protocol, were presented to Dinah in turn. Each was greeted with a direct, unsmiling look from clear gray eyes and a polite acknowledgment in a soft, low voice. Direct questions were answered in an economical fashion, but Miss Elcott volunteered no comments or opinions. Anyone glancing in her direction after a few moments of general discussion would have received ample evidence of Miss Elcott's absence of mind in the faraway expression in those eyes. By the time the ballet, a new production of *Psyche*, came on, Natasha, fearing to call more attention to Dinah's deplorable mental vacancy, had abandoned her discreet efforts to include the girl in the conversations that developed. When the last visitor left the box, she sighed inwardly, resigned to the necessity of having a frank talk with her guest on the delicate subject of her social duty, but tomorrow would be soon enough for lectures. Despite a mild exasperation, Natasha was sympathetic to the spell the beauty of the music and the production had cast over the young girl. It was the kind of magic that could never be quite duplicated by succeeding experiences and she would not dream of tarnishing the memory for Dinah.

Charles Talbot was untroubled by such scruples. Like his cousin he had paid some brief duty visits during the intervals, but he had seen quite enough to form a poor opinion of Dinah Elcott's manners. "Miss Elcott," he began, about to give voice to this opinion while they waited outside the theater for the carriage to pull up in the line.

Natasha, divining his intention, said, "No, Charles," giving him a straight look.

Dinah turned a still-dreamy gaze on Charles. "Did you speak, sir?"

Charles pulled his eyes from Natasha's and raked the younger girl with an impatient glance. "A brief observation of no consequence," he said shortly.

Dinah smiled vaguely and returned to her own thoughts.

Cam, as oblivious as Dinah to any undercurrents, had spotted his carriage now, and he shepherded his party toward the waiting vehicle. Opinions and snippets of news were exchanged by the other three on the drive back to Portman Square, but Dinah contributed nothing. She was in a state of sublime contentment that was not even shaken by Charles's censorious looks, since she remained happily insensible of them.

7

A monotonous humming that occasionally resembled Susanna's second-act song to Figaro was the only sound in the small room where Dinah sat before her easel painting. On a table placed in the light from the long window stood a green glass bowl full of fruit, a scrolled pewter tankard, a small china ornament, and a convoluted brass candlestick minus the candle. A glance over the artist's shoulder would confirm that this odd assortment formed the subject of her work. Though the composition of the disparate items did not pretend to true aesthetic harmony, Dinah did not allow this to trouble her. She was happily intent on developing her skills at handling oil paints, which at this point meant trying to reproduce as many different textural surfaces as she could find among portable household items of painterly interest.

The humming stilled for an instant while Dinah squinted fiercely at the candlestick, trying to reduce its gleaming surfaces to areas of separate color. She reached for a bit more king's yellow and lightened her mix, stroking it into the canvas with tentative motions that quickly became more confident. That was what had been needed. The lines in her forehead behind a gap in her fringe smoothed out and she resumed her humming as she extended her brush toward the smear of umber on her palette.

At that moment the artist's perfect contentment was shattered by the entrance of her abigail, and her frown returned as she glared at the perpetrator of the unwelcome interruption.

"I . . . I beg your pardon, Miss Elcott. I did knock, but you must not 'ave heard me," Sally said meekly. "I 'eard 'umming, so I knew you was in 'ere. Mrs. Talbot sent me to tell you there are visitors in the red saloon and to 'elp you get ready."

Her nose wrinkled at the strong odor of turpentine that greeted her and her eyes assessed Dinah's paint-splattered smock and hands.

Dinah clamped her lips together to prevent rising frustration at having her pleasure curtailed from escaping in the form of ungrateful and injudicious utterances. She deposited her brushes in the turpentine solution without a word, avoiding the temptation to look at the canvas again, and turned to Sally, who rose nobly to the occasion, having had the foresight to provide herself with a clean washcloth and towel, as well as a hairbrush. There were no mirrors in the studio, but this lack did not occur to Dinah, who submitted to her handmaiden's ministrations with docility and complete unconcern for the result.

Sally, working with swift skill, passed a smoothing hand over her mistress's silken tresses and laid down the brush a few moments later, saying with satisfaction, "There now, Miss Elcott, if you'll just slip your arms out of this smelly smock, you'll be fit to meet the queen 'erself."

Dinah had been following the maid's directions mechanically, her mind still engrossed with the recent color experiments. Sally's last words penetrated her abstraction, however, and she swung around, her eyes dilating in horror. "Did you say the *queen*? *Here*?"

"No, no, miss, o'course the queen's not 'ere," Sally assured her, speaking soothingly as to a child. "What would 'er Majesty be doing paying morning calls on 'er subjects? Now, you just give me that dirty old smock you're twisting to pieces afore you get paint all over your 'ands again."

Awareness flowed back into Dinah's eyes, accompanied by a glint of mischief as she handed over the item offending the maid's tidy soul. "It's all right, Sally, my wits haven't deserted me permanently. I was still thinking about my painting and only heard the part about meeting the queen, which you'll allow was enough to frighten anyone out of a year's growth."

"Now, now, there's nothing to be afeared of, Miss Elcott. You just go on downstairs to the saloon. Mrs. Talbot's expecting you."

Sally's bracing words, kindly meant, warmed Dinah's heart but did not succeed in thawing the icy knot of dread lodged in

her stomach as she descended the stairs on lagging feet. It
seemed to her escalating dismay that the knocker on the Talbots' door had not ceased banging since their evening at the
opera. It should have come as no surprise to her that her own
reaction to Natasha's warmth and charm was scarcely unique;
she might have guessed that her new friend was one of the
most popular young matrons in London.

In the past sennight Dinah had been presented to a bewilder-
ing array of visitors, ranging from imposing dowagers whose
piercing stares and pointed questions directed at the newcomer
threw her into a quake lest her awkwardness discredit her hostess, to finely dressed gentlemen with apparantly no other aim
in life than to amuse the lovely Mrs. Talbot with the latest sto-
ries making the rounds of the capital. Dinah's dearth of social
skills would ensure that she was of no more than brief, inci-
dental interest to any of these callers.

Natasha had pointed out that the Season did not really begin
until after Easter, at which time families with daughters to present would swell the numbers of the city's inhabitants. Presumably, these unknown girls would make up the bulk of her
own associates this spring. Knowing Natasha's intent had been
to reassure, Dinah had smiled and returned a noncommittal
murmur. Not even to her sympathetic friend was she willing to
confess her doubts that she would have anything in common
with the majority of young ladies making their bows in London this year.

Outside the saloon Dinah took a deep breath and squared
her shoulders before venturing across the threshold. She had
promised her father she would try to fit in and she owed it to
the Talbots to avoid putting them to the blush for their guest's
inadequacies.

A quick glance around the room revealed that today's crop
of visitors had not even the attraction of novelty to recommend
it. The red-faced gentleman who appeared to have been
packed into his clothes like the stuffing in a sausage was Mr.
Jermyn Adler, a persistent admirer of Natasha's, who affected
a dragging precision of speech that grated along Dinah's
nerves. Natasha was too kind to snub him or to be other than
warmly welcoming to another caller, Lady Maria Huntley, an
aristocratic dragon whose clipped accents regularly ripped up

her entire acquaintance behind a pious but spurious assumption of sympathy for her victims' troubles. Dinah saw with no increase in pleasure that Lady Maria had her nephew, Mr. Benjamin Wickham, in tow. There was nothing to fault in Mr. Wickham's fastidious appearance; his slender form was neatly encased in a brown coat worn over a tan waistcoat, and his snowy cravat was a model of crisp, elegant folds. Stiffly starched shirtpoints halfway up his smooth cheeks and glossily pomaded chestnut locks painstakingly arranged into artistic disorder reflected a high degree of concern for his appearance. Mr. Wickham had inherited his aunt's high-bridged nose but not her acidulated tongue. The question from Dinah's point of view was whether the young man even possessed a tongue. The first time he'd come to Portman Square he'd sat mumchance throughout the visit except when called upon by his loquacious relative to second one of her malicious statements, at which times he would produce an inarticulate gurgle, his manner evolving from sheepish to harassed in the course of the call. Recalling this as she stepped into the room, Dinah wondered that he allowed himself to be persuaded to accompany the dowager anywhere.

Having greeted everyone present, Dinah was about to take a seat beside Natasha when Lady Maria forestalled her by rising and sailing over to that chair herself, saying with the weighty playfulness of a pug dog who thinks he's a kitten that she had no desire to sit bodkin between two young people intent on becoming better acquainted. Dinah had halted in confusion at the dowager's movements, and now she shifted a blank gaze from that lady's knowing face to Mr. Wickham's amiably vacuous countenance before proceeding with downcast eyes to take the recently vacated chair beside this gentleman.

Mr. Adler resumed the story he had been narrating at Dinah's entrance, a tactful move that covered the resounding silence issuing from the reputedly eager pair of young people.

Dinah's eyes were on her clasped hands in her lap a moment later when a light masculine voice at her side said, "I say, what is that odd smell, d'you know?"

Spotting a streak of unmber on her right thumb, Dinah did some rapid mental calculation and replied calmly, "It's probably turpentine. I was painting."

"Painting what?"

"A still life."

"Oh, that kind of painting."

Silence spread between them again. Dinah continued to study her smudged fingers and Mr. Wickham looked off into space. After a moment she angled her head a bit to peek at him from under the screen of her lashes, just in time to witness Mr. Wickham thrust out his lower lip and stretch his neck upward, an unlovely gesture that flattened his already receding chin still further. Under her fascinated eyes he jerked his head to the left and then to the right once or twice before it dawned on Dinah that her neighbor was not sniffing the air for more unpleasant odors but was trying to gain some comfort space within his tightly tied neckcloth. Obviously, he was as oppressed as she by the awkwardness of the situation contrived by Lady Maria. A ripple of fellow feeling caused her to look at him with some sympathy for the first time.

As he met her gaze, relief filled Mr. Wickham's light blue eyes and loosened his tongue. "My aunt seemed to think I ought to meet you. She says being new to town and away from your family, you're likely to be feeling down pin and homesick. Can't see it myself. Why come at all if you're going to be homesick? It stands to reason, better to stay home in the first place. Don't know what she thought *I* could do about if you were."

"Did you ask her?" Dinah interrupted, intrigued by these artless revelations.

"Ask her what?" Mr. Wickham said, startled out of his preoccupation with his grievance.

"What she thought you could do to . . . to ease my homesickness."

Mr. Wickham's gloom deepened. "She said you needed a friend. Said it would help you to learn to converse with a man before being launched full into society. Seemed to think since I've been on the town for years I could teach you. Wouldn't listen when I told her she was wrong. The thing is," he explained laboriously, "that it don't matter that I've been on the town myself. I've never been much in the petticoat line, whatever my aunt might think." He tugged at his cravat unconsciously, marring its perfection. "I've *got* no conversation, no brains either as far as that goes. So, you see?" he finished, looking at her with a hint of desperation.

Dinah saw much more than he intended. She addressed herself to the appeal in his earnest eyes. "Well, I should not let a lack of conversation worry you too much. I've got none either, but the talkers need an appreciative audience, do they not? You and I can both be that. And I do not think you should say you have no brains. It's rather poor-spirited of you."

"It's true, though. When I was at school the other fellows told me so, the masters too," he added as a clincher.

"Well, they had no right," Dinah argued, indignant on his behalf. "You say you've been on the town for years. If you've survived all the pitfalls that abound in the city without coming to grief, I should think that is proof that you have brains."

"That doesn't take brains, not the sort the clever chaps have. It just needs common sense," Mr. Wickham said dismissively, but he was looking more cheerful and seemed finally to have achieved a comfortable accommodation with his neckcloth.

"Can we agree, do you think, that common sense is sufficient between friends?" Dinah asked with a rare smile. "I am persuaded I shall have need of a friend when I find myself cast adrift at Almack's or such places this spring."

Mr. Wickham subdued his innate humility to the extent of conceding that, put that way, friendship did not seem beyond their reach. "Be glad to help any way I can," he offered magnanimously. "If you need a dancing partner or want to escape a crashing bore, I'm your man."

This point having been settled to their mutual satisfaction, the new friends found themselves once again with nothing to say to one another.

Natasha came to the rescue. "Dinah, Mr. Adler was just commenting on the furor in Paris over the recent presentation of M. Arnault's new play, *Germanicus*. I was about to tell him of the letter we received from Aunt Hester this morning." Having gathered the young people into the fold, she turned back to Mr. Adler and explained. "Cam's great-aunt is staying in Paris this spring, and she was present at the Théâtre Français the night the play opened. She writes that they had to send someone there hours early to claim their boxes, so great was the desire of the general populace to be present. Getting permission to present the work of the banished poet has been a cause célébre, since everyone knew the identity of the anonymous author."

"Was Miss Cameron injured in the melee that broke out in the theater?" Lady Maria asked.

"Not at all. She said there was a mad scramble of people trying to leave the boxes, but the actual disturbance was confined mainly to the pit and the stage areas. It began at the end of the play when people in the audience called for the author. Most of those involved in creating the disturbance were assumed to be half-pay officers. Soldiers were sent in to restore order. They took possession of the stage and gradually were able to disperse the crowd, though there were numerous small fights going on."

"How horrible for Miss Cameron," Lady Maria declared with a shudder. "I should have been frightened to death to be trapped in the middle of a near riot."

"Actually, Aunt Hester says she would not have missed the excitement for the world, that it was by far the most interesting evening she has spent in Paris, though she found the play somewhat tedious."

"Well, stands to reason she would if the whole thing was in French," Mr. Wickham said, nodding his head wisely. "Dashed tedious language those Frenchies jabber in, but the old girl sounds like a real game 'un, by George." The terms in which his enthusiastic approval were couched brought a strong expression of disapprobation to Lady Maria's haughty features, while Natasha was hard pressed to retain her composure as she seconded his sentiments with careful gravity. Mr. Wickham, though naturally abashed, took heart from his hostess's sanction. The fiery blush that had risen to his cheeks at his aunt's censure receded, but his contributions to the general conversation dried up from that moment. Intercepting the withering look his starchy relative had bestowed on him, Dinah took pity on the hapless young man and began to draw him out with quiet questions on what she might expect from an evening at Almack's. This proved a fruitful cast since Mr. Wickham was an habitué of that august establishment and was happy to share what he had gleaned from his experiences over the past few years.

When the callers had gone, Natasha said, "It was kind of you to keep Mr. Wickham happily occupied, Dinah."

"I felt sorry for him. I know how it feels to be under the thumb of an elderly tyrant. I never imagined that gentlemen were ever so constrained, though. He must be a very poor-spirited creature."

"Lady Maria is a childless widow. I believe," Natasha said delicately, "that she has let it be known in her family that Mr. Wickham is her chosen heir, so it is not wonderful that he should feel himself obliged to dance attendance on her at times, and cater to her whims to a certain degree."

This was all the hint that Natasha permitted herself, but she noted with satisfaction in the days that followed that it had fallen on fertile ground. Dinah seemed more at ease with the inarticulate Mr. Wickham than any other gentlemen she met in those first weeks, but she could not be described as warmly responsive to anyone outside of the Talbot family. Careful observation of the girl when she'd been presented to strangers had led Natasha to conclude with relief that her guest was not a victim of that painful shyness that rendered social occasions terrifying to some young women. Dinah's calm countenance reflected no fear of new experiences. On the other hand, neither did it reflect an eagerness to pursue any new acquaintances as yet. Hopefully, strangers would attribute her lack of participation to the timidity that might be expected in a quiet girl in her first Season. Natasha suspected this quiet, respectful air masked a bone-deep reserve, an instinctive disinclination to share her inner self with others, at least at the begining of an acquaintance. Her own nature being so open, she was concerned enough to mention her observations to her husband along with her worry that Dinah would miss out on the pleasurable experiences available to girls in her position.

"A girl's first Season is a unique experience, Cam. For the first time in her life, perhaps, she is looked on as someone special; everyone makes much of her, caters to her wishes, treats her with flattering deference. I should not like to think that Dinah will not share in this . . . this coddling, if you will. I don't believe she has had much of that type of coddling since her mother died."

Cam smiled lovingly into his wife's anxious dark eyes. "If

it's coddling she wants, Dinah has come to the right place, for she's certainly found a mother hen in you, my love. And the result is charming," he added as Natasha's lips parted. "The girl has blossomed into an attractive personality under your influence. Justin adores her and she is good company for you, if you could only stop worrying over her future. Dinah strikes me as a young woman eminently capable of deciding what she wants from life."

"I don't think I am worrying precisely, Cam, not about her ultimate future, at least. I simply do not wish her to miss out on the special pleasures of her first Season by giving people the impression that she is cold and reserved."

"Are you certain you are not in retrospect casting a romantic glow over this whole business of a girl's come-out, darling?" Cam asked with a quizzical smile. "Don't forget, I was there three years ago, a witness to the fact that your own bow to society was not so comprehensively delightful as this abstract ideal you have been describing."

"It was different in my case, Cam. Cousin Eugenia and Lucretia resented my presence in their lives. It was difficult to feel oneself always unwanted, but I vastly enjoyed the experience of going to parties and meeting new and interesting people."

"Ah, now we come to the crux of the matter. I should not be at all surprised to find that these things—parties and new people—do not have the same attraction for Dinah that they do for most young women. She will participate in these activities for your sake and because she promised her father, but do you not think, my love, that her real joy comes from her painting, not from people? There do exist those odd souls whose natures *are* cold and reserved. Except for those few persons they love, their delight is not in humanity in general but in some other aspect of living. I am one of those odd souls, and so, I strongly suspect, is Dinah."

"You shan't talk about yourself in that fashion," Natasha scolded, putting her fingers over his lips. Whereupon a laughing Cam gathered her into his arms, effectively ending the discussion.

Dinah's first evening party that spring was a small dinner given by the Talbots for a few old friends and colleagues of

Cam's from the Foreign Office. Natasha was of the opinion that familiar surroundings and small numbers would go some way toward easing Dinah's initial plunge into the social swim. Hearing this, Dinah murmured something that might be taken for agreement and kept her opinion to herself. In an effort not to disgrace the Talbots by her ignorance of world events, she voluntarily gave up one of her precious painting sessions the day before the dinner to pore over the last sennight's newspapers, concentrating on items dealing with news from foreign countries. She even mastered the pronunciation of the name of the new minister from the Two Sicilies, Prince Castelcicala.

On the night of the party, Natasha, dressed in a perfectly plain gown in a deep, vibrant shade of orange, entered Dinah's room while Sally was giving her mistress's hair a final brushing.

"What a magnificent color for you," Dinah approved, spotting her friend in the mirror above the dressing table where she sat. "Mrs. Simmons is quite right; a straight fall of one color does make you look taller, and that gold filigree necklace and gold lacé fan are the perfect accessories. Turn your head," she commanded as a sparkle of gold caught her eye. Natasha obeyed and laughed when Dinah exclaimed, "How clever of you to use a miniature fan for a hair ornament!"

"I must confess that it was not my cleverness but Mallory's that conceived this particular stroke of genius."

"Well, I think Miss Mallory is a genius when it comes to devising styles that make the most of that wonderful dark hair of yours. Your hair must be the envy of all the women in London."

"Don't you believe it. Oh, it has its public," Natasha admitted with a cheeky grin, "but my gypsy coloring has always been considered slightly vulgar in some quarters. Blue-eyed, pink-and-white blondes are still the most universally admired females."

"And I am neither dark nor fair, nor even moderately pretty," Dinah said with a wistful sigh, turning abruptly away from her own image. Her hair swung in a soft cloud before settling into its smooth curve against her neck.

"That may be true, but it is far from the whole truth, Dinah,"

Natasha said earnestly. "You have truly beautiful eyes and a look of cool distinction that many will consider intriguing. And when people get to know you and discover your intelligence and honesty, you will find yourself with more admirers than those empty-headed girls who imagine their vapid prettiness is enough to offer the world."

"You . . . you are very kind," Dinah stammered, ashamed of herself for whining over what could not be changed.

"Not kind at all, merely truthful," Natasha insisted, "though it will take some time before you will recognize the truth of what I have said. Meanwhile, I have brought you this topaz pendant of mine to wear tonight. It should complement the soft amber tones of your gown, which nearly match your hair."

As Dinah rose with a smile of appreciation to allow Natasha to fasten the pendant about her neck, Sally, handing her mistress her small netted reticule, was moved to express her admiration. "The pair of you look just right together with those unusual colors and both of a size and all."

"Why, thank you, Sally. It had not occurred to me before, but I believe you are right." Natasha smiled at the young maid, who ran over to open the door for them.

"I have seated you near Sir Humphrey at dinner, Dinah," Natasha said a moment later as they descended the stairs together.

"Charles's father? Is . . . is he much like Charles?" Dinah tried for a casual air, but Natasha detected the faint trace of uneasiness in her guest's question.

"Oh, Sir Humphrey is the dearest, kindest man one could ever hope to meet. I adore him."

Their proximity to the saloon where Cam awaited them spared Dinah the necessity of pretending to accept her friend's assessment of Sir Humphrey Talbot at face value. Her recent exposure to a sampling of the persons making up the Talbots' wide circle of acquaintances had taught her that Natasha saw something to like in nearly everyone who crossed her path. She really seemed unaware of defects that were readily apparent to one less inclined by nature to credit everyone with a good heart until unmistakable evidence to the contrary made this no longer possible.

In the present instance, however, Dinah was ready to accede

to Natasha's opinion after five minutes in Sir Humphrey's company.

Father and son arrived together. Standing between Cam and Natasha while her hosts greeted their guests and made her known to those she had not yet met, Dinah had time for a cursory inventory of the two men before being presented herself. Her artist's eye detected the similarity of bone structure in the two faces, though Sir Humphrey was a trifle taller and considerably heavier than his elegantly attired son. He was dressed with similar precision and neatness but with less regard for the decrees of fashion and more for comfort and suitability. The vivid blue eyes that Sir Humphrey had passed on to Charles were even more outstanding beneath a full head of silver-gray hair that waved most attractively. Dinah had just time to decide that Charles would possess the same distinction one day when her attention was claimed by the elder gentleman.

"I am delighted to meet you, my dear. I hope you will not condemn me as an elderly flatterer if I say that you and Natasha radiate the glory of a tropical sunset in your lovely gowns."

The smile that Sir Humphrey directed at Dinah contained all the charm of his son's but had much more warmth.

Charles Talbot, watching the proceedings with an air of detached amusement, noted that Dinah's smile for his father was of a shining variety he had not before witnessed from the reserved girl. He was unsurprised to see that it had dimmed to a mere convention when she greeted him a moment later.

"Good evening, Dinah, I cannot hope to equal my father's eloquence, but I shall make so bold as to echo his sentiments. You have risen nobly to the occasion tonight."

"Thank you, Charles," she replied coolly, ignoring the little sting that he had not been able to keep out of his voice. Those direct, candid eyes told him how little she regarded his flattering words. He felt his father's quick look at him and passed on to his cousin.

The dinner party was not the ordeal Dinah had anticipated, thanks in part to the unobtrusive support of Sir Humphrey Talbot. Except for the daughter of one of Cam's colleagues, Dinah was the youngest lady present, but she did not feel as

isolated as was often the case when there was a mix of genera-
tions. During the course of the evening, nearly everyone expressed a conventional interest in her impressions of London,
along with the kind wish that she might enjoy her stay before
moving on to speak to others. She was welcome to listen in to
the far-flung discussions that cropped up among the various
groups constantly dissolving and reforming, and would not
have been afraid to speak up had she possessed an informed
opinion on any of the topics that were touched on.

Miss Sybil Bannister, the other unmarried young lady, was,
like Dinah, teetering on the brink of her come-out. She was a
pretty blonde of that empty-headed persuasion alluded to earlier by Natasha, and became animated only in the presence of
the opposite sex. It was obvious from her sweeping eyelashes
and trilling laughter that she was intent on perfecting her techniques of fascination, and after a few awed moments, Dinah
left her to get on with it unencumbered by the presence of another female.

Dinah was conversing with Sir Humphrey, who had succeeded in slipping beneath her guard and discovering the fact
that she was studying in an artist's studio, when dinner was
announced, and she walked into the dining room on his arm.
When the soup was offered, Dinah shook her head at the footman. "No, thank you, soup always makes my nose run and I
forgot to put a handkerchief in my reticule tonight."

Charles Talbot, seated directly across the table, heard this
artless remark and was diverted but not beguiled. He fixed a
look of narrow surmise on the serene face of Miss Dinah Elcott, who, chancing to look up at that moment, assumed her
blandest expression and reached for a roll. After an instant
Charles turned to his neighbor, the pretty Miss Bannister. He
imposed an expression of flattering attention on his features in
response to her predictable prattlings while his intelligence
performed a task of rapid readjustment in its previous estimate
of the character of Miss Elcott. Charles, priding himself on his
perceptive reading of the character and mood of his fellow beings, did not take kindly to being gulled, especially by a brat
not long out of the schoolroom. He'd recognized that she was
unlike most girls her age, but he'd assumed her occasional
gaucheries were inadvertent, the result of her peculiar upbring-

ing. This little exhibition showed him his error. That little minx was enjoying a private laugh at the expense of people who were too polite to call attention to her lapses from good taste. Was she hoping someone would feel called upon to give her a hint? Would that feed some warped feeling of superiority? Admittedly, some of the minor points of genteel behavior, such as the elaborate avoidance of the name of certain body parts, were artificial and laughable, but it was not the province of a green little provincial to challenge the accepted standards. Presumably she cared not a whit that she would be making a name for herself as a rough diamond, to put it no higher, but her boorish actions would inevitably reflect on Natasha, and that he would not permit. Let Miss Slyboots try a fall with someone who could see through that limpid assumption of ignorance.

Miss Bannister abandoned him to lavish her charm on the man on her right, and Charles did his duty by his other dinner partner, but his thoughts, and sometimes his eyes, tended to stray to the puzzle that was Dinah Elcott. He was on the alert lest she decide to enliven the party with another innocent-looking *bêtise*, but Dinah and his father had their heads together throughout most of the time at table, their absorption in each other aided by the fact that Thomas Malacort, her other partner, was bent on devoting himself to the very good food that was being presented. Charles relaxed his vigilance after a time in the confidence that his parent could be counted on to keep her in check.

He was more than a little curious at the rapport that seemed to have sprung up between his shrewd and cultured parent and Natasha's protégée. He'd only managed a few moments with Dinah himself when the gentlemen rejoined the ladies after dinner. She'd been her usual noncommittal self with him, parrying any questions that were not strictly impersonal. He'd concealed his annoyance and allowed the persistent Miss Bannister to lure him away. Any slight triumph at putting Dinah in her place was canceled by what he suspected was genuine pity in her large eyes as she turned away.

Though he generally liked walking at night, Charles accepted a ride in his father's carriage at the end of the evening.

He took a deep, appreciative breath of the crisp night air before climbing into the carriage.

"That was a most enjoyable evening," Sir Humphrey confided as he sank back against the velvet squabs. "As I get older I find myself much preferring this intimate sort of gathering where one actually has time to converse with old friends."

"Or new ones."

"Yes. I hope I never grow so old that I lose sympathy for the young and refuse to recognize the validity of their point of view."

"I don't expect you will, Father."

Sir Humphrey, touched by the rare note of affection in his son's voice, was moved to continue his musings. "There is more to that little one than to most of the hen-witted females who appear on the scene year after year. Not a beauty, of course, but there's nothing amiss with her understanding, and she knows how to listen, a rare quality in the young. In my opinion, she has a great deal of countenance and a quiet charm that will wear well. I liked the girl."

"Since I am well aware that you have long doted on Natasha, I presume by 'little one' you are this time referring to Miss Elcott?"

"You cannot imagine I meant that Bannister chit with her frenetic attempts at flirtation?" Sir Humphrey said dryly. "She even tried out her wiles on me."

Charles smiled. "She is merely practicing those feminine arts of enticement she believes are expected from pretty girls. She will improve as she finds her feet in society. She is very young."

"Such indulgence of youthful foibles is unlike you, Charles, but I should be happy to think you have mellowed somewhat in your judgments, which have been rather . . . stern in the past."

"Have they? One has one's standards, after all."

"You are not known for even minimal patience with the brainless, my boy, so I am naturally encouraged by your championship of Miss Bannister. Your kinder nature has prevailed in this instance."

Sir Humphrey spoke in gentle accents. In the dimness of the moving carriage, Charles privately acknowledged that his wily parent had scored over him. Even the mildest criticism of Dinah Elcott would look like gross brutality under the circumstances. Besides, he was clear-headed enough about his own failings to recognize the element of pique in his response to Dinah's unconventional behavior this evening. Despite considerable exposure, he had failed to discern the complexity of her character, and he did not like being found wanting in sensibility. How many more layers were there beneath the bland surface she presented to the world? There obviously existed a previously unsuspected sense of humor, perverse though it looked on this evening's evidence. Perhaps the girl had more promise than he had given her credit for. For Natasha's sake he hoped this was true.

8

Charles's bow to Lady Jersey was, according to the recipient, a masterpiece of grace that, she added with an arch look, would not have gained him entrance to Almack's assembly rooms had he arrived even five minutes later. "It's nearly eleven, Charles, and the rules apply to everyone."

"I assure you, Sally, my vanity and presumption stop well short of challenging the benevolent patronesses of Almack's." His own smile was so benign it drew a laugh from the lady as her eyebrows arched upward.

"Developing humility at this late date, Charles?"

"Not at all, but I have never been in favor of wasted effort. I am far too indolent to rig myself out in knee breeches and shoe buckles only to miscalculate the time and earn a rebuff at this sacred portal. I see the rooms are well attended as usual," he added, his sweeping gaze taking in the crowded ballroom where almost as many people sat against the walls or stood talking in groups as were performing on the dance floor.

"The beginning of a new Season is always hectic," Lady Jersey agreed. "The company will thin out somewhat as numerous private entertainments are scheduled in the next weeks."

"Dare one hope that this year's crop will be more distinguished than last?"

"Perhaps you are too nice in your requirements, Charles," Lady Jersey suggested with a hint of impatience. "As in the past, there are two or three real diamonds who will take the town by storm, and any number of charming and pretty girls who will make amiable wives for some fortunate men. There are also a few who show promise of becoming sought after for their wit and conversation when they have acquired a little town polish. I regret to say that your cousins' protégée does not look like becoming one of their number, however," she finished with a pointed glance at the corner where Dinah Elcott sat with three other young ladies temporarily without partners, the only one not participating in what appeared to be a stimulating conversation.

Charles had already spotted Dinah's tranquil figure, physically but not actually a part of the vivacious group. "Despite the vacant expression, Miss Elcott is not unintelligent, but she is sadly unschooled socially. I gather she has led a rather solitary existence until very recently."

"Poor Natasha. That soft heart of hers almost guarantees that she will be lumbered with lame ducks. The girl's father wished her on the Talbots, I hear."

"Actually, I believe Natasha and Dinah have become firm friends in the weeks Dinah has been staying in Portman Square," Charles said coolly, unwilling to assist in propagating a story that featured either girl as a victim of another's manipulations. "They are neighbors in Devon."

"I see. Well, though Miss Elcott is not perhaps in the accepted style, her looks are not impossible; in fact, there is a rather piquant attraction that should appeal to those who eschew the commonplace. If her fortune is respectable, something might be done for her. I don't believe I know of the family."

Charles did not rise to the question in Lady Jersey's voice, saying carelessly, "As to that, you would have to inquire closer to the source." He remained talking to Lady Jersey for another few moments before making his way, stopping for a brief word here and a bow there, to the section where Dinah Elcott sat mentally divorced from the scene about her.

Natasha arrived on the spot in time to see Dinah jump slightly at Charles's greeting. Noting his narrowed eyes and mindful of their interested audience, she gushed, "Ah, here you are at last, Charles. Are you acquainted with these young ladies? No? Miss Slocum, may I present Mr. Talbot? Miss Braithwaite, Miss Anderson, Mr. Talbot is my husband's cousin." She flashed her famous smile along the row of eager girls.

While Charles was busy acknowledging the introductions to

one plain-faced and two mildly attractive females, Natasha unobtrusively pulled Dinah to her feet, murmured a soft excuse, and edged her friend away from the group. The music was winding down and they nearly succeeded in losing themselves among the dancers leaving the floor, but within a minute of finding places across the room, Charles appeared in front of them.

"We meet again, ladies," he said affably.

"Now, no scolding, Charles," Natasha warned. "The first time at Almack's is difficult enough without that."

"My purpose in following you was to obtain a dance from each. Why should you suppose otherwise?" Charles replied, contriving to look wounded.

Natasha smiled. "I'm not dancing tonight, but stay and talk to me while Dinah is on the floor. Cam wasn't able to come with us this evening."

"My cousin had a previous engagement, I apprehend?"

"A late session at the ministry," Natasha stated. "Do you have space on your card for Charles, Dinah?"

"There is one country dance left near the end of the evening."

Charles's eyes narrowed again at the unflattering lack of enthusiasm displayed by Miss Elcott, but any reply he might have made was forestalled by the appearance of a very young gentleman who claimed her for the dance starting up.

Natasha and Charles watched the dancing for a while in silence. Even Natasha's partiality could not command any higher encomium than "adequate" to describe Dinah's performance in the set she had joined, and if she exchanged a single remark with her partner or anyone else, it was not apparent to the spectators.

Hearing a soft sigh at his side, Charles said, "I take it the evening has been less than a howling success thus far?"

"True," Natasha admitted, "but it could have been worse. Dinah isn't a . . . a lively girl in company, but she looks charmingly tonight, and most of her dances have been bespoken."

"If the present one is a fair example of how she comports herself on the dance floor, she won't be so fortunate next time. Most men expect *some* response from their partners."

"I know, but Mr. Butterworth is as shy as Dinah, so it is useless to expect any scintillating conversation between them."

"Dinah Elcott is not shy; she is simply uninterested in her fellow beings, with precious few exceptions. Also, she is too lazy or too self-engrossed to put forth a decent effort to be pleasant."

"That is very harsh, Charles, and it is not true. She simply doesn't know what things interest people or how to go about discovering their interests."

"And does she try? For ten minutes I watched her sitting among a chattering group of young girls like herself and did not see her contribute a single remark. She sat there looking bored the whole time."

"I know," Natasha admitted again, "but you are wrong about one vital thing, Charles. Dinah is *not* like those girls or any other girls she is likely to meet in London. She has no real interest in clothes or parties or young men or marrying."

"Then she had better counterfeit an interest in the immediate future or her lack of manners will put you to the blush every time you take her anywhere."

"The case is not nearly so bad as you make it out to be, Charles. There is nothing amiss with Dinah's manners. When people speak of social or political or cultural issues she listens attentively, but she has nothing in common with most of the girls she will be associating with this spring."

Before Charles could comment on Natasha's lame defense of her guest, someone came up to speak with them. He sensed her relief and berated himself for adding to the discomfort that abominable chit had already caused her tonight. He bided his time until his dance with Dinah arrived, circulating through the rooms, chatting with various acquaintances and, when Maria Sefton caught him in her net, partnering a self-possessed young woman who subjected him to a fifteen-minute monologue on the discomforts of her recent journey from Cumberland. Through the good offices of Lady Jersey, he contrived to meet Miss Dunstan, one of this year's beauties, a stunning green-eyed redhead with a translucent complexion. Unhappily, five minutes of conversation with the glorious redhead was sufficient to convince him that nature's gifts to Miss

Dunstan had been totally expended in the realm of the physical. Her mental acuity proved inadequate to pursue a conversation that jogged even an inch out of the well-worn path of conventional formulas. Fortunately, his place by the beauty's side was hotly contested by a half-dozen panting youths, permitting him to retreat gracefully before the sound of her inanities had time to wipe out the considerable pleasure the sight of her afforded him.

Dinah, who had not been oblivious of Charles's eyes on her during the course of the evening, accompanied him onto the floor in silence, her own eyes wary. She performed her part correctly, but her movements were often jerky, as if the decision had been taken at the last possible instant. Obviously, she was not a natural dancer like Natasha, though practice would increase the ease with which she moved. Likewise, her lack of conversation might be attributed in part to the need for concentration on an activity that was new to her, but after Charles's first few remarks had been greeted with, at best, monosyllabic sounds that could be taken for agreement while her eyes avoided contact with his, he decided the standard of her terpsichorean performance didn't bear out this theory of intense concentration.

"You are shirking your duty, Miss Elcott," he accused softly as they came together.

Her eyes flew to his. "What duty?"

"Your social duty to entertain your partner, of course."

"I don't know how to be entertaining, as you are well aware," she replied defensively.

"Excuses won't serve you here, my dear Dinah. It is not required that you actually *be* entertaining—that would be too much to expect from most people—just that you put forth a minimal degree of effort. For instance, if I begin with a comment on the large number of people present, you may agree that it is a sad squeeze, or argue that you find crowds stimulating, or express a fear that you will be run down in the crush. The banality of the response does not signify. What you may *not* do is assent or disagree in one parsimonious syllable unless you are immediately prepared to introduce a new topic. At this point a judgment on the temperature of the rooms or the quality of the music would be acceptable. I would then express an opinion on that weighty question and it would be my turn to produce a new subject or probe this one for deeper insights. Am I making myself clear?"

"You make conversation sound like a repetitious ritual recited by rote."

"And so it is for the most part. There are precious few pearls of wisdom exchanged on the dance floor, but exchanges there must be, and you must be willing to undertake your fair share of the burden."

"It seems such a waste of time."

"Try to think of it as a necessary and harmless preliminary to possible future encounters that will be more rewarding."

Dinah sighed, unconvinced, and Charles said sternly, "Recollect that you made a promise to your father, and that you have a duty to your hosts to repay their hospitality by not becoming a social incubus. It is obvious that you have been unwisely indulged in the past, my girl, and this is the result."

"Indulged? I?" A startled look came into Dinah's eyes.

"If permitting you to develop a taste for solitude, a disinclination to put yourself out to set others at their ease, and a dislike of sharing your thoughts is not an indulgence, I don't know what else to call it," Charles replied, well aware that neglect and indifference were probably at the root of Dinah's social malajustment but persuaded that easy sympathy was not what was needed to prod her into giving herself a chance to enjoy some varied society. He excused his own lack of compunction in upbraiding her by assuring himself that the tenacious girl possessed an inner core of strength that would keep her firm in adversity. She did not require coddling like a child; she could face up to the truth without sugar-coated adornments.

Dinah was looking at him oddly as they passed each other in the chain a moment later, but she did not resume the interrupted conversation when she joined him again. Catching a glimpse of a dancer with luxuriant red hair whirling by, she said impulsively, "Isn't Miss Dunstan beautiful? How I would love to try painting that hair. It would take half the colors in the paint box to do it justice."

"It would be much easier to paint her mind—a dull dun color would suffice for that," Charles said dryly.

"You've met her?"

"Yes, and was put forcibly in mind of some lines of Congreve's. 'But soon as e'er the beauteous idiot spoke, forth from her coral lips such folly broke. Like balm the trickling nonsense heal'd my wound, And what her eyes enthrall'd, her tongue unbound.'"

"Charles, that's cruel!" Dinah cried, but she had trouble keeping her lips compressed and she would not meet his dancing eyes.

"Do not waste your pity on Miss Dunstan. Unless I am wildly deceived, she is destined to be the toast of the town. Brains would only get in the way of her enjoyment of her success."

"I *think* that is one of those sly remarks you frequently toss off that should be rebutted, except that you do not permit one the time to think them through," Dinah said severely.

Charles allowed himself one smug little smile and led her off the floor to where her chaperone awaited her.

Natasha's anxious glance skittered from one to the other before her face relaxed into a relieved smile. The evening was not going to be an unabated disaster after all. Dinah and Charles appeared to have negotiated an armistice.

Now that the Season was in full swing the ladies from Portman Square spent a considerable portion of their time paying and receiving what Dinah privately thought of as ritual calls. Though much younger than those matrons with daughters to present, Natasha included a number of such families in her wide acquaintance. Her sparkling good nature assured her a welcome wherever she elected to visit, and she was not shy about seeking out young company for her guest. Within a few weeks Dinah found herself on visiting terms with nearly a score of girls, many of whom had brothers or cousins in their train. Never after her first evening at Almack's did she arrive at a social event where there were not at least a few familiar persons with whom to exchange courtesies. Natasha might well have preened herself on this accomplishment had she not recognized that her young charge was not yet on terms of friendship or increasing intimacy with any of her contemporaries. Natasha may have provided opportunity, but she reluc-

tantly came to accept that it was not in her province to pro-
mote friendship.

Charles received an inkling of this when he called in Portman Square one morning late in April. As he ascended the
stairs in Dawson's wake a high-pitched twitter as from a flock
of birds floated down to greet him.

"The ladies are receiving, I hear, Dawson."

"More often than not these days, sir."

Charles's lip quivered at the faint suggestion of pride in the
butler's voice. Obviously the vicarious satisfaction in his employers' popularity more than made up for the extra work involved in toiling up and down stairs to cater to an unending
stream of callers.

The crimson saloon was well-populated with visitors when
Charles was shown in. He counted three attractive young
ladies, two matrons who were no doubt their proud mamas,
and two would-be Corinthians, one in the spotted waistcoat of
the Four Horse Club. Charles had barely responded to the
mass introductions and taken a seat between Natasha and Miss
Moore, the prettiest of the young ladies present, when Dawson
reappeared at the door with Mr. Benjamin Wickham in tow.
Mr. Wickham, though some half-dozen years his junior, was
known to Charles as belonging to a set of young bloods who
generally spent their days in various sporting pursuits and their
nights in gambling clubs. The riddle of the amiable block-
head's presence was solved when Mr. Wickham, having stammered and blushed his way through the necessary
preliminaries, retired to a chair beside Dinah with patent relief
and became submerged in near-total silence.

The twenty minutes or so that elapsed before the various
callers took their leave proved a treasure trove for someone for
whom the oddities of his fellow creatures provided a limitless
source of diversion. It required less than half of Charles's attention to maintain a decent share of the various conversations,
while he set the rest of his mind to the exercise of discerning
the reasons for their presence from the behavior of his fellow
guests.

The young ladies had naturally been brought by their mothers, but his guess was that Lady Moore had been no more than

her daughter's accomplice, while Mrs. Smithson had probably been the driving force in steering her girls to Portman Square.

Even without introductions anyone with two eyes could have supplied the last names of the young ladies. Lydia Moore, who appeared to hang on Natasha's every word, possessed her mother's extravagant brown curls and wide-set blue eyes and was similarly tall and slender. The two could have been mistaken for sisters had peevish temper or discontent not set aging lines into Lady Moore's countenance. These lines were much in evidence as she launched into a detailed complaint of the inadequacies of all drapers' shops in the area for the edification of Mrs. Smithson. This large, good-natured lady listened with exemplary patience, supplying sympathetic platitudes whenever the petulant interlocutor paused in her diatribe. The blond Smithson daughters, also good-natured and bidding fair to equal their mother's girth in time, plied Natasha with questions about the opera. Tonight was to be their first operatic experience and they were agog with anticipation, their delight spilling over into generous smiles for everyone present.

It took Charles only a few moments to learn that the two budding Corinthians were old friends of the Smithsons, having gone to school with the son of the family. One was apparently smitten with the elder sister and eventually succeeded in winning her attention away from the general discussion. His abandoned friend began a conversation with Mr. Wickham, who had as yet offered no more than a few words to Dinah, sitting a little apart from the rest, setting stitches in what looked like a baby's cap. Several times during the length of the call Dinah responded briefly to a direct question from Natasha or Mr. Wickham, and that was the extent of her participation by the time Dawson showed everyone out.

Charles, having accepted an invitation to lunch, remained behind. Dinah had risen to shake hands with the departing guests, and she would have slipped out the door had not Natasha begged, "Would you entertain Charles for a few moments, Dinah, while I run up to the nursery to check on Justin?"

Dinah sank back into her chair and picked up her needle again.

As the door closed behind Natasha, Charles said silkily,

"You have pretty hands, but I fear I don't find it particularly entertaining to watch a woman embroider, though I can see that you do it very skillfully."

"Shall I play for you on the pianoforte?" Dinah offered as if humoring a child. "Then you may watch my hands and be entertained by music at the same time."

Charles acknowledged the hit with a grin. "So you do possess at least one publicly valued feminine accomplishment? Do you sing too?"

"No."

"You relieve my mind. It has always been my contention that there is a surfeit of young-lady performers in this town. Why not tell me instead what you think of the young ladies who just left?"

"What I think of them?" Dinah seemed at a loss.

"All three struck me as amiable and pleasant," he prompted.

"Oh, yes, certainly."

When nothing more was forthcoming, Charles exercised patience and continued to probe delicately. "Are these the girls you have become most intimate with this spring?"

"I have not become in the least intimate with anyone this spring."

"Except Natasha?"

"Except Natasha," she agreed.

"I am persuaded Natasha hoped to see you make friends among the younger set. The girls who were here today seemed well-disposed to be friendly. Do you have some objection to accepting their friendship?"

Dinah had been gritting her teeth during Charles's poorly disguised interrogation, and now she turned on him. "Surely your powers of observation are not so impaired that you failed to discern that those girls were here to see Natasha, not me."

"And do you have a right to resent that, you who refuse to make the slightest effort to win people to you?"

"I do not resent it," she said flatly after a throbbing silence.

Had Charles not been raking her unrevealing features with a burning blue gaze, he would have missed the quick spasm of pain that had appeared in her eyes before she reasserted her habitual control. Insight and compunction shafted through him. "I'm sorry," he said gently. "I was wrong to imply that

you are jealous of Natasha's popularity. I know that isn't true
But it is a form of jealousy, or possessiveness certainly, to try
to keep the loved one all to oneself."

A dull flush stained Dinah's cheeks as she met his eyes
bravely for a second before dropping her gaze to the hands in
her lap. She was massaging the first joint of the middle finger
of her left hand between the thumb and forefinger of her right
in an unconscious twisting gesture that betrayed her agitation
A film of unshed tears lent her eyes an opalescent quality as
she took a shuddering breath. "I've never had a friend of my
own before," she said humbly, conceding the validity of his
charge.

Charles, who had taken pleasure on occasion in tilting at the
extraordinary control that seemed to betoken a cold, passion-
less nature, found himself more shaken than he would have believed possible as he glimpsed the desolation behind her
admission. Even worse, he was possessed by an insane compulsion to cry out against what he sensed was Dinah's unquestioning acceptance of such bleak deprivation as her lot. He
could not do that, not here and now at any event, when her
composure was already precarious, thanks to his ham-handed
assault tactics. His own self-knowledge told him Dinah would
repudiate a clumsy offer of sympathy; he had just realized that
they had that prickly sort of pride in common.

"Well, you have a good friend now in Natasha," he said, determinedly matter-of-fact, "but there are things in this world
that can only be held in open hands; if you try to clutch them
tightly they ooze out between your fingers. It would also be
the height of stupidity to deny yourself the possibility of other
rewarding associations. Artists in particular cannot afford to be
small-minded unless they are content to paint only rocks and
trees and inanimate objects."

"You do not believe, then, that emotional attachments can
cloud an artist's objectivity?" Dinah asked, mustering a small
smile, though her eyes were grave.

"Being of the world sharpens the eye and deepens the in
sights into the human heart," he declared, pontificating
grandly in the hope of erasing the lingering shadows in her
lovely gray eyes.

When Natasha returned to the saloon a few minutes later, Charles and Dinah were embroiled in a lively argument on the ideal relationship of the artist to his world. She beamed a smile impartially upon both, delighted with this evidence of a better understanding between two difficult personalities.

9

If his grimacing wince was to be believed, the solid thumps of the knocker must have reverberated through the body of the elegantly clad gentleman standing on the Talbots' doorstep. His right hand, encased in a kid glove whose delicate hue matched a dove-gray coat of the finest Bath suiting, left the knocker and hovered in the vicinity of his meticulously arranged neckcloth before dropping to his side.

After a few seconds, the silence beyond the black-painted door seemed to threaten the caller's resolution, for he glanced rather wildly around and had actually taken a half-step backward when he heard the steady tread of someone approaching the entrance door. The gentleman hastily retucked a mother-of-pearl-handled walking stick under his arm and essayed a nervous smile as the door was opened by the Talbots' butler.

"Good afternoon, Dawson. Are the ladies in?"

"I'm sorry, Mr. Wickham, but Mrs. Talbot is out and Miss Elcott is occupied in her studio. Would you care to leave your card?"

Answering this simple question was apparently beyond Mr. Wickham's powers at that moment, if indeed he heard it. He shifted his weight from one foot to the other and stared helplessly up at the butler before confiding with a rush, "Well—er—actually, Dawson, I don't want to see Mrs. Talbot—I mean, it is really Miss Elcott that I would like to see . . . privately . . . for . . . for just a few minutes, if . . . if I may?"

During this disjointed address, Dawson was struck by the full glory of Mr. Wickham's skintight yellow pantaloons, which were carefully coordinated with a yellow silk waistcoat, the large emerald tiepin nestled among the chaste folds of his neckcloth, and the proliferation of fobs hanging below his coat. The implications of all this splendor, combined with a high color and more than ordinary difficulty in articulating, were instantly clear to the butler who, being of a kind and romantic nature, took pity on the young man's plight. Not by a flicker of an eyelid did he betray his understanding of the situation.

"If you would like to step into the morning room, Mr. Wickham, I will ascertain whether Miss Elcott can spare you a few minutes. This way, sir."

Dawson's tact was rewarded by a rather sickly smile and an appreciable lessening of the tension in Mr. Wickham's shoulders as he suffered himself to be led to a ground-floor room at the back of the house. The butler opened the door to a small apartment and stood aside to allow the caller to enter. There was a fraught moment of indecision while Mr. Wickham waged an internal war against a craven urge to flee, but eventually he advanced into the room. Dawson left him standing in the middle of the Axminster carpet clutching his gray beaver, his eyes fixed on the closing door, his expression that of a man staring down the barrel of a gun.

There was no reply to Dawson's knock on the door to the studio. After a polite pause he tapped again lightly and proceeded to open the door to check that Miss Elcott had indeed removed herself to some other part of the house. To his surprise the room was very much occupied. Dinah Elcott, her back to the door, was engaged in trying to capture on canvas the beauty of an alabaster vase filled with deep red roses, and such was her concentration that she remained oblivious of his presence until he cleared his throat softly.

"Ahem, I beg pardon for the intrusion, Miss Elcott, but Mr. Wickham is in the morning room and desires a word with you if it is convenient."

The involuntary jerk of the hand holding a paintbrush proved she had heard him, but at first the artist only leaned closer to the easel, intent on painting in a small detail. Her left hand waved vaguely out at her side. "Just a minute, please, Dawson. Ah, that's better." Satisfied, Dinah sat back from her canvas and looked over her shoulder. "Now, what did you wish to tell me, Dawson?"

"Mr. Wickham has called to see you, Miss Elcott. He is waiting in the morning room."

Dinah scowled. "Why did you not tell him we aren't receiving today?"

"I did, Miss Elcott, but I am persuaded Mr. Wickham has a particular desire to speak with you privately."

"Could you not ask him to come back tomorrow, Dawson?" she begged in wheedling tones. "I am right in the middle of this painting and it is going so well."

"So I see, miss. Are you painting the roses Mr. Wickham sent you?"

A pregnant pause followed this innocent question. Dinah's rainwater-clear eyes searched the butler's respectful face. "Would it be considered uncivil in me to deny myself, Dawson?"

"Not uncivil precisely, but perhaps a trifle ungracious."

Dinah cast a glance of longing at her unfinished painting and sighed deeply. "Very well, I'll go down to Mr. Wickham." She plunked her brush into a turpentine solution, rose, and whipped off her painting smock, pulling it over her head when she couldn't reach the buttons easily.

"Shall I send Sally up to help you?" Dawson asked, eyeing her crumpled housedress and tousled hair.

Dinah looked up from scrubbing a turpentine-soaked rag across her paint-smeared knuckles. "No, thank you, Dawson, I'll be coming back here directly when Mr. Wickham leaves so there's no point in changing clothes."

Dawson, watching her cursory efforts to make herself more presentable, said hesitantly, "It may be that Mr. Wickham has something of a particular nature to discuss with you, Miss Elcott."

Dinah gave him a careless nod. "So you said." She shook out her skirts, changing the pattern of the wrinkles without removing any, ran her fingers quickly down the length of her hair, and set off for the doorway in a businesslike fashion. "Thank you, Dawson," she said, unconscious of the odd mixture of amusement and resignation on his thin face. She passed him and ran lightly down the stairs.

"You wished to see me, Mr. Wickham?" Dinah entered the

morning room briskly, her hand extended to the man who leapt off the sofa at her approach.

"Ah—er—yes, Miss El—er—Dinah."

Mr. Wickham's nostrils were twitching and he gripped her fingers rather tightly. Dinah tugged her hand free and said with a cheerful smile, "I fear that is turpentine you smell. I have been painting. Shall we sit down?"

She seated herself on an armless Chippendale chair across from the sofa and waited placidly while Mr. Wickham seemed to waffle a bit over a choice of location. After a moment he elected to return to his former place on the rose damask sofa, nearly sitting on the hat he had placed there before he noticed it.

No one spoke for a moment. Then Mr. Wickham, nervously glancing at the expectant girl sitting motionless, her hands in her lap, took a deep breath and plunged. "Miss El—Dinah, er—I *may* call you Dinah?"

Dinah nodded.

"Thank you. My friends call me Ben."

He paused, and Dinah obediently echoed "Ben."

The first step successfully negotiated, Mr. Wickham was emboldened to continue. "You must have noticed, Dinah, that I have grown fond—very fond of you in these past weeks and—"

"You have?"

Dinah's patent surprise seemed to disconcert him. "Dash it all, of course I have! Don't I always come and sit by you whenever we meet?"

"I thought that was because I don't make you talk."

This deplorable piece of frankness threw Mr. Wickham completely off his stride. "You don't make it easy on a fellow to get through this," he said, an accusing note creeping into his voice as he arched his neck free of the constricting folds of his neckcloth.

"Get through what?" Dinah began, and then sat up straighter in her chair, her eyes dilating as comprehension finally dawned. "Mr. Wickham, are you . . . ?" She shook her head as if to clear it. "You *cannot* be asking me to *marry* you?"

"Why not?" he demanded, clearly affronted by her display of astonishment. "I told you I've grown fond of you."

"You're not in love with me," she said flatly, fixing a demanding pair of eyes on his.

Unable to sustain her challenging regard, and wilting visibly under it, Mr. Wickham said in an aggrieved tone, "Who said anything about love? One gets over that sort of foolishness very quickly. Happened to me once when I first came to town. Dreadfully uncomfortable feeling while it lasts, let me tell you. You wouldn't like it. The thing is, must get married eventually, so why not me? We get along fine together and—"

"Mr. Wickham, was it Lady Maria's idea that you should offer for me?"

"I don't—" He stopped, sensing a trap, then conceded. "Well, it might have been her idea initially, but . . . but the notion grows on one the more one thinks about it." The harassed look that accompanied this assurance belied the sentiment expressed.

"Then don't think about it," Dinah advised, getting to her feet and thus compelling her visitor to rise also. "Mr. Wickham, I am deeply sensible of the honor you do me in wishing me to be your wife, but I must decline your flattering offer. I'm afraid we would not suit, and in any case, I don't believe I want to marry."

Mr. Wickham's mental processes were not swift, but eventually he arrived at the correct conclusion. Looking at the composed girl with desperate concentration, he said slowly, "You mean you won't have me? You are turning me down?" he added, determined to get it right.

"Yes, but I do hope we can still be friends," Dinah said with a straight look as she offered him her hand.

Mr. Wickham, gathering up hat, gloves, and walking stick, gave this proposal careful consideration as he took her hand. He said magnanimously, "Well, I don't see why not, if you wish it."

Sitting at her easel a few minutes later, Dinah was unable to recapture the contentment that had been hers before Mr. Wickham's fateful call. The truth was that her conscience was not entirely clear with regard to that gentleman, though she had tried to be kind and conciliatory once she'd guessed the reason for his call. Certainly it was a kindness to stop him before he'd laboriously delivered a formal petition—memorized in all likelihood—for her hand, but she was troubled by a sense of social impropriety or, if not quite so bad as that, at least a social ineptness at not having guessed the situation in time to avert the inevitable chagrin a man must feel at being refused.

Should she have offered him refreshments? she wondered, nibbling on the end of her brush as she stared unseeingly at the canvas. Did the demands of hospitality supersede the natural desire to cut short a meeting attended by embarrassment for both parties? What was the proper protocol for a lady receiving a marriage proposal anyway? It was information she'd never thought to require. She would have to ask Natasha. No, of course she would not ask Natasha. Where had her wits gone? There was no need for anyone to know what had transpired in the morning room today.

On the heels of this thought came the conviction that Dawson, in the mysterious fashion peculiar to good butlers, had divined Mr. Wickham's intention and had tried subtly to prepare her for the interview. A reluctant smile tugged at the corners of Dinah's mouth as she recalled Dawson's gentle hints that she might wish to freshen her appearance, while she, all uncomprehending, had blithely applied turpentine instead of French scent to her grubby and unprepossessing person. Poor Dawson had gone beyond his duty on her behalf to no avail. Her smile faded as a mental image of Benjamin Wickham replaced that of Dawson. Poor Mr. Wickham deserved better after having nerved himself up to propose. On the other hand, she decided, there was no call to descend to a maudlin state of misplaced pity. Mr. Wickham had admitted he wasn't in love with her. His terrible aunt had put him up to this foolishness. He would recover quickly from any problematical disappointment her refusal might have caused him and go back to enjoying a comfortable state of single blessedness for a little while longer, at least until Lady Maria lined up some other unsuspecting girl in her sights.

As for herself, Dinah reflected, bending toward her canvas with a brush newly touched with vermilion, she had never wished or expected to receive an offer of marriage, but perhaps every girl should have the experience once in her life. It was actually somewhat gratifying to know that she had had her chance to marry. On this conclusion she dismissed the incident from her mind and attacked her painting with renewed vigor.

Dinah was wrong in supposing Mr. Wickham's was the only proposal of marriage she would ever receive. In the next two weeks she received two more offers, and gratification was not the emotion uppermost in her breast.

Though neither beautiful nor vivacious, Dinah had rarely found herself without a partner at Almack's weekly balls or the numerous private dances given in the spring. Her performance improved with practice to the point where she considered dancing a mildly pleasurable activity and one, moreover, infinitely to be preferred over sustained talk. In this arena she continued to make a dismal showing, having no flair for amusing quips, no taste for mordant humor or sarcasm *à la* Charles Talbot, and a positive dread of prosy pontificating that came from being raised by Lady Markham. Despite these conspicuous drawbacks, Dinah achieved a degree of popularity with the masculine element that was envied by a number of less successful girls, something that would have puzzled her had she ever noticed it. If she'd given any thought to the circumstances of their company being frequently sought by a variety of gentlemen, she'd have attributed this phenomenon to Natasha's charm and extensive acquaintance among the *beau monde*. As it happened, Dinah's inner attention was often engaged elsewhere when her corporeal being was surrounded by chattering people, and she utterly failed to appreciate the distinction being conferred on her, just as she failed to recognize that she was the object of occasional malicious speculation originating from the disappointment of some less favored young ladies and their ambitious mamas.

Dinah had taken Charles Talbot's strictures against a too-jealous reliance on Natasha's friendship to heart. Within the limits of her reclusive temperament she had exerted herself heroically in response to get upon closer terms with some of the more agreeable young ladies of her acquaintance, with the result that she paid the occasional call unaccompanied by her friend, and sometimes went shopping or walking in the Park with one or another of her contemporaries. If she found these outings more tedious than enjoyable and continued to feel herself a somewhat alien species from other girls her age, she kept these heretical sentiments to herself. Her reward was Natasha's pleasure in what she thought was Dinah's increasingly comfortable assimilation into the society of her peers.

Charles Talbot in his favorite role of observer of his fellow creatures' peculiarities noted and silently applauded Dinah's efforts, the more so because, unlike Natasha, he was not deceived into believing this introverted girl was following her own personal inclinations in submerging herself more deeply in the social swim.

Charles also noted Dinah's increasing popularity with the opposite sex and derived no little amusement from watching the maneuvers of various gentlemen vying to engage her attention. He was not entirely unprepared for the lack of success that attended the lion's share of such attempts. His privileged position in the Talbot *ménage* had provided an opportunity to witness the intricate workings of Miss Elcott's mind. She put on no airs, but her simplicity was still deceptive. He knew that behind that calm, attentive—sometimes unnerving—regard, Dinah was often absent in spirit, busy reducing her surroundings to visual symbols for painting, or simply following her own train of thought, perhaps prompted by a random remark that captured her interest. Her would-be suitors, not possessing the key to Miss Elcott's mental complexity, were baffled to find that any imagined progress they'd made, as measured by her seeming compliance and good will, was often negated by her inability to recall even their names at the next meeting. Dinah's vagueness seemed to be proof against the practiced gallantry of the town's most successful beaus. She carried her own protection with her.

Charles's innate cynicism did not allow room for doubt that the news of Dinah's status as a prospective heiress had gotten abroad. The girl possessed neither the beauty nor the provocative charm to attract the sort of men who were paying court to her at present. Unfortunately, the crowd around her was all too likely to discourage the honest, steady type of suitor who would make her a good husband. This would be more serious, of course, if Dinah were bent on finding a husband like most of her contemporaries, but Charles had gradually come to accept her flat declaration of disinterest in marriage as a truthful

representation of her ideas on that subject. Whether this decision of her intellect accurately reflected her innermost feelings—assuming she had any such feelings or enough
self-knowledge to interpret them—was something upon which
he did not feel qualified to express an opinion. A tiny corner of
his mind refused to accept that Dinah was such an unnatural
female as to consider the married state repugnant in itself, but
that reluctance on his part might well be attributable to masculine vanity. Still, he thought he had learned enough about her
to theorize that Dinah had a low opinion of her own worthi-
ness as a female. She possessed a strong belief in her artistic
talent and her ability to overcome obstacles in pursuing her
chosen path, but that was a vastly different matter. He based
his assumptions about her lack of feminine confidence on casual remarks Dinah had let drop about her life in Devon that
added up to a picture of a child whose physical needs always
had been attended to by servants while her existence had been
largely ignored by those most closely related to her.

His idle speculations about Dinah Elcott might turn out to
be pure fustian in the end, but they entertained him while he
observed and chronicled the attempts of some of England's
most egregious fortune hunters to make themselves agreeable
to one of the Season's richest matrimonial prizes. For the most
part, Dinah's chilling vagueness preserved her from intense
gallantries, so there had been no need for Cam to take any action *in loco parentis*, not that his cousin had seemed inclined
toward intervention. When Charles had presented him with a
partial list of the hopeful swains in Dinah's train, Cam had
taken the sanguine view that Dinah's good sense would prevail
without the necessity of his playing a heavy-handed role to
save her from bestowing her affections and expectations on a
fortune hunter.

"Only while her heart remains untouched," Charles had retorted. "As with all females, her good sense will desert her the
instant she fancies herself in love with one of these golden-
tongued flatterers, and then the damage will be done. You
won't be able to prevent her from getting hurt."

"Is it your considered opinion that Dinah is in imminent
danger of losing her heart to one of her ineligible admirers?"
Cam had asked.

"Not at present, no," Charles had been forced to concede, annoyed with himself for having given his cousin the smallest opening for one of his superior smiles. Cam had gone on to thank Charles gently for his generous concern in the matter of their visitor's ultimate happiness.

"It doesn't signify, Coz; it's all in the family, after all." Charles had managed a negligent little wave of his fingers, though he'd had to unclench his jaw to speak at all. After this conversation he had resolved to ignore the developing situation, a sensible resolution that he was forced to break within a few days.

He had escorted Dinah and Natasha to a private ball in his cousin's stead. Natasha had been her usual outgoing self in the carriage, but he'd gained the impression that there was a distinctly cooler edge to Dinah's manner toward him. It crossed his mind that the chit might be indulging a fit of pique because he did not choose to swell the ranks of those competing for her attention. She had never totally relaxed her wariness in his presence, however, which cast doubt on this facile explanation for her coolness, but he quickly dismissed it from his mind in favor of enjoying himself with some old friends whom he hadn't seen in town this spring.

It was late in the evening when Charles, returning alone from the supper room with the courteous but belated intention of checking on the welfare of his ladies, spotted Dinah coming toward him. Her quickened pace, faintly pink cheeks, and glittering eyes were sufficient indication to one who knew her well that the self-contained girl was in the grip of an uncharacteristic agitation of spirits. She averted her eyes and would have passed him with no more than a nod had not Charles stepped into her path. Dinah pulled up short and raised determinedly blank eyes to his, silently waiting for his explanation.

Though he admired the swift command with which she mastered her expression, he was not led into the error of believing he'd been mistaken about her emotional state, and it was with genuine concern that he inquired, "Are you all right, Dinah? Is there something I can do for you?"

"Thank you, you've done quite enough already," she replied with a sudden bitter twist to her lips. "My throat is dry. If I might pass, I'll get myself a glass of punch in the supper room."

Charles's eyes had not left her face. The flush had died down and she'd obviously regretted the cryptic accusation because she'd instantly offered an innocuous explanation for her appearance. He said smoothly, "You must permit me to procure a punch cup for you, my dear Dinah." Since these polite words were accompanied by a firm grip on her arm, Dinah could not do else but go with him unless she chose to create a scene.

He steered her to an empty table and kept one eye on her while he filled her order, having no illusions about her disinclination for his company. "Now, what is this all about?" he invited as he handed her the glass and seated himself beside her.

Dinah concentrated on sipping the contents of her glass. "It's nothing. I told you, my throat was dry."

"Don't fence with me, Dinah. You implied that I am somehow responsible for your flustered state, which is *not* due to a dry throat. What have I done to annoy you? I cannot apologize properly until I know my crime," he added with a sudden smile of pure friendliness.

For a second Dinah's veiled hostility melted and then she looked away from him, her face a frozen blank again. "You are talking nonsense," she insisted, sipping her punch.

"Very well, since you prefer innuendo to direct dealing, we'll leave the subject of my putative offense for the moment," he said briskly. "What sent you rushing down to the supper room unescorted and in a state? Surely a lady as popular as your charming self could command any number of gentlemen eager to attend to her wishes."

"Oh, yes," she flared, coming off her high horse in the face of his sarcasm and turning eyes full of burning reproach on him. "My odious popularity, which you have assured will plague the life out of me. I have just been compelled to endure a declaration of undying affection from a man who doesn't even know the color of my eyes and who became sullen and argumentative when I turned down his insulting offer in far more civil terms than it merited. What's more, that was the second such proposal this week, and I only narrowly managed to stave off another by hiding in the cloakroom for forty-five minutes at Lady Silton's musical evening on Tuesday."

"I fear such impetuous persecution is often the lot of a female who attains the enviable status of a Toast of the Town."

Charles's light tones, at variance with hard blue eyes, served to further inflame Dinah's passions. "I'm glad you are pleased with the result of your little joke, sir. If you hadn't broadcast the fact of my father's wealth around town, I would have remained in happy obscurity and I might even have been able to enjoy some of the Season's events," she cried, glaring at him.

"You are mistaken in attributing any public knowledge of your father's circumstances to me. Not one word on this subject has passed my lips since your arrival in London."

"You are the only person apart from the Talbots who knew," she argued, but uncertainty had crept into her face and voice as she stared into his icy, controlled countenance.

Charles rose from his chair and bowed stiffly. "I am not in the habit of having my word doubted, but since you do, there is nothing further to be said. I will remove my objectionable person from your presence immediately."

He strolled away in a leisurely fashion, leaving the white-faced girl sitting alone at the table, miserably aware that a disaster of no small proportions had just occurred.

The drive to Portman Square was accomplished in an atmosphere made heavy by Dinah's inability to fully conceal her distress despite Charles and Natasha's tactful conversation designed to obscure this fact. Natasha wasted no time in worming the entire story of the dismal evening from her friend when she followed her to her bedchamber that night. She was dismayed at the sudden unhappy turn of events, but it was not in her power to smooth things over for Dinah. She too had privately wondered if Charles's loose tongue had been the instrument that had created the queue of prudent admirers vying for the girl's attentions, knowing he was quite capable of deriving cynical satisfaction from observing the disingenuousness and hypocrisy of his fellows. On the other hand, she had never known Charles to disown his actions, nor was it like him to deliberately hurt a vulnerable person like Dinah. She soothed the unhappy girl as best she could and made her drink hot milk before tucking her into bed with the well-intentioned advice to

put the whole affair out of her mind until morning, when th
situation would look less bleak.

Natasha was less confident of a happy resolution of the af
fair when she repeated the essentials to Cam the next mornin
at breakfast, which the two shared in private, Dinah not havin
put in an appearance.

"I thought they were finally beginning to like each othe
but obviously the suspicion that Charles told people her cir
cumstances out of pure mischief has been festering in Dina
for some time or she would not have hit out at him like tha
last night. She is miserable, poor child, no longer convinced o
his guilt but equally unable to accept his denial wholeheart
edly. I am not absolutely sure of his innocence myself, and i
is an uncomfortable feeling to doubt one's friends' veracity.
have never doubted Charles before."

Cam reached across the table and gripped his wife's hand
smiling at her troubled expression. "My deplorable cousin ha
brought this on himself with that damned malicious humor h
delights in, but I must say in his defense that I have neve
known Charles to lie to save his skin. That would go agains
that fierce pride of his. Don't fret yourself to ribbons over this
my love. I'll speak to Dinah. I rather think the news of he
being an heiress can be laid not at Charles's door, but at mine
at least indirectly. A few weeks ago Lady Featherstone wa
quizzing me closely about Elcott's identity, claiming she knev
a family by that name and wished to find out if it was the sam
one. I didn't think much about it at the time, but now that yo
tell me that MacKenzie was one of the men who offered fo
Dinah, it begins to fall into place. He is Lady Featherstone'
younger brother, a spendthrift and gambler who has been look
ing for a rich wife to support his expensive habits for years
The other one you mentioned, Martin Doubleday, is cut from
the same bolt of goods, and the two are thick as thieves
Charles warned me about the caliber of some of the me
buzzing around Dinah. It seems I have been grossly neglectfu
of my duty toward her, but I'll see that I accompany you a
often as possible from now on. We can't have that poor gir
harassed by all the gazetted fortune hunters in London."

* * *

Cam was as good as his word. He sought out Dinah for a private talk that very evening and contrived to make himself available for escort duty for most of the private entertainments his wife and guest attended. Dinah's court was diminished by some of the more notorious fortune hunters, for which she was most grateful. She retained enough of her former popularity to ensure that she had plenty of masculine company during their outings, and might have been quite content with her lot except for one glaring source of discomfort.

Dinah had been both relieved and dismayed to learn of Charles's innocence in the matter of acquainting the *ton* with her status as an heiress. A persistent twinge of soreness deep within at the thought of his knowingly injuring her healed itself at that juncture. Unhappily, her dismay at her unjustified accusations was not able to find an outlet in apology, for Charles did not come near Portman Square in the week that followed their quarrel. Nor did she so much as set eyes on him at any of the parties they attended during that time. When she did at last espy his lithe figure displaying superior waltzing form on Almack's dance floor, she was too far away to catch his eye. During the next few hours she did not once succeed in reducing the distance between them enough to permit their eyes to meet despite starting in his direction on three separate occasions. Once when she was dancing herself she spotted him in earnest discussion with Natasha, but he had disappeared by the time her partner returned her to her friend's side.

By the end of the evening even someone as socially backward as Dinah had to realize that only a great deal of skill in avoidance tactics had prevented her from coming face-to-face with Charles. She went home that night feeling diminished and unhappy but no less determined to get the necessary apology behind her, even if Charles rejected her efforts to repair their damaged friendship.

10

"Charles, may I speak to you for a moment, please?"

Dinah had chosen her moment well. Charles wa[s] standing with his back to her, chatting with Lady Cooper an[d] Lady Jersey. He could not refuse her request without settin[g] those active tongues wagging. Not that it even occurred to h[im] that he might refuse outright to speak with her. Charles wa[s] never other than a gentleman despite his barbed tongue. Whil[e] she smiled nervously at the two august personages regardin[g] her with mild interest, Charles made his excuses, taking he[r] elbow to lead her toward a small alcove partially screene[d] from the improvised dance floor by a row of decorative pal[m] trees. There was a backless gilded bench with an upholstere[d] seat of gold damask in the alcove, and Charles guided her to i[t.] He remained standing, which immediately set her at a disa[d]vantage, but Dinah did not possess the kind of pride that foun[d] this galling. She looked up at him beseechingly, noting wit[h] regret the absence of the indulgent good humor that had cha[r]acterized his attitude toward her until their quarrel.

"Charles, I am terribly sorry," she said in a rush, grippin[g] her hands together. "Cam told me it was he who inadvertentl[y] let it out about my expectations. He told Lady Featherston[e] who my father is. Her brother was one of the men who pr[o]posed to me. Please forgive me for not believing your word. I[t] was very bad of me, but I . . . I don't know you as well as Ca[m] does," she finished on a pleading note.

Charles's remote expression gradually thawed in the face o[f] Dinah's sincerity. An alert look came into his eyes when sh[e] spoke of Cam. "So my cousin knows me well, does he?" he re[-] peated, an odd note in his voice.

Dinah nodded. "Cam said you are as irritatingly mischie[vous]

vous as a cartload of monkeys but that you would never lie to escape the consequences of your actions." Emotions too fleeting to pin down came and went in Charles's eyes as the sense of her words sank in.

"It seems he does know me," was all he said on that subject, but as he looked into Dinah's anxious face his austere expression softened. "I'm sorry too, Dinah. Considering the way I teased you about your prospects in the beginning, it was sheer presumption to expect you to take my unsupported word that I had not been having malicious fun at your expense. Shall we strike the past and start again as friends?"

She took the hand he extended to her and allowed him to pull her to her feet, smiling shyly. "Thank you, I would like that."

He shook her hand solemnly, then placed it on his bent arm and led her back past the palm trees. Sensing her lingering discomfort, he said to put her at her ease, "How are the painting lessons going? Are you and Martin Crossman getting to know one another better? He is a fine artist but not really interested in people, I fear."

"The lessons are wonderful," Dinah said, adding with a little chuckle, "as for Mr. Crossman, he still calls me 'Miss Er' and always looks surprised to see me enter his studio, even after six weeks of tuition."

"Do you still spend Monday and Wednesday mornings in Long Acre?"

"Yes, unless Natasha needs me for some special reason."

Dinah was looking relaxed and content by the time they reentered the main section of the room. Charles smiled at her and they turned to seek Natasha.

When the couple passed beyond hearing range of two silent men on the other side of the screen of trees, the man in the dark coat said, "Well, there she is, not much to look at but not so simple as she looks either."

"Thanks, Doubleday. I'm in your debt," said the other.

"Not unless you make more headway with Miss Indifference than I think you will," the man in the dark coat declared carelessly. "The girl's not like most females; in fact, she's got a deuced odd kick in her gallop. I suppose you want me to present you?"

"Quite the contrary, old son. If she's twigged you, you're the last person I'd wish to present me, if I may say this without fear of giving offense?"

The older man grinned. "You may say what you damn please. I'm not a sensitive soul."

"Who is the man with her? They looked to be rather well acquainted."

"That is Charles Talbot. It's his cousins the girl's staying with for the Season. So far as I know, Talbot has never pursued any female with serious intent. He's a supercilious blighter with a damned nasty tongue in his head under the guise of smiling civility. I daresay he has never found a female who measures up to his exacting standards."

"A healthy fortune can whitewash a lot of faults. And the girl has a certain piquant appeal. She's not just in the common style, I'd say."

"Truer words were never spoken as far as your last statement is concerned. I wish you luck in storming the fortress. Shall we head into the card room?"

His companion assented to this suggestion and the two men abandoned their post behind the palm screen.

Dinah ran down the steep stairs, her portfolio banging against her thigh. Suddenly she turned to say something over her shoulder to Mrs. Evans, coming along behind her, and ran smack into a solid wall of flesh and bone. Her balance overset, she'd have fallen ignominiously had not the person she'd bumped into put out two strong hands to steady her. When she got her balance back, Dinah looked up into a pair of concerned brown eyes.

"I . . . I beg your pardon, sir. That was stupid and clumsy of me. Did I hurt you?"

A rich chuckle sounded in the region of her ear as the man on the step below her, still holding her upper arms, said, smiling down at her, "How could a fairy creature like yourself hurt a huge hulk like me? It's you I am anxious about. Are you quite certain you are all right? Perhaps you should sit down for a moment to regain your breath. I've jolted you badly, I fear, clumsy oaf that I am."

During this gentle monologue, Dinah continued to stare up

into the face of her rescuer, a bemused look in her eyes as she assimilated the fact that here was the epitome of masculine perfection a few inches away from her—closer, in fact, than a dancing partner, for he still held her by the arms. She became aware of the clean, pleasant aroma of his skin, the warmth in his eyes, and the rapid beating of her heart in the time it took for him to ease her acquiescent form down onto a step. The solidity of the wooden stair beneath her and the sound of Mrs. Evans voicing her concern snapped Dinah back to the reality of the situation. She tossed her head and bounced up, dislodging the man's hands as she clutched her portfolio more securely and smiled at him.

"I am completely unhurt, I assure you, sir, just a trifle winded for a second. I must thank you for saving me from a fall. The accident was entirely my fault in any case. I was not looking where I was going." She drew back near the wall as if to allow him passage room, saying, "Were you going up the stairs?"

"Yes, if that is the studio of Martin Crossman above us. I am interested in studying painting under a good teacher, and Mr. Crossman has been recommended to me. Are you an artist too?" he asked, eyeing her portfolio.

"Just a student at present," Dinah replied, returning the stranger's friendly smile.

"We must not keep this gentleman from his appointment, my dear," Mrs. Evans chimed in, bringing Dinah to a belated sense of the unconventionality of the present situation.

"Of course not," she agreed, moving down a step with a farewell nod to the man, who had politely removed his hat. "Thank you again, sir. Good-bye."

The ladies continued on down the stairs without further delay, but Dinah could not resist swiveling her head for one last look when she reached the bottom. The tall, handsome gentleman was standing exactly where she'd left him, staring after her with a warmth in his eyes that caused her pulses to accelerate again. Hastily she removed her glance and person from the building.

Natasha had not returned from a visit to an old friend of her mother's when Dinah arrived back in Portman Square. The woman, who suffered from a severe arthritic complaint that rendered her housebound, had expressed a wish to meet her dear friend's grandchild, and Natasha, never loath to show off her darling, had brought Justin to Kensington. In the half hour before luncheon would be served, Dinah hurried to her workroom as was her custom. Once there she ignored the unfinished canvas on the easel, electing instead to make some rapid pencil sketches.

After fifteen minutes and several torn sheets of paper, she put down the pencil and propped a sketch in front of the painting on the easel. Her puckered forehead as she stepped back and surveyed the drawing was evidence of dissatisfaction with her work, which was a recognizable portrait of the young man she'd bumped into on the stairway of Mr. Crossman's building.

Certain features had burned themselves into her memory: the beautiful golden-brown eyes with their look of warmth and the cleft chin beneath smiling lips, but the entire incident had probably lasted no more than a minute or two, even though time seemed to have stopped while they looked into each other's eyes. She'd gotten the shape of the face wrong; she couldn't recall whether his brow was wider than most. All she knew was that for a short time she'd beheld the personification of masculine beauty in the flesh. Until today she'd considered Cam Talbot with his perfectly carved features the handsomest man of her acquaintance, but Cam could not boast of a head of guinea-gold curls or skin bronzed by the sun . . . nor did he have an intriguing dent in his chin. Of its own accord, her pencil deepened that shadowed area in her sketch, then moved up to thin the line from cheekbone to chin. That was closer to the original but still not right.

The luncheon bell rang, and Dinah removed the drawing from the easel, tucking it safely into her portfolio. How frustrating to know the portrait must remain inaccurate, since she would never see the handsome stranger again. She was aware of a disproportionately acute pang of disappointment at this situation.

Dinah's disappointment on this head was destined to be of a temporary nature, however, for she met the gentleman again within a sennight.

She saw him the instant she opened the door to leave Mr.

Crossman's building. He was about to enter at the same time, his hand extended toward the doorknob as she pulled it open from inside. He was even more handsome than she remembered, thanks to a brilliant smile that displayed to advantage a perfect set of white teeth.

"What luck that we should meet again! I had not dared to hope for such good fortune," the gentleman cried in undisguised delight. He raised his hat and stepped back to allow Dinah to come outside.

Her pleasure, every bit as great as the man's at the serendipitous workings of fate, was contained behind a polite little smile, though her eyes, did she but know it, were glowing with excitement. Her reply was very matter-of-fact. "How do you do, sir? Are you going up to Mr. Crossman's studio? Have you been taken on by him as a pupil?"

"Not yet. He was too busy to speak with me the first time I came, so you see me here again to make another try."

"You do not have any of your work with you?" she asked, clutching her own portfolio closer.

"No. I thought I'd wait until I gained some idea of Mr. Crossman's feelings in the matter of taking on pupils. But how is it that you are alone?" he inquired, glancing back at the closed door. "Did your companion—chaperone?—not accompany you today?"

"Oh, yes, but she had an errand, so she went on ahead."

"Then you must permit me to escort you to your home."

"Thank you, sir, it is very kind of you to offer, but there is no need. Mrs. Evans will be waiting for me at the chemist's shop on the next corner with our carriage."

"Then I shall escort you to this shop."

"I could not put you to the trouble, sir. Besides, you were on your way to see Mr. Crossman."

"We did not have a fixed appointment, however. Please, for my peace of mind, accept my company. I would feel most uneasy knowing you were unaccompanied even a short distance in this section of town. I really am quite respectable," he added with his delightful smile as Dinah hesitated.

"Oh, of course . . . I did not mean to imply . . . Very well, then, I should be glad of your company," Dinah said quickly, concerned lest she had seemed rude.

"And I shall be honored with yours," was the gallant response as the stranger took her portfolio from her and offered his arm, which she accepted with a shy smile.

They walked a few paces in silence before the gentleman gave a soft laugh. Dinah looked at him questioningly.

"It occurs to me that in default of a third party to do the honors I shall never find out your name without committing the solecism of introducing myself . . . if you will permit this breach of etiquette, ma'am?"

Dinah was not proof against the charm of the smile that accompanied this request. She gave a small nod, which was all the encouragement needed.

"I am Godfrey Bellingham, very much at your service indeed, and now it is your turn."

"How do you do, sir. My name is Dinah Elcott," she replied like a polite little girl brought into the drawing room to meet her parents' friends.

"Dinah," he replied slowly, as if tasting the sound on his tongue. "I like that. It's unusual and it suits you. You are unlike any girl I've ever met."

"I assure you, sir, I am a distressingly ordinary female," Dinah replied, the color in her cheeks fluctuating under the open admiration in Mr. Bellingham's light brown eyes.

"I hate to appear argumentative at the very beginning of our acquaintance, but you are not at all ordinary," he insisted with pleasant firmness. "For one thing, I know of no other young woman who is studying under a well-known artist. How did this come about?"

Encouraged by his obvious interest, Dinah began to speak about her passion for sketching and painting. What started as a brief history on her part turned into a lively exchange of ideas as she finally encountered a man who did not see anything strange or unfeminine in her desire to perfect and use her talent. Even Charles had protested at first and flatly declined to help her enroll in a life-drawing class except under very restrictive conditions. She learned that Mr. Bellingham's main area of interest was landscape painting, and he confessed that he had no aptitude for drawing the human figure, adding ruefully that he knelt in humble reverence before those fortunate beings who possessed this skill.

All too soon the corner where the pharmacy was located loomed up before them, with the Talbot carriage waiting outside. By tacit agreement, they slowed their steps to prolong the present pleasure.

"I . . . we cannot just say good-bye forever when we have so much to talk about," Mr. Bellingham said, adding diffidently, "that is, if you would like to continue our acquaintance as much as I would."

Dinah answered the question in his eyes. "Yes, of course I would. Could you not come to call on us? It is obvious that you are a gentleman of refinement."

His lips twisted wryly for a second before he said, choosing his words with care, "It is certainly true that there is nothing in my background that would preclude friendship between us, but I fear your parents would be shocked, and rightly so, at such unconscionable presumption on my part. We have not been properly introduced. In fact, they might consider with some justification that I had accosted you and taken advantage of your innocence in speaking to you at all."

"It wasn't like that," Dinah said calmly. "I am staying with friends who are not at all stuffy or high in the instep, but perhaps it would be better—more *convenable*—if we could discover a mutual acquaintance."

He grasped at the invitation in her words. "That is a capital notion, but there is no time today. Will you be at Mr. Crossman's next week at the same time?" When she confirmed this with a nod, not forward enough to confess that she spent two mornings per week with the artist, Mr. Bellingham produced an elated laugh and said with a twinkle in his eyes, "Then you will have a sennight in which to invent another errand for Mrs. Evans, and I shall spend the time making a list of my most prepossessing acquaintances in town. I believe I see Mrs. Evans coming out of the chemist's shop now, so I shall return this to you and make myself scarce to avoid any embarrassment for you."

He moved so quickly that Dinah found herself holding her portfolio and staring at his rapidly retreating back before she could protest that she would not be at all embarrassed to present him to Mrs. Evans. She turned reluctantly and resumed her trek, mentally selecting the best phrases to explain the

quite unexceptionable circumstances under which she had accepted Mr. Bellingham's escort.

As it turned out, Mrs. Evans, on emerging from the shop,
had glanced first into the carriage to see if her charge had returned, and by the time she spotted Dinah, Mr. Bellingham
was lost in the distance. There seemed to be no real reason to
bother with complicated explanations after all.

Happily, Mrs. Evans was not one to chatter excessively, for
Dinah's head was chock-full of the recent exhilarating experience. She was content on the homeward drive to recall in detail the delightful discussion she'd had with Mr. Bellingham,
forgetting for once her customary interest in the many varieties
of human life they passed en route. Instead, she mulled over
every nuance, tried to recapture each shade of meaning in his
charming voice and beautiful eyes. She was confident that this
time she would get his likeness down accurately on paper if
she attempted it as soon as she got home, while his image was
fresh in her visual memory.

Dinah acknowledged to herself that she preferred solitude
for once over Natasha's companionship. Thinking of her hostess, her elation dimmed just a little. Should she mention the incident to her friend? Her instinct was to hug the delightful
episode to herself at present. In all likelihood she was attach-
ing too much importance to a pleasant but casual and essentially meaningless interaction. Her conversation with Mr.
Bellingham had arisen quite naturally out of unusual circumstances. He had probably dismissed it—and her—from his
mind as soon as he turned the first corner. It had no lasting sig-
nificance and was not worth relating to Natasha. That would
be to lend the affair an importance it did not warrant.

This line of careful rationalization convinced Dinah to say
nothing to her friend about Mr. Bellingham. She tried but did
not quite succeed in convincing herself that the odds were all
against a friendship developing from such an unconventional
beginning. Mr. Bellingham had said he could not call on her in
Portman Square as a result of their irregular meeting. An inner
voice reminded her that he had also strongly intimated that he
intended to see her again. For the moment she was content to
cherish the possibility of a continuation of their acquaintance,

but she was utterly resolved to keep this hope pushed to the farthest corner of her mind.

In the days that followed, Dinah conscientiously kept to her resolve, expelling the image of Mr. Bellingham whenever it intruded—as happened with disconcerting frequency—into her awareness. As a corollary to this endeavor and a sop to her conscience, she concentrated on focusing her attention more strictly than was her wont on the numerous social situations in which she found herself during the course of a typical week. The result of this policy was that her brain actually recorded a larger proportion of the inanities and outright nonsense that generally bounced harmlessly off her eardrums.

There *must* be more rational conversations taking place somewhere in this vast city, she thought with a silent scream one evening at a private party, repressing with difficulty an overpowering urge to jump up and run out into the cool night air, away from this stifling exchange of regurgitated banalities. At that moment her glance collided with that of Charles Talbot, walking away from a trio of gentlemen, two of whom she could now identify as prominent Members of Parliament. In less than a minute he had coolly cut her out of the pack of young people on the smiling excuse that she was in need of some gentle exercise. She accepted his arm with alacrity and strolled off, her restlessness palliated by the physical freedom. She exhaled a breath of relief and said gratefully, "Thank you, Charles."

"I'm always happy to rescue a desperate, glassy-eyed female in the hope that she might be inveigled into a delicious flirtation to ease her boredom," he returned lightly, his keen glance at odds with his habitual indolent grace.

Dinah chuckled in genuine amusement but demurred. "Sorry to disappoint you, sir, but the art of flirtation is yet another social accomplishment I lack."

"It is one that can be acquired with the proper tuition. I believe I might claim a modest success in this arena if you care to put yourself in my hands—ah, not literally, of course," he added with an exaggerated leer that won him a spontaneous smile.

"Thank you for the kind offer, but it is my unalterable belief that flirtation is an innate not an acquired talent."

"Foiled again," he declared cheerfully, "and it seemed suc' a promising approach too. Feeling better?" he asked a momer later. "What brought on this attack of the megrims?"

Her smile faded and she looked away from the kindness i his face. "I fear I am simply not a gregarious person. I don' feel comfortable in a group exchanging meaningless platitude by rote."

"No, you are not a social animal," he agreed, "but the con ventions have their uses. They keep people at a safe distanc and prevent 'meaningful' communication. We'd all be at eac' other's throats otherwise."

"A rather cynical attitude."

He shrugged. "A matter of interpretation. I prefer to think o myself as aware of the underlying realities of life."

Dinah was still digesting this when Charles returned her t Natasha. He traded amusing banter with Natasha and an el derly matron for a few moments before withdrawing with final smile for the quiet Dinah.

The critical day did at last arrive and with it Godfre' Bellingham at the end of a class of life drawing that earned a inattentive Dinah more criticism from Mr. Crossman than i all the lessons that had preceded it. This, added to the guilt knowledge that she was behaving badly by sending Mrs Evans off on a trumped up errand, ensured that Dinah did no emerge from the studio in the most equable spirits.

Guilt and uncertainty vanished in the face of Godfrey' open delight in her appearance. Suddenly there was so much t say to each other and so little time in which to do so. Time be came their enemy that day and remained unrelentingly inimi cal over the next fortnight as the two traded life histories an explained themselves in tiny, regulated increments.

Dinah and Godfrey met by prearrangement following eac' of her twice-weekly art lessons, but they could not stretc' these stolen intervals much beyond fifteen minutes without in volving Mrs. Evans in what had inevitably become a conspir acy, not against any person but against a malign combinatio of circumstances that decreed friendship between them un seemly at present.

At the first meeting that could rightly be called an assigna tion, Dinah had brought forth the names of more than a half dozen young men in Godfrey's age bracket, the mid-twenties, but he could not claim acquaintance with any, nor was he upon calling terms with any of the families closest to the Talbots. The hopeful light died out of her eyes at this seemingly insurmountable barrier to putting their growing friendship on a conventional footing, but Godfrey rallied her flagging spirits, insisting that it was only a matter of time before they hit upon someone they could press into service on their behalf.

It was Godfrey's ardent persuasiveness on this head that enabled Dinah to overcome her scruples and agree to continue their secret meetings. While she was with him her doubts as to the propriety of their actions receded to the far background under the influence of his potent charm. He swept her along on a heady wave of elation and optimism, which only gradually ebbed when she was away from the intoxicating influence of his certainty that matters would turn out as they desired. When she confided her fears to him at their next meeting he teased her gently, calling her an adorable little coward and promising that what looked like insurmountable problems were destined to resolve themselves in their favor.

Dinah was happier than she'd ever been in her life, conscious of happiness as an entity, a condition like health to be enjoyed by those fortunate enough to have had it bestowed upon them through no meritorious efforts of their own. When she was with Godfrey her blood raced through her veins and joyous laughter continually bubbled from her lips. Gazing at his beautiful face, seeing the warmth in his eyes for her alone, was the visual equivalent of feasting in a baronial banquet hall, a superabundance that nearly overwhelmed the senses.

Contrarily, just getting through the long days when she could not see him required heroic feats of discipline on her part to keep from betraying her consuming desire to be elsewhere with someone else. That would have been sufficiently unsettling without being simultaneously bedeviled by torturous guilt at the deceit she was practicing on Natasha, whom she loved and to whom she was deeply indebted for making this wonderful experience possible. All her emotions seemed to be in a heightened state at present, and what was worse, she ricocheted from euphoria and optimism to lethargy and despair like a billiard ball caroming around a table. In her saner mo-

ments she recognized that such exaggerated states could no
long endure. Surely this frantic fluctuation would be tempere
as soon as her friendship with Godfrey—at this point she re
fused to call it by any other name—became an accepted part o
her life.

11

"Charles, what a nice surprise! It seems ages since we've set eyes on you."

Charles basked in the pleasure radiating from Natasha's dark eyes and raised the hand she extended to his lips. "The discomforts of traveling over corduroy roads are of trifling moment in exchange for a welcome like this. I should be sorely tempted to repeat the exercise were it not for the necessary loss of your company in the meantime."

"Idiot!" she said, laughing at his exaggerated gallantry. She released her hand and patted the chair at her side, an invitation he lost no time in accepting.

"Cam told me you have been down at Seven Oaks supervising the planting for Sir Humphrey this past fortnight."

"Yes, my father finds traveling increasingly onerous these days, so I offered to spare him this trip."

"And so you should. Seven Oaks will be yours one day. It's more than time that you took some of the burden of running the estate from your father's shoulders."

"One of the things I have long admired about you, dear heart, is your uncompromising honesty," Charles murmured, "devastating though it often is to my *amour propre*."

"Well, we never have stood upon ceremony with each other, have we, Charles? Perhaps that is why our friendship is so strong; it is based upon truth."

"I would not dream of disputing with you, since you are so enamored of your theory," Charles replied softly, an enigmatic smile touching his lips for a second. He acknowledged the greetings of those persons sitting closest to Natasha and glanced idly at the couples circling Almack's dance floor. "I assume your charge is somewhere in that throng?"

"Yes, she is wearing green tonight."

Even as Natasha spoke, Charles spotted Dinah's unadorned silky hair, conspicuous among the elaborately dressed heads adopted by most of the females on the dance floor. She was clad in a simple gown the tender green of new willow leaves and was gliding effortlessly around the perimeter of the floor in the decorous hold of a rather spotty-faced youth wearing a coat with outsize silver buttons.

"Her dancing has improved out of all recognition lately," Charles observed.

"Yes. All that was wanting was a little application and the confidence that comes with practice. She is very lithe and quite strong for her delicate build. I have devised an exercise routine to help her keep her muscles supple here in the city where she cannot walk for hours each day as she does at home."

Charles's eyes remained on Dinah as the music ended and her partner escorted her in their direction. "Who is responsible for the new confidence—certainly not that spotty youth?"

Natasha laughed. "She is looking very blooming these days, is she not? But you are mistaken if you think a man is responsible. Dinah has never displayed the least hint of partiality for any of the men who seek her out. Quite the opposite; she is rather bored by all of them."

"Nevertheless, I do not mistake, my dear Natasha; only a man could have put that radiance in her eyes," Charles retorted in a low-voiced aside as he rose to greet the couple who were approaching them.

Dinah bestowed a friendly though absent-minded smile on Charles and allowed, when he asked, that she had one dance left, a waltz.

"Ah, a milestone. You have received permission to waltz from the benevolent goddesses who superintend the rites at this sacred shrine," he remarked in portentous tones.

Dinah smiled unself-consciously. "At long last. I should not wonder if the hostesses had all trembled lest I should trip my partners and cause widespread disaster on the dance floor."

"I trust all danger of such a harrowing prospect is past, Miss Elcott?" he queried with mock anxiety.

"I shall quite understand if you would like to withdraw your invitation, sir."

"Minx." Charles grinned at the wide-eyed look of innocence she gave him and tapped her cheek with a careless finger before excusing himself to speak to an old friend who had just come up to them.

His dance with Dinah was near the end of the evening. At intervals during the next two hours, Charles found his glance seeking her out, assessing her attitude toward her partners with piqued interest. He saw nothing to support his earlier contention that Dinah's new maturity and yes, radiance was not too strong a word, were attributable to romantic feelings for someone. And reciprocated feelings at that, despite Natasha's denial. As the implications of this line of thought came home to him, a slight frown settled over his features. Why was her chaperone being kept in ignorance of Dinah's interest in one of her suitors? The two girls were most compatible; indeed, Dinah gave the impression of having a case of hero worship in her regard for Natasha. What was the chit up to?

Charles's bland expression gave away none of the conjectures seething in his brain when he collected Dinah for their waltz. He was too experienced a hand to pounce on her, an action guaranteed to drive the always-reticent girl into full retreat. He let several minutes go by in comfortable silence before making the most innocuous beginning.

"May I compliment you on your performance in the waltz, Dinah? You have become a first-class partner, very responsive to my every move."

"Thank you, Charles. Cam has been so obliging as to practice with me on occasion at home."

Charles detected an undertone in the sweet voice and laughed as he whirled her safely out of the path of an aggressive pair determined to have the outside perimeter all to themselves. "So it still rankles that *I* was *not* so obliging, does it?"

A tiny dimple that had escaped his notice until now quivered at the left corner of her mouth as she airily denied the charge, ending with a meek declaration that she was truly honored to be deemed worthy to partner him.

"Now you are in danger of getting above yourself, my child," he said indulgently, but the expression in his eyes sharpened as he gazed into her upturned face sparkling with demure mischief. "Not so long ago you claimed to have no talent for flirtation. Whom have you been practicing on, I wonder?"

She stiffened for an instant and nearly lost step. "I? No one. I never flirt." The generously curved lips were pressed together and a hint of defiance stared out of smoky gray eyes.

Charles sighed theatrically. "It grieves me that you should take me for a flat, my girl," he said in mild accents.

"Now you are talking nonsense," Dinah insisted, looking away from him.

Charles did not press her. Her defensiveness had confirmed his suspicions in his own mind, but he was not so green as to expect an admission that she was nursing a tendre for someone. He switched to a neutral topic and kept his comments to a minimum for the rest of their dance, thanking her gravely for the pleasure when he returned her to Natasha. It seemed to him that she regarded him a trifle uneasily, but he affected not to notice as he bowed and walked away.

Charles shrugged away a teasing sense of unease. The state of Dinah Elcott's emotions was nothing to him. It stood to reason that sooner or later one of her persistent horde of suitors would make an impression on the girl. She had sense enough to see through the worst of the lot, but she and her healthy fortune were almost certainly destined to become the property of some man despite her talk of pursuing a career as an artist.

Over the next few days Charles had the opportunity at several social events to observe Dinah's demeanor in the presence of more than half a score of eligible and interested gentlemen. As Natasha had said, she demonstrated not the least sign of favoring any of her admirers above the others, something he found vaguely disquieting, considering that she still wore the unmistakable look of a girl on the brink of falling in love.

On Thursday afternoon the nagging little mystery of Dinah's recent radiance was cleared up beyond the shadow of a doubt.

Charles, having an errand on Piccadilly Street, was on foot. He had sent his groom off with the curricle on another commission and was enjoying the first really warm spring day. He swung around the corner onto Dover Street and stopped abruptly, causing a portly gentleman to plow into him. Apologies were muttered, resentfully by the other man and somewhat absently by Charles, who maneuvered himself behind this generous human shield, his eyes fixed on a couple standing on the flagway not thirty feet ahead.

Dinah Elcott was talking animatedly to a tall, well-made young man whom Charles failed to recognize. Without stopping to rationalize his action, he stepped into the shadow of a print shop doorway, turning partially away, and when the pair began to walk away, followed them, keeping several persons in front of him as he did so.

Charles had ample time in the next ten minutes to propose and examine possible explanations both for his quarry's conduct and his own as he trailed after the unsuspecting couple. It required no special adroitness to remain unobserved, since Dinah and the stranger spared no attention for their surroundings or any of their fellow humans sharing the lovely afternoon with them. They were completely absorbed in each other. From his vantage point behind them as he caught interrupted views of their profiles, Charles could sense the closeness between them. These two knew each other very well indeed.

This realization startled Charles and set questions rioting in his mind, the principal one being the identity of the young man. How had he and Dinah become so friendly without the developing relationship becoming a matter of comment in her circle? It was true that he'd been away for a fortnight recently, but he'd heard no talk on his return, quite the contrary. Natasha had categorically denied any interest on Dinah's part in any of her suitors. Which left the possibility of a secret attachment, since attachment there very definitely was—the evidence was here in front of his eyes.

Charles slowed his idling pace even more as the pair ahead paused on the curb waiting to cross the street. A moment later he followed them into Berkeley Square. He gave no thought to their destination; his eyes and mind were fixed on the girl in the charming straw bonnet with its light blue ribbons. He had thought he knew her well; he would have taken his oath that her nature was too straightforward to stoop to duplicity. Obviously he'd been wrong, for there was no way this happy little scene could be taking place without some deception on her

part. If she were jauntering about the town on a man's arm
without the vestige of a chaperone or even her maid in attendance, then she had told lies to get here today. This was the
way the wretched girl repaid Natasha's care and sacrifice.
Well, Miss Dinah Elcott was about to discover the essential
truth to the old adage that the way of transgressors was hard.

Dinah and her escort were going into a building up ahead.
Charles looked about him, having been too intent on his pursuit up to this moment to care where he was. Gunters. They
were going to refresh themselves with some of Gunters' famous ice cream. He waited outside a moment or two, giving
them time to settle themselves comfortably before strolling
into the popular establishment himself.

His prey were seated close together at a small table, still totally engrossed in each other. Charles took a moment to observe the man and groaned inwardly. He'd already noted the
tall, athletic figure and fashionable attire from the back, and
now he beheld a face that must be every young girl's *beau
idéal*. With her artist's appreciation for visual beauty, Dinah
would be putty in this man's hands if he were half as clever as
he was handsome. Summoning up an air of smiling bonhomie,
Charles advanced on the unconscious couple, sending a
purring voice ahead of him.

"Dinah, what a delightful surprise! I trust I find you well on
this lovely afternoon. But how foolish of me; it would be obvious to a blind man that you are in fine fettle, positively ravish-
ing."

The words were addressed to the girl, but Charles's covert
attention never wavered from her companion, a wise precaution since the furious consternation that leapt into the man's
eyes at being discovered was mastered in an instant, after
which only the polite inquiry suitable to the most innocent occasion showed on that handsome countenance.

Charles extended his hand to the girl sitting in petrified silence, the picture of guilty embarrassment. The hand she gave
him with palpable reluctance was cold and trembled in his. He
supposed it was a point in her favor that she was not yet an accomplished deceiver. She still had not uttered a sound, and
Charles, smiling benevolently, said as if to a backward child,
"Won't you present me to your escort, my dear?"

"Of . . . course," she said in a stifled voice. "This is Mr. Bellingham. Godfrey, may I present Mr. Charles Talbot."

The men shook hands with every evidence of pleasure and Mr. Bellingham indicated a chair nearby, saying politely, "Would you care to join us, Mr. Talbot?"

Charles beamed a smile that embraced both his companions, noting that Dinah still looked as if a snake had poked its head out of a basket she had opened. "Thank you, just for a moment, then. I have an appointment shortly." He pulled the chair closer and sat down, addressing Dinah's companion in amiable tones. "I gather you are newly arrived in town, Mr. Bellingham?"

"Why, no," the other replied with the caution of one scenting a trap. "I have made London my headquarters for the last year or two."

"Oh, really?" Charles looked surprised. "It is just that I thought I knew all Dinah's friends," he confided with an apologetic little shrug, happily impervious to any atmosphere of constraint.

"We . . . we only have known each other for a few weeks," Dinah said, rushing into the breach. "You have been away recently, Charles."

"That's true, I have. Where did you meet—at Almack's?" he asked as one determined to uphold his end of a trivial conversation.

"No." Mr. Bellingham seized the reins. "We met at Mr. Martin Crossman's studio—a wholly delightful happenstance," he added, flashing an intimate smile at Dinah that had Charles curling his hands into fists under the table. He kept the smile fastened to his lips.

"Delightful indeed. Almost as though a kindly fate had intervened in the affairs of two mortals," Charles suggested silkily. "I am devastated to have to run away before we have a chance to become acquainted, Mr. Bellingham, but as I believe I said earlier, I have an appointment elsewhere, and one's word is one's word after all."

Charles had gotten to his feet during this long-winded explanation, casting his eyes idly around the room as he did so. Now he brought his puzzled gaze to Dinah, saying with questioning intonation, "I don't believe I see your maid, Dinah."

"She . . . she is doing an errand for me—"

"Miss Elcott and I ran into each other by chance a few moments ago on Dover Street," Mr. Bellingham said easily, "and I persuaded her to allow me to give her some refreshment on this warm day while her maid finished their shopping. I shall, of course, see her safely reunited with the girl when we leave here in a few minutes." He had risen also and now offered his hand in farewell.

"It seems that fate is still active on your behalf," Charles drawled, his expression benign as he shook the other man's hand before bowing to the stricken girl. "I'll leave you in good hands, then. Your servant, Dinah. You'd best eat that ice cream before it melts," he advised kindly, waving toward the unappetizing remains of her treat as he took his leave of the happy pair.

Natasha was seated at the desk in her morning room writing a letter to Cam's Great-aunt Hester when Dawson showed Charles in.

"You are abroad bright and early this morning, Charles," she observed jauntily as he came toward her. "If you continue these matutinal habits you will be in danger of losing Grigson."

"Grigson has already tendered his resignation three times this year in protest at one or another of my actions which did not meet with his approval, and he knows he is in grave danger of having it accepted if he does so again any time in the near future. I came early in the hope that I might be before the crowd on your regular 'at home' morning."

"This sounds intriguing. You have something of a special import to discuss, Charles?"

"Yes, dear heart, but not for once with you. It is Dinah I would like to speak with if she is available."

"Dinah is upstairs in her studio. Do you wish to be private with her?" Natasha's expressive face was full of curiosity, but his as usual gave nothing away.

"Yes . . . unless . . . Has she told you that we met accidentally yesterday?"

"No, no, she didn't mention that, Charles."

"I see. Then yes, I would appreciate a few minutes of her time, after which I shall try to satisfy your curiosity."

Natasha nodded, her eyes thoughtful. "Very well, Charles. Why don't you go on upstairs to her studio now? I don't expect we shall have any callers for close to an hour or so."

Charles sketched a bow and went out of the room without another word. He'd had over twelve hours in which to examine yesterday's discovery of the attachment between Dinah and Godfrey Bellingham. His initial anger at her deception, mostly on Natasha's account, had long since dissipated and had been replaced by concern for the younger girl's welfare. His relationship to the Talbots did not entitle him to a say in Dinah Elcott's courtship or marital arrangements. Nor was her happiness his legitimate concern, but he was making it his business, as of yesterday.

Charles had learned a lot about Dinah over the past two months, enough to know that she was peculiarly vulnerable in this area, having never really felt herself important to those who had the care of her after her mother died. It was not surprising that she should believe herself undesirable except for her expectations, and the fact that she had quickly become the object of fortune hunters only reinforced this belief. If Bellingham was another of the same ilk, he could do her irreparable harm because it was clear that with him she had lowered her guard. As Charles saw the situation, it would be up to him to establish Bellingham's credibility before Dinah fell all the way into love with the fellow. He hadn't the least doubt that she was partway there already, so haste was essential.

An unusual air of purpose sat on Charles's countenance as he rapped on the workroom door.

"Who is it?" Her voice beyond the door sounded startled. There was a brief silence after he identified himself; then she called, "Come in," with tangible reluctance.

As he entered, a flustered Dinah was in the process of removing an unfinished still life from the easel. "I was afraid it might be Natasha at the door. This is a surprise for her and I don't want her to see it until I have it framed."

This, the item underneath the canvas she was holding, was a large pen-and-ink drawing consisting of a head-and-shoulders portrait of baby Justin in the center, surrounded by sketches of him in typical attitudes tucked into each corner. In the left corner the child was pictured sitting on the floor, legs widespread, playing with his toy soldiers. Dinah had succeeded in capturing the exquisite concentration of childhood in this and the other poses she had selected.

Fascinated, Charles came right up to the easel, chuckling at the sketch of the toddler with his hands on the floor and his bottom in the air as he righted himself from a fall. He studied the composite drawings in silence, taking his time about it. Finally, he turned to the anxious-eyed girl standing behind him.

"This is brilliant work, Dinah. You've caught his spirit of independence and the competence with which the little imp masters his small world, as well as succeeding in the anatomical correctness. You've made tremendous progress in two short months. I am very impressed. And the whimsical poses you've chosen for this picture are just what will most delight a doting mother. It's safe to predict that Natasha will be thrilled with her surprise gift." The glow that had come into Dinah's eyes at his unstinting praise faded rapidly as Charles added, "Did you hope it might make up to her for your other surprise?"

Dinah's eyes fell but not her pointed chin. "What do you mean?" Still holding the unfinished oil, she walked across the room to add it to a stack of canvases leaning against the wall.

"You would be ill-advised to fence with me, my girl. Does Natasha know about Godfrey Bellingham?"

"Not yet," she admitted reluctantly, then went on the attack. "But as you must have seen with your own eyes yesterday, there can be no possible objection to our . . . friendship. Godfrey is always the perfect gentleman."

Nothing in Charles's closed countenance suggested agreement with her description, and his words were sternly uncompromising. "That remains to be seen and is beside the point in any event. There is a great deal to object to in the secret nature of your acquaintance and the fact that you are meeting him clandestinely, thereby deceiving your trusting chaperone and putting your reputation in jeopardy."

"You don't understand," Dinah cried, resorting to the age-old complaint of youth oppressed by the tyranny of its elders. "It wasn't like that at all! We didn't set out to deceive anyone.

I don't even know how matters got to this stage," she finished, the defensiveness draining out of her, leaving her pale and unhappy.

"Suppose you tell me how it all started," Charles suggested softly, taking instant advantage of the very human need to justify one's actions. "How did you meet?"

"Godfrey told you yesterday. Our meeting was wholly accidental."

"At Mr. Crossman's studio?"

"Ye . . . Yes."

He noted her hesitation and probed further. "Did Martin Crossman introduce you?"

"No, it was an accident in every sense of the word. I wasn't looking where I was going and bumped into Godfrey on the stairway as I came from my lesson. He saved me from a bad fall."

"So you naturally thanked him."

"Naturally."

Prying information from Dinah Elcott was about as easy as extracting teeth, Charles decided, smothering his impatience as he persisted. "And having thanked him, you proceeded to exchange identities and embark on a series of secret assignations? When did this accidental meeting take place?"

"A bit over three weeks ago, and we did *not* 'embark on a series of secret assignations,' " Dinah declared hotly. "You are deliberately misconstruing the situation. We did not even exchange identities that day. I never expected to see him again."

"Let me guess—was there a second happy accident that brought you together again?"

"Yes, and you need not say it in that sneering fashion as if you did not believe me. It could not have been anything but accidental; we did not know each other's names then. It was at our second meeting that we introduced ourselves."

"This second meeting, was it also at Mr. Crossman's building?" At her nod, Charles asked if Godfrey Bellingham was also a pupil of Mr. Crossman's.

"No, but he had hoped to study with him. That is how we happened to meet that day."

"And why was he there the next time you met—that second happy accident?"

Dinah ground her teeth audibly. "For the same reason. Mr. Crossman had been too busy to speak with him the first time, so Godfrey returned to try again."

"And was so fortunate as to encounter your charming self again but was *not*, if I've understood you correctly, fortunate enough to be taken on by Crossman as an art student?"

"No. Godfrey's interest is primarily in landscape painting and they decided, he and Mr. Crossman, that it would be better if he studied with someone who concentrates in this area."

"I see. Meanwhile, you and Godfrey, having struck up an acquaintance, continued to meet—ah, accidentally?"

Dinah flushed. "You needn't be sarcastic, Charles. After the second meeting, we did . . . arrange to meet after my classes, but it was never for more than fifteen minutes at a time until yesterday. That was the first time we had met anywhere but in front of Mr. Crossman's studio."

"Just as a point of interest, did you bribe Mrs. Evans to keep quiet about your ripening acquaintance?"

She glared at him. "That's unfair, Charles—at least, it's unfair to Mrs. Evans. She knows nothing about Godfrey and me except for that first day." As his eyebrows climbed in skepticism, she admitted sheepishly, "I always send her in the carriage to the chemists' shop in the next block to buy various items while I am gathering my materials together at the end of my lesson. That's how Godfrey and I have been able to snatch a few moments to talk twice a week."

"Good Lord, you must be able to stock a hospital by now," Charles said with a shout of laughter. His face softened as he looked at the ashamed and unhappy girl. "Why could you not have asked young Bellingham to call on you here, you foolish child? It would have saved you a lot of misery and guilt and put your friendship on a normal basis, assuming he is not totally ineligible, of course. Is he a cit?"

"No," Dinah said, lifting her chin. "His birth is gentle and his family, though not wealthy, are comfortably circumstanced in Hampshire. Godfrey is a younger son, however, so his prospects are not bright, not that I care anything for that! I did ask him to call, and he wishes to, but Godfrey says the Talbots would think him presumptuous and forward to claim acquaintance when we were never properly introduced, and if they forbade him to call again, what should we do? We haven't dared to take the risk. We have been trying to discover some mutual acquaintance who might be willing to speak for him in front of Natasha and Cam, but there seems to be no one," she finished on a despondent note.

"Cheer up, my child, your problem is solved. You and Godfrey do have a mutual acquaintance who is prepared to speak for him to Natasha and Cam."

"Who?" Dinah demanded, wide-eyed.

"Why, your humble servant, of course," Charles replied, making her an elegant leg.

12

As Charles explained to Natasha a few moments after leaving a still-unbelieving but cautiously ecstatic Dinah in her studio, it was too late to prevent the inexperienced girl from forming a tendre for Godfrey Bellingham. The best they could hope for was to investigate this gentleman's background and establish his general eligibility. He postulated that it was preferable to have the young man under their eye while the affair was developing than to try to put a rein on Dinah that would inevitably strain her friendship with Natasha.

Natasha saw the force of this argument but was concerned for her friend's ultimate happiness. "Is this Godfrey Bellingham presentable, Charles?"

Charles's laugh was mirthless. "He's a veritable Adonis, and there's nothing to cavil at in air or address either; in short, a young girl's dream prince."

Natasha brightened. "Well, it might just all be true. There is such a thing as kindly fate, you know. It won't really signify if he isn't a matrimonial prize in the worldly sense as long as he cares for Dinah. It sounds as if their meeting was truly accidental. If they have no acquaintance in common he cannot know of her circumstances." A thought struck her and she said doubtfully, "Of course he will learn about her expectations soon enough if he is introduced into her circle of friends."

"There's no help for that. My guess is that, for all her talk of friendship, these two have some sort of understanding already, perhaps even consider themselves betrothed."

"Oh, dear, has it gone that far?" Natasha looked dismayed at first, then said thoughtfully, "If this is true, it is good in a way, is it not? It proves that his is a disinterested attachment, not one based on hope of material gain."

"It does *if* the whole affair is the 'accident' both parties portray it to be."

"How could anyone ever prove otherwise?"

"Aye, there's the rub."

"You sound as though you wish the accident story *could* be proved false, Charles." Natasha's voice held a question and her eyes searched her dear friend's face.

There was an unusual grimness about the set of his mouth as Charles replied slowly, "To the contrary, I wish it could be *proved* true for Dinah's sake, but there is no hope of that. It must always be based on Bellingham's word that his presence at Martin Crossman's building on the fateful day had nothing to do with Dinah." All expression was wiped from his face and voice as he added, "The odds are at least ten to one that Dinah Elcott will be married for her fortune. It is thus with every heiress even should she be an Incomparable. At least with Bellingham, Dinah will be getting the man of her choice."

"That could be even more tragic," Natasha said soberly.

"I suspect that is one of those profound feminine utterings beyond the grasp of the masculine sensibility," Charles declared, rising from his chair. "It's time I was off. Tell Cam I'll find out what there is to know about Bellingham. Don't be too hard on the penitent when she comes down to make her confession," he added carelessly. "She has been flagellating herself over her treachery toward you for a fortnight or more."

"Of course I won't be hard on her," the tender-hearted Natasha protested indignantly. "Thank you, Charles. I am most grateful for your intercession."

He gave a quick wave of his hand and took himself off to find Dawson and retrieve his hat and gloves.

Natasha and Dinah spent a slightly tearful half hour together, at the end of which Natasha had nearly succeeded in convincing her guest that she was not the wickedest, most ungrateful beast in nature. It was agreed that unless Cam objected they would send Mr. Bellingham a card for the modest dance the Talbots were giving in Dinah's honor the following week, though the invitation would have to be extended in person after Dinah's next painting lesson since she had only the vaguest idea that his lodgings might be somewhere in St. James's.

The few days that must elapse before her Monday lesson
with Mr. Crossman passed in an agony of anticipation for
Dinah, her elation at the sudden marvelous turn of events
clouded at intervals by an almost-superstitious dread that some
pending though inconceivable disaster would befall Godfrey,
causing him to vanish into thin air before the good news could
be imparted to him. Perhaps this necessary waiting period was
even more trying for the loyal Natasha, who was called upon
to lend a sympathetic ear and extend a calming influence as
each gruesome new improbability suggested itself to the anxious girl. After weeks of secretiveness, Dinah was in the grip
of a compensatory compulsion to confide all her thoughts and
fears to her patient friend. That none of these confidences included an explicit admission that Dinah had fallen in love with
Mr. Bellingham was a point that did not escape Natasha's attention, though she could not say with certainty whether this
was the last precious secret unconsciously guarded in the heart
until a formal declaration from the loved one made public dis-
closure possible, or simply meant that Dinah had not yet progressed to this final stage of self-knowledge. Natasha herself
was in no doubt that her friend had tumbled into love with the
unknown Mr. Bellingham and she was suffering qualms on
Dinah's behalf, alternately anticipating and dreading Charles's
report on the young man.

When Charles came to see Natasha during Dinah's Monday
art lesson he did not bring the conclusive vindication of Godfrey Bellingham that she had hoped for, but at least he had
come across no really damaging intelligence. He had questioned Martin Crossman about his imputed conversations with
Bellingham concerning possible tuition but found it impossible
to hold a satisfactory discussion with the artist when his mind
was involved with a technical problem relating to his art. He
thought he recalled someone asking about painting lessons recently but, far from supplying a description, could not even remember if the inquirer was male or female, young or old, and
he was very vague about a time frame. Charles had abandoned
the idea of getting corroboration from this source and had concentrated on discovering what he could about the young man's
associations in town.

It seemed that Bellingham was not so entirely unacquainted

with people in Dinah's circle as he had claimed. Charles had checked with some of the younger men and found several who knew of him, though differentiating between recognition and friendship. He had apparently lived on the fringes of society for several years, too impecunious to claim automatic inclusion but possessing the indefinable attributes of good looks and sufficient breeding to be accepted by similarly sports-minded youths as a companion in pursuits of this nature. Though ineligible for Almack's and the better clubs, he could wangle invitations to larger, less select parties where extra men were desirable providing they were presentable. Whether he had in fact known of Dinah's existence and contrived to meet her was something Charles had been unable to ascertain. Nor could he know if Bellingham had lied about being unacquainted with any of the men Dinah knew without asking the girl directly for the names she had submitted when the couple was trying to discover a mutual acquaintance to introduce him into Natasha's drawing room.

On the positive side, nothing discreditable was known about the young man's character and activities that would automatically disbar him from friendship with an innocent girl. He boxed at Jackson's, culped wafers at Manton's, placed wagers on horse races at Tattersall's, and spent his evenings in gambling hells, but so too did most of the men she had met in London. So far as was known, Bellingham had managed to steer clear of the moneylenders, stretching a small income to indulge his chosen pursuits. If Natasha had questioned him more closely, Charles might have added that Bellingham's conduct in the petticoat department was either above reproach or a model of discretion, because no talk of any adventures with the West End comets had reached his ears in the course of his inquiries.

"So Mr. Bellingham's only crime is the accident of birth that makes him ineligible to aspire to the hand of an heiress," Natasha said, summing up the findings.

"His only provable crime at any rate," Charles agreed.

"But you still have reservations about his suitability on some other count?" she persisted.

"Since any reservations I might have must be on an instinctive—and therefore suspect—level, it would behoove me to keep them to myself," Charles replied with finality, gathering up his hat and gloves, which he had not turned over to Dawson on his arrival.

And so Mr. Godfrey Bellingham gained the coveted entrée to the Portman Square residence of one of the leading lights among the younger government circles.

It would have required an older and much sterner female than Natasha to resist the powerful attraction of Mr. Bellingham's physical presence, allied as it was to a pleasant, unassuming demeanor and well-bred manners when he called upon her the morning after the first meeting with Dinah since Charles had discovered them at Gunters. He disarmed her right at the start by saying as he bent over her hand, "I feel strongly that the first words out of my mouth should be an abject apology for the way I have treated you, Mrs. Talbot, in persuading Dinah to keep our meetings secret. Regardless of the extenuating circumstances, it was shabby treatment and I humbly beg your forgiveness."

"What extenuating circumstances might these be, Mr. Bellingham?" Natasha asked.

Mr. Bellingham looked discomfited for a second until he glimpsed the twinkle in his hostess's lovely dark eyes, whereupon he laughed. "Feelings that blinded me to the dictates of propriety," he admitted. "It was entirely my fault that Dinah did not tell you of our friendship."

"It was as much my blame as yours, Godfrey," Dinah protested. "I am not a child to have others decide what is right or wrong for me."

"Shall we apportion the fault equally?" Natasha suggested with a smile that took the sting out of the words, "And resolve that from here on there will be no cause for anyone to question the propriety of your conduct?"

The eager assent of both parties ushered in a new stage in the developing attachment between Dinah and Godfrey. Natasha made him feel welcome in her drawing room and Dinah blossomed under the spell of his infectious charm. If she'd harbored any secret misgivings that his interest in her might cool when other, prettier girls were included in the company, those fears were soon put to rest. Godfrey's smile was delightful and his manners could not be faulted, but no one observing him in company remained long in doubt as to where his interest centered. His eyes sought Dinah's in a crowded room and the two exchanged unspoken messages that had nothing to do with the general topic under discussion at the moment. His smiles for Dinah likewise were intimate and exclusive.

These were halcyon days, and Dinah came alive in a way no one had thought her capable of, with the possible exception of Charles Talbot, who had prodded and poked her in a figurative way from the onset of their acquaintance, though with infrequent and evanescent success. It would not have been totally out of character for him to preen himself a little on the perspicacity of his judgment, but Charles did nothing of the sort. It could not be that he failed to notice the improvement in Dinah, because he kept close tabs on her in an unobtrusive manner. Whatever he noticed he kept to himself.

On the evening of her dance, Cam and Natasha presented Dinah with an intricately fashioned bracelet of tiny pearls set in gold flower-shaped links. Surprised and speechless at first, she could only gasp, "This is for me? It is the loveliest thing I ever saw, but . . . but you shouldn't have. You are giving the dance for me, though I have no claim on your generosity. It . . . it is too much."

"Don't be idiotish, love," Natasha scolded as she took the bracelet from the box in Dinah's limp hands and proceeded to fasten it around one trembling wrist. "This is just a little memento of what we hope will be a memorable evening for you. And it would not do for you to look tear-stained for your party, you know," she added as Dinah's eyes filmed over.

"I'll treasure it always." As she glanced into their smiling faces, Dinah blinked moisture from long lashes and sniffed inelegantly.

Cam whipped out his handkerchief and they all began to laugh. "Wait here," Dinah begged. "I have something for you also."

She dashed up the stairs and returned a few minutes later carrying a framed picture. When she turned it around to face them there was a short silence before Natasha sucked in a breath and promptly burst into tears.

"Oh, Dinah, this is Justin just as I love him most, all the funny little things he does—Cam, isn't this the most wonderful gift? Th . . . thank—" Her voice became wholly suspended by tears as she threw her arms around Dinah and kissed her warmly.

Cam removed the frame from Dinah's slackened grasp and continued to study it while the two women, their arms around each other's waist, watched him. "I had no idea you were so talented, Dinah," he said at last. "This is an excellent piece of work as well as being personally priceless to Natasha and me. May I add my thanks to hers?" He leaned forward and kissed Dinah on both cheeks before adding, "If you would be willing, I would like to commission you to paint a portrait of Natasha. I have long wished for one but haven't known which artist to choose. Now I do know. What do you say?"

Dinah's eyes were starry with delight. "If you really mean it, Cam, I would love to try to paint Natasha."

Natasha laughed and hugged her. "You may live to regret those rash words, Dinah. I am not overly fond of sitting still; you will probably find me a terrible model." She wrinkled her pert nose at her husband.

It was Dinah's turn to laugh. "You do not imagine that Justin sat still for me, do you? I have literally scores of unfinished drawings of him."

"You have? May I see them first thing tomorrow morning?" Natasha squealed, her eyes alive with pleasurable anticipation.

It was at this happy moment that the first guests arrived. The orchestra Natasha had hired could be heard tuning up in the larger of the two main saloons that had been readied for dancing. With a hand under the elbow of each, a proud Cam urged his ladies into position to greet their guests.

Though Dinah could not hope to rival Natasha's dramatic dark beauty, he considered she was in her best looks tonight, dressed in a gauzy creation of a soft purplish-blue that sparkled with brilliants with each movement of her lithe body. The elfin charm of her gamine features was enhanced by a wide smile that displayed her perfect teeth. Tonight he had difficulty in summoning up an image of the colorless, unsmiling waif who had arrived on his doorstep less than three months ago. That girl had been diffident, unsure of her welcome, and fearful of the ordeal that awaited her. He could only marvel at the happy, confident young woman who stood here this evening greeting their guests with pleasant composure.

His glance moved on to Natasha's vibrant face and his heart performed its now-familiar quick step. He would never grow accustomed to the miracle of love that was Natasha, or cease to be grateful for her generous spirit and dogged persistence at a time when his own emotional cowardice would have denied them any chance of love. This same generous spirit had presided over Dinah Elcott's metamorphosis this spring.

In the next moment Cam had to amend this complacent analysis when Mr. Godfrey Bellingham was announced. Obviously a significant portion of the credit for Dinah's transformation belonged to the handsome young man who advanced into the room and bowed over Natasha's hand before bestowing an intimate smile on Dinah, who looked as if candles had been lighted behind her eyes. Cam frowned, a bit shaken by this glimpse of transparent joy with its concomitant vulnerability. Could this genial-looking young man be trusted not to abuse the feelings so blatantly on offer to him? Cam's keen eyes could discern no clue in Bellingham's appealing facade or pleasant manner as he responded to his host's welcome.

Dinah's was not the only glance that followed Godfrey Bellingham as he gave way to the next arrivals. One of these was Charles, and Cam's eyes locked with his cousin's as the latter's glance returned from marking Bellingham's progress into the main saloon. The laziness Charles simulated was conspicuously absent from that bright blue gaze. For once Cam derived comfort from the fact that Charles was on the alert. His cousin was fond of Dinah in a casual way and he would not stand willingly by and see her run into danger, though Cam accepted that there were some dangers willing champions had no power to avert.

The object of the Talbot cousins' protective impulses, serenely unaware of any possible threats to her present happiness, thoroughly enjoyed her party from start to finish. Dinah floated in a bubble of delight throughout the evening, dancing and laughing with most of the guests, but always conscious of Godfrey's attentive presence. Though propriety dictated that he could only have two dances, he took her down to supper and remained discreetly on the fringe of any group of which she was a part, a maneuver that permitted an occasional exchange of smiles and unspoken messages. He was a perfect dancing partner, as she had known he would be, and their dances were blissful intervals too quickly ended.

The only sour note in an otherwise harmonious evening was sounded by Charles Talbot. Her dance with Charles came early in the evening. He complimented her on her looks and her dancing with that air of amused condescension she always found irritating, but she ignored this and used the opportunity to thank him again for his role in bringing Godfrey into favor with Natasha and Cam. He brushed her thanks aside, no better pleased with her gratitude than she'd been with his compliments. After this they circled the floor in a rather bristling silence interrupted at regular intervals by impersonal remarks from Charles's vast social repertoire that required no more than a "yes indeed" from Dinah. By the end of the dance she was filled to bursting with righteous indignation and resentment, only to have the accumulated animus whoosh out of her as from a pricked balloon when Charles gave her a smile of such singular sweetness that she stood blinking after him in disbelief until Godfrey came to claim her for their first dance, after which Charles vanished from her thoughts. He returned with a vengeance a few hours later.

Supper with Godfrey was a wonderfully happy occasion. Afterward she could not even call to mind the persons who had shared their table, they had been so wrapped up in each other, sitting closely together in a world that contained only two. They were reluctant to return to the ballroom when the first strains of the orchestra drifted down to them. When they left the dining room it seemed perfectly natural to stroll back toward Natasha's morning room rather than to the staircase. The door was open and they went inside. Dinah was oblivious to anything save her inner excitement as Godfrey pulled her gently into his arms. No thought of propriety or resistance entered her head as she stared mesmerized into his compelling golden-brown eyes.

Her first kiss would surely have been a thrilling event had she been granted the time to savor it, but she was barely past the initial shock of feeling a man's lips pressing against hers when an annoyingly familiar voice from the doorway caused her to leap back in guilty confusion and whirl around.

"It grieves me to cast stumbling blocks in the path of true love, but this really won't do, my dear child. Someone could walk in here at any moment."

The owner of that soft, silky voice, Charles Talbot, lounged against the doorframe in an indolent attitude that echoed the ineffable boredom written on his features. At that moment it would have afforded Dinah immense satisfaction to erase the insulting expression from his face with the palm of her hand as a most uncharacteristic rage exploded in her brain. She actually took an impetuous step toward the door, her hand upraised, before sanity rushed back and she stopped, appalled at her loss of control.

Charles straightened and strolled into the room. "Very wise, my dear Dinah. I find second thoughts are often best," he murmured. "May I humbly advise you to compose yourself and go back up to the ballroom? Your next partner will be looking for you. Now, Dinah, and alone," he added with a touch of steel under the silk as her eyes flashed an appeal to Godfrey, who had remained frozen in place, his handsome countenance wiped clean of all feeling. "I would like a word with Bellingham."

Dinah still hesitated for the space of a heartbeat; then, at Godfrey's nod, dashed from the room.

She performed her part in the next two dances through sheer rote as her brain roiled with anxiety over what had taken place between Godfrey and Charles. Both men had reappeared in the ballroom—separately—within five minutes of her return. It was a small measure of relief that neither gave any outward indication that anything unpleasant had transpired, but she fidgeted with impatience until Godfrey claimed her for their second dance of the evening.

At first Dinah found Godfrey's unclouded smile reassuring, but when he proceeded to propose a drive to Kensington Gardens in the next day or two, she stared at him in disbelief. "Never mind that, Godfrey. Tell me what that officious, overbearing Charles Talbot had to say about something that was none of his affair. Was he horridly sarcastic?"

"Actually he behaved rather decently, didn't come the high

and mighty over me at all. He explained that since your father had entrusted your safety and welfare to the Talbots they felt honor bound to see to it that your name does not get bandied about the town. And he was dead right, of course. I was greatly at fault for luring you into that room. Even though I've been longing to kiss you for weeks, I should not have done it."

Dinah had been listening with active annoyance at Charles Talbot's effrontery in assuming some sort of mantle of guardianship over her, but Godfrey's confession caused her to forget her spleen. "Have you really, Godfrey?" she asked softly, shyness preventing her from meeting his ardent glance for more than a second.

"You must have guessed how I feel about you," he replied, pulling her a bit closer than decorum permitted for a measure or two, "but from now on, everything must be done by the book." Gazing down into her glowing eyes, Godfrey brought himself up short. "I should not have said that, any of it," he declared with a touch of bitterness. "I haven't any right to aspire . . . my circumstances are less than modest. Last week it didn't seem to matter, but a few minutes ago, during that last dance, I overheard a remark that made me—" He stopped and stared searchingly at her upturned face.

"What remark did you overhear?" she prompted.

"Someone made a laughing reference to 'the heiress' and he was looking directly at you. Is it true? *Are* you an heiress?"

"Yes, and it doesn't signify in the least."

Her calm self-possession lighted a spark in his amber-brown eyes. "Bless you, my dearest," he said softly, gathering her closer again, "but it certainly will signify to those who have your interests at heart. Your father will not consider me a fit candidate for your hand. You may choose from the most prominent families in England."

"Nonsense. I am not a snob and neither is my father."

The music was winding down then and there was no further opportunity for conversation of a personal nature for the remainder of the party. Godfrey pressed her hand in a most reassuring fashion when he made his adieus. Charles sketched her a mocking bow and sauntered out, typically unapologetic about his gratuitous intrusion into her private affairs.

After a relaxed post-party gossip with Natasha and Cam,

who were pleased at having hosted a successful evening and touched by their guest's gratitude, Dinah drifted off to bed in a haze of contentment. As she slipped between lavender-scented sheets, she was full to overflowing with a buoyant joyfulness and excitement that was entirely outside of her experience. And to think that she had protested against coming to London! Looking back at the person she had been three months ago, she felt the liveliest contempt for her craven reluctance to leave the shelter of her dull existence. Even if she'd never met Godfrey, she would have gained immeasurably by the forced exposure to a great number of people. It did not matter that relatively few of them were persons for whom she felt any degree of affection or intellectual kinship. She had learned that there was something of interest about most humans. This knowledge was bound to make her a better artist in time. Her progress in her artistic studies alone made this London sojourn invaluable. And her friendship with Natasha made it warmly gratifying.

As for Godfrey's presence in her life, she was almost afraid to examine the joy his friendship brought her. It wasn't something to be pondered but to be savored. Sleepily she began to enumerate their tentative plans to meet in the immediate future. She was looking forward to driving with him for the first time, and there was to be an *al fresco* Venetian breakfast later in the week given by Lady Pelting. After meeting Godfrey when they had called in Portman Square two days ago, Sarah and Margaret Pelting had prevailed upon their parent to include him among the guests. Natasha had enthusiastically described the grounds of Riverside Manor, which extended down to the Thames and were beautifully landscaped. Dinah fell asleep picturing herself strolling on Godfrey's arm along the riverbank.

13

"You look beautiful in that color."

Godfrey's whispered words to Dinah as Natasha walked over to the mirror to put on her bonnet brought a pleased blush to the girl's cheeks that rivaled the clear coral hue of her muslin gown. In the past fortnight Dinah had progressed from a state of complete indifference about what she put on her back to one of overriding concern for her toilette, complicated by a helpless vacillation that was the despair of her abigail. Her one aim was that her appearance should do Godfrey credit. The problem lay in her inability as yet to look at her own physical being with the same analytical eye she brought to her artistic studies. Years ago she had dismissed her face as being permanently uninteresting, but now she was more than willing to employ any aids that might increase its appeal for Godfrey.

Dinah replaced Natasha in front of the mirror, tying the coral ribbons of her straw bonnet under one ear as she had been taught, before accepting her white cashmere shawl and white lace parasol from Godfrey's hands with a smile. This was the day of the Peltings' Venetian breakfast, and Godfrey was to accompany the Portman Square ladies in the Talbot carriage. Charles Talbot was also to be among the guests at Riverside Manor, but he had elected to drive himself in his curricle.

As the three paraded out to the curb where the carriage awaited them, Godfrey complimented the women on their promptness as well as their appearance.

It was a rare perfect May morning, the sky a rich canopy of blue unsullied except by the occasional short-lived drift of wispy cloud. The weather was so delightful that Natasha mourned their incarceration in a closed carriage even for the short half hour drive westward along the river, but she was the only one to find any aspect of the day less than perfect. Her companions had no quarrel to pick with any arrangement that permitted them to enjoy each other's company. The threesome conversed with the ease of old friends, thanks to Natasha's and Godfrey's well-developed social sense. Dinah was content to follow where the others led.

The Pelting estate was as beautiful as Natasha had promised. The house was a good-sized villa in the Italian style, with stuccoed walls and stone balconies, but few of the guests expected to spend any time inside on such a day. Wide glassed doors at the back of the house opened onto terraces and gardens that offered lovely views of the slow-moving river. Velvety lawns dotted with decorative trees sloped gently down to the water's edge.

As they moved out onto a broad terrace, Dinah's eyes widened at the sight of three long tables draped in pink linen set out in the shade of spreading beech trees just coming into full leaf. Sparkling crystal, fine china, and silver epergnes filled with fruit and flowers made the pink tables a treat to the eyes.

Sarah and Margaret Pelting detached themselves from a chattering group of young people to welcome the new arrivals and urge Godfrey and Dinah forward just as Charles came up to offer his arm to Natasha, who wished to speak with Lady Pelting.

Two hours later, several dozen happy, replete guests, having topped off a Lucullan feast with early strawberries and champagne, began to stroll over the extensive grounds in pairs and small groups, leaving the laziest members of the party to remain in the shade on the highest terrace. An energetic cluster of coatless young men was engaged in a game of quoits, watched by an appreciative audience of girls looking like spring flowers in their pastel muslins and posy-bedecked bonnets. After they had watched the contest for a few minutes, Godfrey proposed a stroll along the shore to Dinah, who accepted eagerly.

"I'll need to go back up to the terrace for my parasol first,

Godfrey. The sun has become quite strong and there are not many trees along much of the river path."

Godfrey wouldn't hear of her toiling back up the hill and set off himself to fetch the parasol she had left under her chair. Dinah remained with the other girls for a moment or two before deciding to take a peek at the formal gardens they had passed on the way to the sweeping lawns where the young men were involved in their contest. She strolled uphill slowly, drinking in the beauty of the grounds and relishing the warm caress of the sun between her shoulder blades. She took a deep breath of the scented air, pungent with the aroma of watered shrubs and rich, moist earth. She could almost imagine herself alone in the gardens as she wandered down grassy paths between trimmed hedges, such was the sense of being enclosed in a private world that the outer wall of hedge provided. A continual buzz of sound from the quoits game penetrated the formal garden without in any way disturbing the peace within. She would have liked to linger longer but knew Godfrey would soon be returning with her parasol.

As Dinah approached the tall hedge enclosing the gardens, a vaguely familiar voice on the other side called out, "Well met, Bellingham. I take it that dainty object you are carrying belongs to the heiress?"

"Yes, this is Dinah's parasol. How are you, Doubleday? It has been a while since we've met."

Dinah had quickened her step at the mention of Godfrey's name, knowing he must be on his way to find her, but she stopped in confusion on hearing him give a name to the person whose voice had struck a familiar chord. She had not realized Godfrey and Martin Doubleday were acquainted.

"You've not seen me because you've been avoiding the hells of late. Very prudent of you," Mr. Doubleday went on to say in a jovial voice. "Let me be the first to congratulate you on your conquest, dear boy. I admit I never believed you'd make any headway with the aloof Miss Elcott when I pointed her out to you last month—obviously I underestimated the effect that pretty phiz of yours has on the fair sex. No hard feelings. You've run rings around the rest of us and walked off with the prize. Shall I look to see an announcement in the *Gazette* momentarily?"

"Nothing is settled yet. Dinah and I get along very well and the Talbots have accepted me, but Elcott may cut up stiff when he learns that his daughter wishes to wed a penniless nobody."

"That is entirely possible. It never pays to count one's chickens before they've hatched, but I saw the way she looked at you when we were at the table earlier. Tail over top she was, no doubt about it. Wouldn't have thought she had it in her; she was mighty cool with the rest of us."

"She's a nice girl. I am quite fond of her, which is not to say that I'd choose to become leg-shackled at five-and-twenty if I had a handsome independence, but one must seize opportunity when it presents itself. By the way, I appreciated your tact in not approaching us earlier. I've not told Dinah we have any acquaintances in common."

"Think nothing of it, dear boy. I'm not one to queer another's pitch. I had my touch at the golden goose early on. She wouldn't have me."

"Yes. Well, I must go, Doubleday. Dinah will be wondering what has happened to delay me."

Even the echoes of the men's voices had faded before the girl on the other side of the thick hedge moved a single muscle, and when she did it was only the ones in her eyelids.

Dinah squeezed her eyes closed to shut out the sight of that living green wall looming in front of her. She must *do* something; she could not stand in this spot forever like a graven image. Nor could she sink into the ground and let the pain wash over her as she longed to do. She was at a party in company with scores of strangers. She would be expected to chat pleasantly with these people. Godfrey was looking for her— *oh, Godfrey!* Her rigid muscles jerked spasmodically. She must get away; she could not face anyone; she must *hide*!

"I have spoken your name three times—"

Dinah gave a stifled shriek and spun around to stare wildly at Charles Talbot, who had come up behind her.

"What is wrong? You look ghastly." Charles sprang forward as Dinah seemed to crumple. He flung an arm about her, noting the trembling of her entire body. His voice gentled and his arm supported her weight. "There is a garden seat a few feet behind you. Shall I carry you?"

He could not see her face, but the bonnet gave a negative

shake, the straw brim scratching against his shoulder. He kept his arm firmly about her and guided her over to a wrought-iron bench which, he saw thankfully as he pushed her onto it, had a back rest. She sat, head bent a little forward, her hands lying limp in her lap.

"Look at me, Dinah."

After a second she obeyed, and Charles winced inwardly at the absence of life and hope in her eyes. "I assumed you were unwell, but it isn't that, is it? What has happened?"

The bonnet dipped again, leaving just a line of dark lashes visible against her ashen cheeks. Her gloved hands were now clasped together.

"You don't have to tell me anything, Dinah. I'll fetch Natasha, shall I?" There was still no reaction from the lifeless girl, but a susurration of distant speech and an occasional trilling laugh seeped into the quiet garden, a reminder that this oasis of privacy could be invaded at any moment. "Will you be all right while I go for Natasha? Someone could stroll through here at any time," he said in warning. "I saw Bellingham wandering about a moment ago carrying your parasol."

Dinah gasped and leapt to her feet, staring up at him frantically. *"No*, don't leave me alone, Charles!" She clutched at his arm with fingers like talons.

"So your precious Godfrey is responsible for the state you are in," Charles said grimly, his earlier sympathy evaporating. "A lover's quarrel, in fact. May I respectfully suggest that you cease hiding away like a wounded doe and set about making it up with him, since he is riding in your carriage today? I see no reason why Natasha should be subjected to an uncomfortable drive home sitting bodkin between two sulking lovers."

During the course of this unsympathetic speech Dinah's apathy was replaced by active terror, and she tightened her clutch on his sleeve when he would have twisted away from her. "Please, Charles," she whispered desperately, "do not leave me. I cannot face Godfrey. He . . . he *knew* about me!"

Shocked comprehension chased contempt from Charles's face. Icy blue eyes thawed as they gazed into imploring gray ones, shimmering with moisture. "Are you absolutely sure of this?"

She kept her chin up and her eyes wide open, fighting back

the threatening tears. "I overheard him talking with Martin Doubleday on the lawn beyond that big hedge. He—Mr. Doubleday—mentioned that he had pointed me out to Godfrey last month. He congratulated Godfrey on his conquest. Godfrey said he was quite . . . fond of me but would not choose to marry if he were ri . . . richer." Her voice died away and two tears spilled over onto her cheeks.

Charles took out his handkerchief and dried them, saying with soft, urgent clarity, "I hear people in the section over to our right beyond those shrubs. You are not going to succumb to the vapors, do you understand, Dinah? I will get you away from here, but you must do exactly as I say. Take my arm and we'll find Natasha."

"B . . . bossy Charles," Dinah said with a valiant attempt at flippancy, but her softly curved mouth trembled pathetically.

"You, my child, have never learned to accord the proper respect to your elders. Shall we go?"

Dinah laid a shaking hand on the arm offered and concentrated on winking away the tears already crowding behind her eyelids as Charles led her back through the formal garden toward the terrace, slipping his arm about her waist briefly when she stumbled.

As they came in sight of Natasha on the upper terrace talking with two gentlemen and the wife of one of Cam's colleagues, Charles shot Dinah a narrowed glance. She'd removed all traces of recent tears with her gloved fingers and seemed to have regained her composure. Her pallor couldn't be helped and might actually lend strength to his story. He halted their progress a few feet away from the group and sent a wordless message to Natasha, who slipped away from her companions with a smiling excuse. She came toward them, her eyes widening in concern as she looked more closely at Dinah.

"Dinah has developed a blinding headache, Natasha. I think she ought to leave as quickly as possible."

"Of course, Charles. I am so sorry, my dear. I'll make our excuses to Lady Pelting."

As Natasha headed for the group surrounding their hostess, Charles stopped a passing servant and asked him to order the Talbots' carriage brought around immediately. He steered Dinah into the cool dimness of the central passage of the villa to remove that distinctive coral dress from the view of anyone approaching the terrace. Natasha joined them a few moments later and they walked together toward the front of the house, where the porter opened the entrance door for them as a carriage was heard coming along the driveway.

No one had said a word during this time, but now Natasha stopped suddenly on the top step and turned to Charles. "I almost forgot. Godfrey Bellingham came with us today, Charles. Will you make our apologies to him and see that he gets a ride back to town?"

"I plan to drive him back myself."

"Charles, please don't—" Dinah's pleading voice broke off, her wan face full of alarm.

"Don't what?" he asked in a fierce undertone. "Don't tell him what has occurred? Do you want him sending flowers to the supposed invalid and camping on your doorstep? Do you wish to play out a dramatic scene of dismissal—or forgiveness?"

Dinah flinched away from his anger and swayed on her feet. Natasha put a supporting arm around her and guided her down the steps.

"Charles, please don't," she said quietly, unconsciously echoing Dinah. "Can it not wait a bit, whatever it is?"

"Very well." Charles's lips clamped shut and he turned away to open the carriage door and let down the steps. As he took Dinah's arm to assist her, she looked straight into burning blue eyes, her own full of appeal.

"Tell him if you must, but I couldn't bear it if there was . . . trouble between you," she said, her voice faltering.

Charles's lips twisted wryly and the flame burned down in his eyes. "He has to be told and the sooner the better, but you need not fear it will be a case of pistols for two at dawn."

Her eyes fell and she climbed into the carriage without another word. Natasha followed with a brief word of thanks to Charles, who closed the door and signaled the coachman to start.

After a long five minutes during which Dinah sat entirely motionless, staring blindly out of the window, Natasha broke her self-imposed silence to say, "You know I want to help in any way I can, love, but I won't ask you any questions if you tell me not to."

Dinah turned a desolate face toward her friend and saw the sympathy and affection in Natasha's eyes. The brittle control she had imposed over herself shattered and she dissolved into silent tears, putting her hands up to cover her face.

After a minute or two of witnessing this abject misery while Dinah's thin body swayed with each motion of the carriage, Natasha crossed over to the other side. She gently removed the younger girl's hat before putting her arms around the shaking shoulders. Dinah cried into Natasha's shoulder for long enough that the latter was wishing she had brought along a vinaigrette, but finally the sobs subsided and Dinah sat up again, apologizing in a shaky voice.

Natasha soothed her and offered a handkerchief for mopping up, unmindful of the damp patch on her own gown as she waited with exemplary patience for whatever explanation Dinah was moved to supply.

Eventually the whole story came out, the overheard conversation, Charles's timely appearance on the scene, and the masterly way he had removed the shattered girl from Riverside Manor without giving their fellow guests any gossip to chew on. Much of it Natasha had to piece together herself, since Dinah displayed a very natural tendency to diverge into the realm of her feelings of disbelief and betrayal. Natasha let her ramble on where she would go, only interjecting a sympathetic murmur occasionally. By the time they arrived back home, Dinah's initial shock and grief had been poured out and examined and she had achieved a state of resigned acceptance of the end of her fairytale courtship.

"Where is she?"

Natasha sighed and put down her pen as Charles walked into the saloon. "Exactly where she's been almost every waking hour for the past two days—upstairs in her studio."

"How is she?"

"Resigned." Natasha sighed again and left the desk to take a chair near the sofa, waving Charles to its twin on the opposite side of the tea table. "I'd be less concerned about her if she were furiously angry at Godfrey for what he did, but she isn't.

She says he is no worse than any of the others who courted her for her fortune, which is blatantly untrue—at least, he may be no worse than the rest, but what he did was far worse because he knew she trusted him, and he betrayed that trust. What breaks my heart, Charles, is that Dinah accepts that no man could ever want her except for her money. She believes this rubbish, and I cannot convince her otherwise, though I have argued myself blue in the face."

"Of course not, dear heart. You have the disadvantage—in this instance only, I hasten to add—of being female. It will take a man to convince her that she is desirable in herself."

"I *know* that," Natasha retorted, a touch snappishly, "but at the moment there is no man available to play that role, and if there were, she would not believe him either."

"She will in time."

Natasha eyed her old friend without favor. "There *is* no time. She is talking about returning to Devon immediately."

"Now that I cannot allow," Charles replied with no lessening of the cheerfulness Natasha was beginning to find insufferable.

"And pray how will you prevent it?"

"You may safely leave the details to me. After extricating her unscathed from that Venetian breakfast, I have no intention of permitting her to supply the town's gossips with fodder by this present cowardice. You were absent from Almack's on Wednesday and did not put in an appearance at Lord Evander's *soirée* last night. It has to stop."

"Where are you going?" Natasha asked as he rose from his chair and headed for the door.

"Upstairs for the moment. I'm going to take Dinah driving in the Park at the fashionable hour."

"She won't go."

"Oh, yes, she will."

"She's very unhappy, Charles. Please be gentle with her," Natasha begged as he reached the door.

"I have no intention of being gentle with her," he responded, closing the door behind him.

Dinah called out that she was too busy to see him when he knocked on the door of the workroom, but Charles walked in anyway. "Good afternoon, Dinah." Ignoring her angry silence, he made a swift visual survey of the room.

She was clad in a painting smock and stood at the easel holding a palette, but the paint on it looked nearly dry. Underneath the still life on the easel he spotted a thin edge of paper. When he lifted the canvas, Dinah made a grab for the pastel drawing beneath, but he was too quick for her, twitching it out of her reach with his left hand as he replaced the still life with his right.

"This isn't a bad likeness," he said judiciously, holding the sketch of Godfrey Bellingham out at arm's length, "just as shallow and two-dimensional as the man himself."

With an inarticulate growl of protest, Dinah snatched the drawing out of his hands and slapped it facedown onto the table behind her. "What do you want, Charles?" she demanded, looking aggressive and unhappy at the same time.

"I was sure you'd be panting to learn what passed between your erstwhile suitor and myself on the drive back to town the other day."

"I am not in the least interested," she denied, turning away from his penetrating gaze.

"Very well."

The silence lasted perhaps two minutes and was of the nerve-racking variety. "Was he . . . surprised?" Dinah asked, feigning indifference as she glanced over her shoulder.

Charles looked up from the painting he'd been pretending to study. "That he'd been found out? Naturally. Disappointed too at the failure of his plan to secure his future." He saw the pain in her eyes and continued slowly, "To do him justice, it was never Bellingham's intention to hurt you, Dinah. He *is* fond of you. He really believed he could get what he wanted and make you a good husband too, which proves he is stupid, but he is not a monster of depravity or any baser than most men."

"You are trying to defend his conduct," she accused with angry disbelief.

"Not at all," he denied coolly. "I am trying to explain his rationale for his conduct."

"He *lied* to me! Everything he said was a lie!" She stalked over to the window and stood with her back to him. "He said my skin is like flower petals." The muffled words were laced with scorn.

"Perfectly true, it is."

She whirled around. "What did you say?"

"Your skin *is* like flower petals." Charles strolled over to her and ran a knuckle briefly down her cheek. "White peonies, to be precise."

Dinah's eyes grew huge with confusion, and Charles cupped her chin in his long fingers. "Listen to me with your intelligence, my child, not your wounded pride. The fact that Bellingham was a fortune hunter does not negate the truth. If he said you were the most beautiful woman in the world, *that* would be a lie. But even then," he amended, his bright eyes holding hers captive, "one has to acknowledge that beauty is in the eye of the beholder, and love is often blind, which is not entirely a bad thing."

"Have you ever been in love, Charles?"

"Once." He released her chin and produced his mocking smile, but she refused to be intimidated this time.

"What happened?"

"She married someone else."

"Oh, Charles, I am so sorry." A tear slid down Dinah's cheek and he wiped it away with his thumb before stepping back.

"Don't waste your sympathy. I got what I deserved."

"What do you mean?"

"In the arrogance of youth I was saving myself for an heiress, not that the girl I fancied would have had me in any case. She had already bestowed her heart elsewhere, though she didn't yet know this on the level of her intelligence."

Dinah's eyes had widened again. "Are you telling me *you* were a fortune hunter, Charles?"

"An unsuccessful one, as my continued bachelorhood attests."

"I don't think I believe you. You would have been too clever to be discovered as Godfrey was."

"How well you think you know me, child. I suppose the truth is I could never actually bring myself to the sticking point."

"And I know why," Dinah declared.

"Would you care to share your wisdom with me?"

"You've never found any female without blemish," Dinah said with a malicious satisfaction. "Nothing short of perfection will do for you."

Annoyance showed on Charles's face briefly, but he declined to cross swords with the revitalized girl. "We must explore this fascinating theory at a more convenient time," he drawled, "but for now, I have come to take you driving in Hyde Park."

Dinah shrank back literally, once again the woebegone creature he had interrupted at her brooding. "That is kind of you, Charles, but I couldn't," she said, averting her eyes.

"Of course you can. Recollect that I shall be doing the driving. All you need do is sit beside me, look pleasant, and bow to any acquaintances we meet."

"No, please, Charles, I know you mean well; but I . . . I am going back to Devon shortly. I am not cut out for a social career."

"Now, you listen to me, my girl. It's true you've taken a knock, but no worse than happens every day to the young and trusting. It is part of life and one doesn't stop living because of it. All it takes is a little courage to carry on. I thought you had more bottom than to go crawling back to that sterile existence in Devon."

"I don't want a social career, don't you understand? I never did," she insisted, two spots of color flaring along her cheekbones.

"Disabuse yourself of the idea that what you want is the primary concern here. You made an agreement with your father, who then involved Cam and Natasha to the extent that they submerged their own lives in a generous effort to give you this Season. Is this how you propose to repay them, by running away with your tail between your legs?"

"The Talbots will be happy to have their house and their lives to themselves again," she cried, hating him with a passion.

"And will they be happy to have people whispering and speculating about why you disappeared when it was known you were to be fixed in town for the Season? Will Cam be happy to know you have reneged on your promise to paint

Natasha's portrait?" He walked over to the door and opened it
before she could reply.

"Don't just stand there wringing your hands. I will give you
precisely twenty minutes to don your smartest driving costume. If you are not in the saloon by then, I'll come up and
dress you myself. And do something with your face; you look
terrible," he added before closing the door behind him.

14

A charmingly garbed but inwardly seething Dinah subsequently joined Charles in Natasha's saloon, taking ten minutes longer than her allotted dressing time as a matter of principle. Charles, suave and smiling, seemed not to notice. Nor when they circled the Ring behind his beautifully matched and mannered chestnuts did he appear to notice that his companion was very much on her dignity, responding to all overtures like a lifeless charicature of the well-bred young lady of fashion. Had Dinah deigned even once to look directly at her escort, however, she'd have seen that he was hard pressed to discipline a smile on several occasions. Charles's limited capacity for forbearance was not too severely tested, since Dinah was unaccustomed to looking at the world through a self-centered focus; indeed, she found it wearying to filter all sensation through an artificial conception of how a young lady should behave. It was also too wearying for one of her sweet nature to bear a grudge for long. By the time Charles deposited her on his cousin's doorstep, she had relinquished her grievance enough to give him a natural smile on parting.

Once forced back into society, Dinah found it less of an ordeal than she had feared. She had actually been seen only a few times in Godfrey's company, not often enough for the tattle mongers to have gotten their teeth into a juicy story. One or two people questioned Godfrey's absence in her hearing, but for once Dinah's reputation for vagueness served her well. No one found it difficult to believe Miss Elcott had simply forgotten his existence as she had that of other men who had approached her during the Season. The trial she had dreaded most, coming into forced proximity with him unexpectedly, did not happen. Godfrey Bellingham might have vanished from the face of the earth for all she knew to the contrary.

If some small part of Dinah secretly hoped for another meeting with the man who had opened her eyes to the attraction between the sexes, she kept this yearning to herself. She accepted that there was no going back to the cozy cocoon of unawareness in which she had dwelled before Godfrey had lured her into the adult world. Nevertheless, she could still choose to turn her back on this world of tantalizing but perilous possibilities and concentrate her considerable energies on developing her artistic talents.

For the most part Dinah did just this in the period succeeding the debacle of the Peltings' Venetian breakfast. Her main focus was Natasha's portrait, and this project provided all the challenge she could ask for as an antidote to a broken heart. Dinah had never attempted to paint a portrait before and was well aware of the difficulties involved. Any hesitation was merely for Cam's sake, however. Her confidence in her abilities as an artist was diametrically opposed to the unsureness that inhibited purely personal dealings.

After discussing his preferences with Cam, Dinah decided against anything that smacked of the formal or the imposing in the mood or setting of the portrait. Natasha, who had little personal vanity, was delighted to eschew formal garb, jewels, and elaborately dressed hair, and chose to pose at her favorite desk wearing a simple round gown, her riotous black curls confined by a ribbon. The only stipulation Dinah made was that the gown be white; she was intrigued by the contrast with Natasha's warm, rich skin tones. She had the desk moved into her studio where the light was always reliable, and experimented with draperies for a background, finally settling on maroon velvet for texture and vibrancy.

Over the next few weeks the two young women spent a significant portion of their time together in the bare little studio, though two hours was the outside limit of Natasha's tolerance for physical inactivity on any given day. They both came to value this peaceful period free from distractions and the demands of other people. Their conversation, generally sporadic, ranged far wide—from the philosophy of governments to the most trivial of daily domestic happenings. Though neither was aware of the process, their friendship changed and sent down strong roots during this period. Initially it had been based on Dinah's admiration for Natasha and gratitude for her kindness, a rather one-sided affair, which was not surprising, given Dinah's total lack of self-confidence. The romantic disappointment she had suffered had broadened her experience and enlarged and deepened her capacity for human feelings. Awkwardly at first, she opened her mind and heart to her friend with the unlooked for result that the balance of their relationship altered, becoming more equal. Natasha related some of her uncomfortable experiences during her own coming-out Season in much greater detail. It gradually dawned on Dinah that her friend's enviable ability to deal amicably with all types of people had been developed over time and with effort, rather than being a perfect gift bestowed on her at birth along with her marvelous gypsy coloring.

The revelations that most confounded Dinah were Natasha's candid references to the difficult early period of her marriage. Living in the Talbots' home, Dinah could not fail to sense the deep love and trust that flourished between the pair. She would never have guessed that the marriage had weathered a rocky beginning. With the new freedom of their increased intimacy, she overcame her reticence and expressed this thought during one of the portrait sessions. Natasha answered readily.

"Cam is not intuitively knowledgeable about women like his cousin. He had some misconceptions about our sex that colored the way he interpreted my behavior in the beginning of our acquaintance, and he was sent to Vienna too soon after our marriage for us to have reached a good understanding."

"Do you think Charles understands females better than most men?"

Natasha nodded. "Most assuredly. More than is quite comfortable for us at times."

"Lift your chin a bit, Natasha," Dinah directed. "Yes, that's better."

Quiet reigned for a few minutes while Dinah struggled to get the line of the chin accurate, then she said rather hesitantly, "I don't believe I am betraying a confidence by telling you that Charles calmly claimed that *he* is—or has been—a fortune hunter. Was he roasting me or is it true?"

Natasha chuckled. "It's no secret that Charles has made rather a habit of saying outrageous things for the shock value. I could name at least two well-dowered young ladies in the past two Seasons who would have jumped at an offer from him. Perhaps the proof lies in the fact that he is still unwed at thirty."

"I told him he is still unwed because he has never found the perfect female. I cannot conceive of Charles's settling for less than perfection, can you?"

Natasha's smile faded and she said thoughtfully, "I am persuaded the truth is simply that Charles has not met anyone whose welfare is more important to him than his own; in short, he has never really loved anyone."

Natasha spoke with the authority of close friendship, but in this particular instance she was quite wrong.

Dinah was not the only person to undergo a cataclysmic revelation during the Peltings' lawn party. Charles Talbot had never really accepted Godfrey Bellingham at his own valuation. Attractive though Dinah was in an unconventional style, she was not the girl to inspire the sort of love-at-first-sight reaction that Bellingham would have people believe had been the case with him. Charles feared that Dinah was laying herself open to future unhappiness by her headlong plunge into romance. A disinterested observer might be expected to find reassurance in the couple's near-total absorption in each other in the period immediately following the Talbots' acceptance of Bellingham. Charles, though he prided himself on clearheaded judgments, found this closeness cloying and even irritating as an observer, a reaction he was careful to keep to himself since he had difficulty justifying it logically. He refused to examine and analyze his attitude, another departure from the normal, telling himself he was simply tired of being embroiled in Dinah Elcott's affairs. One way or another, he seemed to have spent the entire spring smoothing her path into society, a thankless task, given her disinclination for society of any sort. It was time to pull back from that circle and devote himself to other interests.

Then had come that terrible moment in the formal garden at Riverside when he had beheld Dinah's ravaged face and felt something twisting violently in his stomach. Her pain had somehow become his own, and it would have given him immense pleasure to knock Godfrey Bellingham's perfect teeth back down his throat.

The implications of such elemental feelings had so shocked him that he had resisted them with denial and anger. Dinah Elcott couldn't be more unlike the type of female that appealed to him if she had been specifically designed as its antithesis. She was completely indifferent to her sartorial appearance and no more than tolerably well-favored at best. Her manner and her conversation lacked sparkle; she was inept, not to say *farouche* in delicate social situations, disastrously candid in her opinions, and bored by the things that were of interest to the vast majority of her sex. She was immature, unworldly, and he questioned her capacity to care deeply for another human being, despite this youthful infatuation with Godfrey Bellingham's *beaux yeux*. The list of her imperfections was endless, and he *couldn't* be in love with her.

Caution had always been Charles's watchword in everything. This feeling that only he knew how to safeguard Dinah's fragile self-regard was most likely nothing more than a delayed attack of quixoticism as he left his youth behind him.

By dint of repeating this sensible explanation several times while he was masterminding the cringing girl's flight from the lawn party, Charles succeeded in persuading himself that he could not be in love with a pathetic creature like Dinah Elcott. What really infuriated him was that there was no *need* for her to be so needy. She was more rational and quicker of understanding than most of her contemporaries. A little application on her part, a little timely concentration on the world around her, and she would be as capable of coping with life as the next person. But would she apply herself? Would she concentrate? Not Dinah Elcott. She stuck out her chin, then looked hurt when someone accepted the invitation and smacked her. Perhaps she wanted a keeper, but this definitely was not a role Charles coveted on a permanent basis.

Unfortunately, this carefully constructed edifice of logic shortly collapsed upon Charles's head like a house of cards when he was unable to banish Dinah from his thoughts after putting her into Natasha's tender care. Her face as he had last

seen it haunted him. It was a dear little face with a singular
charm for him now that he had learned to read her mood by
the subtle variations that appeared on what was to most people
a habitually emotionless facade. He never wanted to see that
look of desolation in her eyes again.

Charles arrived at Almack's early that evening, prepared to
lend his assistance in easing Dinah through her first social engagement after Godfrey's betrayal. He prowled around the
rooms until he was convinced she did not mean to put in an
appearance. He was not entirely surprised that she could not
muster the courage to show her face so soon. It would have
been a severe trial even for the most spirited girl, and the Lord
knew Dinah did not answer that description. When she did not
attend the Evanders' rout party the next evening, however,
Charles decided it was time to take a hand. He had no intention of sanctioning such craven behavior, broken heart or no.

Charles arrived at Portman Square the next morning still believing his actions were motivated by strict altruism and an
avuncular affection for Dinah that did not cross the boundary
into romantic interest.

The stormy interview in her workroom destroyed this final
illusion for all time. He'd resisted a passing impulse to tear up
the chalk portrait of a godlike Godfrey, knowing, as Dinah still
could not, that Bellingham's defection was not of lasting importance. For all her talk of meeting him first as a fellow artist,
Dinah's attraction to Godfrey Bellingham had always been
based on a strictly physical appeal. It was understandable, perhaps inevitable, that an inexperienced girl should weave romantic fantasies about a handsome young man at least once in
her life.

Charles found his role as family friend and adviser more
difficult to maintain when he tried to assuage Dinah's sense of
betrayal and hurt as she reevaluated everything Godfrey had
ever said to her in the light of his prior knowledge of her circumstances. This compulsive self-torture was also understandable but should not be prolonged. Who knew better than
Charles the sheer wanton waste of hugging one's injuries—
real or perceived—at others' hands to one's bosom, thus depriving oneself of the emotional vitality needed to forge ahead
with life? He tried to communicate this to her on an intellec-

tual level because, apart from the Bellingham episode, Dinah was essentially a cerebral creature. Easy sympathy would only enable her to stay anchored in her determined slough of depression.

Looking back over that encounter later, Charles could only hope he had succeeded in his efforts, which had been greatly impeded by his own unlooked-for reaction to Dinah's unguarded emotional state. When he'd held her chin in his hand and gazed down into those extraordinary eyes of hers—not just beautiful of design and color, but reflective of the integrity and purity of her soul—it had taken real nobility to resist a burning desire to kiss her until he blotted Godfrey's image from her mind. His senses had clamored a warning tocsin in time and he'd stepped back, dousing the flame, only to find the urge reanimated, more strongly, a moment later when she had shed a tear in sympathy for his past unhappiness. At the instant he'd wiped away this tear with his finger he'd accepted the reality that his feelings for Dinah had mysteriously evolved into those a man cherished for the woman with whom he wished to share his life. They existed on all levels, but the level that was engulfing his person at that moment must be denied any satisfaction if he wished to win her affection. Having been burned once, Dinah would be extremely chary of giving her heart again.

Plotting was central to Charles's character, and he promptly called upon this aptitude in planning a campaign to woo the unsuspecting girl. The fact that Dinah regarded him somewhat in the light of an indulgent though critical elder brother could be turned to his advantage. She might resent the criticism, but she was in the habit of freely commanding the indulgence, and once she'd gotten over her anger at his seeming heartlessness about her failed romance, she'd return unthinkingly to her dependence on his assistance.

Charles took the precaution of stationing himself in his curricle outside Martin Crossman's studio on the day of Dinah's first art lesson after the fiasco of the Peltings' party on the off-chance that Godfrey Bellingham might try to insinuate himself back into her good graces by catching her alone and pressing an apology upon her. He saw Dinah's surreptitious glance up and down the street as she appeared with Mrs. Evans and was pleased that she looked relieved, whether at seeing himself or at not seeing Bellingham was not vitally important at that stage.

Under the circumstances Dinah could not choose but accept Charles's offer to drive her home, so she handed her portfolio over to Mrs. Evans, who would ride in the waiting Talbot carriage, and allowed Charles to haul her up into the curricle.

"You have a smudge of verdigris paint on your right cheek," Charles observed when she had settled herself on the seat.

"While you are splendidly turned out as usual," Dinah responded, casting an appreciative eye over the blue coat that fit his shoulders like a glove and turned his eyes the intense blue in the heart of a flame. "Are you certain your reputation can stand being seen with the likes of me? I probably reek of turpentine too."

"We'll whip up the pace to stir the air and keep to the back streets, which should take care of both problems," Charles said, taking the corner in fine style.

Dinah sighed. "I never can get a point the better of you. You have an answer for everything."

Charles's smile was not without sympathy. "Is that how you see me, as some sort of tormentor to be triumphed over?"

"Of course not, Charles." Dinah looked penitent. "I am very sensible of the many kindnesses you have done me from the beginning of my stay in London. I know I have not always seemed grateful at the time, but—"

"But you were incensed at being treated as a negligible child and annoyed at my officiousness," Charles finished, flashing her his mocking smile.

"I suppose so." Dinah ducked her head. "I must seem very childish to you," she said in a subdued tone.

"A bit immature, perhaps, which is not at all the same thing. Your mind and spirit are not childish, Dinah. Recollect that I have the advantage of a full decade of experience beyond yours, all of it on the town. Do you agree that it might be illuminating to explore the reasons you choose to cross swords with me so often?"

"Do not imagine I am so green as to be lured down that path," Dinah said firmly. "Do you never get bored with the life you lead, Charles?"

"Frequently in the past few years. If you are delicately hinting that it is more than time I mended my lazy ways, I agree. I have nearly decided to do something productive with my life, but that is also a topic for another day. Tell me how the painting lessons go."

Dinah sensed a real interest on his part and they embarked on an animated discussion that touched on several aspects of painting.

"Cam tells me that you were used to enjoy painting as a boy, Charles. Did you ever consider pursuing this interest?"

"Yes, but I realized early on that my abilities were sadly inferior to my ambition. For one thing, I haven't your skill at depicting the human form. At best I have a fair sense of design and spatial relationships and an affinity for color harmonies. Occasionally when I am at Seven Oaks I try my hand at scenic painting, but the results are invariably disappointing. I do somewhat better at architectural drawing."

The discussion continued in an artistic vein for the rest of the drive to Portman Square. Dinah glanced around her in surprise when the horses stopped. "Goodness, I had no idea we were almost home." She looked straight at her companion. "Thank you for coming for me today, Charles. It was kind of you to be concerned." Before he could deny or deprecate his motive, she continued with the air of someone making a discovery, "You know, it is the oddest thing, but I have just this minute realized that although Godfrey approached me by pretending an interest in painting, we never talked about art at all after that first day." Color surged into her cheeks. "You must think me an utter fool."

"I think nothing of the sort. Don't turn away from me, Dinah. We are well beyond being carefully polite with each other, if indeed we ever passed through that particular stage, which I cannot recall. You and Bellingham had other equally important conversations. The problem was that he was a fraud, not that you were a fool. How many girls could have resisted that handsome face and physique, allied as they were with a winning manner?"

Dinah smiled at him, her momentary embarrassment gone. "He certainly was beautiful, but perhaps a bit of a slow top intellectually," she added in a considering way that had Charles concealing a grin as he watched her descend agilely from the curricle.

The new rapport between Charles and Dinah continued uninterrupted by the periodic antagonisms that had marred their relations earlier. Fortunately, Charles's position as an intimate of the Talbot household enabled him to see Dinah frequently without calling attention to their friendship. For both their sakes he was determined to avoid giving rise to any speculation that coupled their names. He was resigned to conducting a protracted courtship, if not a war of attrition, having a fair idea of how high were the walls Dinah had erected around her heart in the wake of Godfrey Bellingham's deception. The least suspicion of pursuit on his part and she would revert to the defensive stance she had adopted at the beginning of their acquaintance. He had brought that upon himself initially by indulging his ignoble impulse to taunt her, something he needed to keep reminding himself when he raged in private at Godfrey Bellingham for leaving her so mistrustful of her own appeal at present. Dinah had had need of defenses around her tender heart most of her life. He knew the magnitude of what he was seeking in trying to persuade her to abandon them voluntarily and give her heart into his keeping. He had blotted his copybook early and often. Why should she suppose that he would be the one she could best trust to cherish the gift?

Dinah proved resilient on all other fronts. She did not overtly mourn Godfrey Bellingham's absence, she continued to pursue her studies with enthusiasm, and she disguised her basic disinterest in the social round with more skill. Her temperament was largely pacific, but she could rear up on her hind legs when sufficiently goaded, as Charles had discovered to his enduring delight.

Lady Maria Huntley descended on one of Natasha's "at home" mornings, this time without her nephew. She had not called since Mr. Wickham had tendered his unsuccessful offer of marriage to Dinah. It soon became apparent to that young lady that Lady Maria was still smarting from this rejection of her favorite. She made several acidulated comments on the sort of young women who toyed with men's affections to embellish their own reputations as belles. Since Dinah had not told anyone of Mr. Wickham's proposal, Natasha remained in the dark about the target of these particular vituperations. Dinah sat serenely sewing, seemingly as unenlightened as the rest of the company, which included Charles and the Pelting sisters. Frustrated at her failure to make any impression on the object of her wrath, Lady Maria moved her chair closer to Dinah on the pretext of admiring her embroidery. Dinah docilely submitted it for scrutiny, curious as to what Lady Maria might find to criticize in the complicated white work she was doing on madras muslin in imitation of costly bobbin lace.

The dowager grudgingly conceded its merit but advised Dinah strongly to give up such intricate work before she ruined her eyes and developed a squint. "You should try some of the new Berlin work patterns, my dear Miss Elcott. They come already stamped with attractive designs that can be quickly worked. Ackerman's has beautiful wools in a wide range of colors. I am persuaded you will find them delightful to use."

"I am sure I should, Lady Maria," Dinah agreed sweetly, "except that I would never be able to face my aunt, Lady Markham, again if I took up a type of needlework she holds in the greatest contempt. I fear she is quite unreasonable on this subject, being herself a very skilled practitioner of all the more . . . all the older styles of embroidery."

Dinah listened with great politeness to a harangue on the necessity of keeping up with new inventions and the dangers of becoming archaic in one's outlook if one never left the country or allowed the fresh breezes of new ideas to circulate freely. She produced an inaudible murmur whenever Lady Maria paused expectantly, and continued to set stitches in the exquisite little neck ruff she was embroidering.

When Lady Maria took her leave at last, Charles paused by Dinah's chair after bowing her out. "I gather from that edifying little performance that the old dragon succeeded in whipping Wickham up to offer for you," he observed pleasantly, his expression quizzical.

Dinah gave him a level look but returned no answer as she continued to ply her needle with unimpaired serenity.

Charles grinned. "I'll say this for you, my child. In your own quiet way you are more than a match for the likes of Lady Maria Huntley."

"And the likes of Charles Talbot?" Dinah widened her eyes in exaggerated innocence.

"Now, that would be overweening presumption and would certainly invite disaster."

"Or, at the very least, one of your famous setdowns," she replied pertly, rewarding him with a brief appearance of the elusive dimple beside her mouth.

"The wages of impertinence," he agreed, preparing to take his own leave. He invited Dinah and Natasha to accompany him to the Royal Academy showing later in the week and went away, moderately satisfied with his morning's work. Dinah was comfortable in his company, and while she never sought him out specifically, she always greeted him with mild pleasure these days.

On the other hand, Charles acknowledged as he stepped onto the pavement a moment later and headed toward Oxford Street at a brisk pace, there was no slightest indication that his careful little love was beginning to find him indispensable to her happiness. So far he had not been privileged to receive any of those soft looks she had lavished on Godfrey Bellingham a few weeks ago. Of course he could not claim the same resemblance to a Greek god as Bellingham either, he conceded without rancor, but that was not really the point. Dinah had consciously buried that side of her nature until recently and would not easily set it free again. He actually owed Bellingham a debt of gratitude for bringing her sensual side to life at all. It had been a glimpse of what Dinah could be if she loved a man that had awakened his own dormant romanticism. It had been a long time since a woman had meant more than a temporary source of diversion to him. He had not expected to find such integrity and purity of heart again. If he wanted the promise of what he'd once seen in Dinah's luminous eyes, and he most assuredly did, then he would simply have to possess his soul in patience.

15

As spring stretched toward summer, Dinah remained unaware of the change in Charles's feelings for her. She blithely greeted his presence at nearly all the events she attended and accepted as a matter of course that he would dance with her at least once and take her into supper if she was not already promised to someone else by the time he approached her. If she'd possessed the typical feminine obsession with personalities—which she clearly did not—she'd have assumed he was keeping a protective eye on her in his self-appointed role of temporary guardian. The truth was that she took his presence completely for granted; he was simply a member of her current family circle.

Charles was under no misconception that Dinah had begun to attribute his attentions to a personal and romantic interest in her, nor did he permit himself to harbor any illusions that she would welcome such an interest at the present time. Though there were occasions when he longed to give matters a push in the right direction, he kept to his resolve, exercising all the patience of a good fisherman who knows that it is sometimes necessary to play out quite a lot of line before reeling in his catch.

Considering her patent indifference to all her would-be suitors, there had been remarkably little diminution in Dinah's court over the weeks of the Season. Assorted swains hopeful of wedding her father's money still swarmed around her at social gatherings. She danced and chatted with them all—which with Dinah meant mostly listening—and took her place in Natasha's saloon on visiting days, but she was rarely inveigled into the park, either walking or driving, citing the demands of her painting as her reason for turning down most invitations.

This left the rather public forum of Almack's or private receptions and balls in which the most determined suitors could plead their case. She became fairly adept at gliding from one partner to another before any talk of a private nature could be attempted. Charles's timely appearance spared her embarrassing scenes on more than one occasion. Though Dinah never referred to this in his hearing, Charles was too awake on all suits to miss the implications, and it afforded him private amusement that Dinah was that rare creature, a woman who did not prattle about her conquests.

One evening, early in June, Charles came forward to claim his dance with Dinah at Almack's just as the music was starting up. He had failed to spot her tiny figure in the middle of a knot of gentlemen. The knot opened as he approached and disgorged Dinah on the arm of a well set up young man with curly dark hair and a pair of merry brown eyes.

"Ah, there you are, Dinah. This is my dance, I believe."

"A good try, old chap, but the name on Miss Elcott's dance card is Thurgood," said the curly-haired gentleman.

"Our dance together is the *third* waltz, Charles," Dinah added, making a move to go around Charles, who promptly planted himself in her path.

"Exactly, my dear Dinah. I am relieved that you have not forgotten."

"But this is only the *second* waltz."

"It grieves me to correct a lady, but I believe you'll find it is the third."

"But I promised this dance to Mr. Thurgood."

"And to me."

"Oh, dear, I am so very sorry, but what is to be done?" Dinah produced a creditably helpless look and awaited developments.

Mr. Thurgood laughed and bowed to Charles. "I'd invite you to step outside to discuss the matter, Talbot, but alas, it is after eleven. They would not let us back in, and someone else would walk off with the prize."

Charles's mocking smile came into play. "It's as well for me in that case, for I abhor fisticuffs—such a deplorably barbaric exhibition—not to mention having a strong aversion to bloodletting, especially when the blood is mine."

"Coming it a bit strong, Talbot," Mr. Thurgood said with a grin. "It's no secret that you've no objection to bloodletting if it's done with thirty-odd inches of steel."

"Ah, but fencing is not merely a sport but an art form requiring skill and intelligence, unlike boxing, which glorifies all man's most brutish instincts."

"And demands as much speed and more skill and strength than fencing," Mr. Thurgood rebutted.

Here Dinah intervened, saying judiciously, "I suppose we could all three sit down and I could listen to a reasoned debate on the virtues of various sports instead of waltzing to that infectious music." Limpid gray eyes gazed from one man to the other.

Charles laughed and threw up his hands. "That would indeed make us brutes, my poor child. Since I am the older and wiser, I shall sacrifice myself and withdraw in favor of the young element, with, however, the proviso that I may collect my lost dance at a time of my choosing. Your servant, Miss Elcott . . . Yours, Thurgood."

Dinah's eyes followed Charles's retreat until a tug on her hand brought her around to face Mr. Thurgood, who swept her onto the dance floor. "I didn't know Charles liked to fence," she said. "It has always been my impression that he detests all forms of sport."

"Don't be taken in by Talbot's avowed disdain for any activity that might dirty his hands," Mr. Thurgood replied carelessly. "It's true he doesn't much care for hunting or boxing, and he sees no point in driving races despite being a first-class whip, but don't let him gull you into believing he lacks competitiveness. He's positively deadly with a small sword, as quick as a cat on his feet, runs rings around larger men who should have the advantage of a longer reach, and he has wrists and nerves of steel."

"Charles?" Dinah stared into her partner's eyes, flabbergasted.

"Strange, ain't it? Most men are more likely to puff off their accomplishments on the field of sport than in the realm of the arts. It takes a contrary sort like Talbot to wish to leave the impression that he never takes his eyes off a painting or raises his head from a book all day." Mr. Thurgood shook his head, ex-

pressing mystification, and abandoned the subject of Charles
Talbot's peculiarities in favor of describing his newest acquisi-
tions to his partner—a matched pair of high-stepping grays
with whom he expected to beat a long-time rival in an important race.

Dinah listened with feigned interest, making appropriately
admiring noises, but her real attention was centered on trying
to reconcile the new picture of Charles Talbot that had
emerged in the last few moments with the man she had been
associating with since her first hour in London. The only thing
that had sounded familiar was Mr. Thurgood's use of the word
"contrary" to describe Charles's character. Charles did take a
perverse delight in confounding people. It was an uncomfortable trait and what she liked least about him, along with an indefinable air of superiority that was both irritating and
somewhat intimidating. He would have people believe he
thought nothing more important than the set of his coat and the
perfection of his cravat, but Dinah had noticed, without taking
too much account of the fact, that Charles never seemed to fid-
dle with his neckcloth or cuffs or check his appearance in a
mirror as she had frequently seen other men do. His intellect
and personality were so compelling one tended to overlook his
physical presence, which was not so striking, except for elec-
tric blue eyes that were twice as alive as anyone else's. He was
not much above the average in height and not overtly muscular. His features, while perfectly pleasant, held no special distinction, though she liked the way his finely grained skin
stretched tautly over high cheekbones. He would be difficult to
paint, she thought suddenly, because his looks did not tell
much of the story.

Of their own volition Dinah's eyes sought out Charles's person that evening as if she were seeing him through the eyes of
a stranger. It gave her a slightly shivery sensation to think of
him being as deadly with a sword as with his blistering tongue.
She also acknowledged a slight feeling of pique that she had
not known this vital fact about the person, next to Natasha,
with whom she had spent the most time during her London sojourn.

Charles didn't approach her again that evening which, upon
reflection later in her bedchamber, Dinah decided was a very

good thing. She might have challenged him to discover why he had never thought to inform her about this important side of him, an impertinent impulse that would have exposed her to his cutting wit. Having been on the receiving end of a few of his patented setdowns, she was happy to have averted this one, she decided as she crept sleepily between the sheets.

Dinah's perceptions of Charles Talbot changed after that evening at Almack's. He had always occupied a significant portion of her time; that was none of her doing, simply the result of his close association with Cam and Natasha. Now, almost imperceptibly at first, he began to occupy her mind also. Where before she had greeted his approach with slightly wary pleasure, she now began to take note of his arrival at various events, then to watch for it, and by insensible degrees to speculate on whether he would attend, and if not, where he might have chosen to be in preference, and with whom. When she caught herself engaging in this foolish activity, Dinah took herself severely to task. Charles Talbot's comings and goings were surely none of her affair. If she should feel a personal preference for his society the explanation was not far to seek: she had known Charles longer and was more at ease with him than with most gentlemen. Besides, his conversation was much more varied and interesting than anyone else's. There was nothing complex or hidden about that.

There was another Talbot whose company Dinah always greeted with unaffected pleasure, Sir Humphrey Talbot. In the months she had been in London she had met Charles's father on some half-dozen occasions, and never did he fail to single her out for a pleasant chat. Consequently she actually did look forward to his dinner party during the first week of June without the mild trepidation with which she generally greeted such events. She preferred the company of people who traveled in government circles to that of the purely social types; their conversation tended to be intrinsically more interesting to her, though long-winded bores could naturally be found in any group.

Natasha always acted as Sir Humphrey's hostess when he entertained. She and Cam were prodigiously fond of his uncle, an affection that was obviously returned in full measure. Dinah tried not to envy them the familial closeness that was missing in her own life. It was with a trace of wistfulness that she referred to this after dinner when the gentlemen had rejoined the ladies in the drawing room. After standing talking to a group of seated ladies for an extended period, Sir Humphrey excused himself and came over to Dinah, sitting himself down beside her on the sofa with a sigh of relief to be off his feet.

They had only been chatting for a moment when Charles appeared with a glass of cordial that he pressed into his sire's hand, saying, "I don't mean to interrupt your tête-à-tête, but I am persuaded you can use a stimulant at this point in the evening, sir."

Sir Humphrey accepted the glass gratefully. "Thank you, my boy. This is very welcome, as is your delicacy in not disturbing our tryst."

Dinah noted a similar twinkle in the eyes of father and son before hers trailed Charles as he joined a cluster of men nearby who were discussing the labor unrest in the Midlands. She turned back to the elder Talbot, saying impulsively, "It is wonderful to see the very real affection that exists between you and your son, sir."

"I feel fortunate beyond my desserts," Sir Humphrey replied. "There was a time when I feared I had lost all chance of a harmonious relationship with my son, so badly had I bungled matters in his boyhood and youth."

"Oh, I am persuaded you did not do anything so very wrong, sir," Dinah exclaimed in sympathy.

"My intentions were always of the purest, but I was woefully ignorant of my son's feelings and blind to the effect my clumsy policies were having on him." Seeing the sympathy in Dinah's eyes, Sir Humphrey went on slowly, "You have no doubt noticed a certain . . . coolness between Charles and his cousin and perhaps wondered at it?"

"Yes," Dinah answered simply.

"That is also the result of my well-meant meddling. Cam was only twelve when his father, my younger brother, died at sea. In a spirit of misguided zeal I tried in some measure to take his father's place in my nephew's life, which in practical terms meant throwing the two boys together much more frequently than in the past. They had never been particularly compatible once Charles outgrew the hero-worshiping affection he bore his cousin as a small lad. Cam was older, bigger, stronger—it was to be expected that he would take the lead in all the physical sort of activity in which young boys delight. I should have foreseen that Charles would bitterly resent a situation so damaging to his self-esteem."

"I believe it is the nature of boys to be very competitive," Dinah said earnestly, "no matter how their parents try to prevent such behavior."

Charles, casting an occasional glance at the twosome from his position a few feet away, saw the look of tenderness on his father's face as he patted Dinah's hand, and wondered what had occasioned it.

"That is no doubt true, my child," Sir Humphrey was saying, "but I blame myself for not seeing the hurt beneath the natural boyish resentment and envy of his cousin, especially after my wife died a couple of years after my brother's death. Charles adored his mother and grieved deeply. My wife was a lovely person and my own loss was acute, but I should not have let it blind me to what Charles was suffering. I did not notice at the time that he gradually . . . withdrew from everyone on an emotional level. By the time I realized what was happening, he had become an aloof adolescent who kept everyone at arm's length by means of an abrasive wit and an uncaring attitude that he paraded in public so successfully that it became almost a second skin. I had hoped that he would follow me into the Foreign Service, but he soon let it be known that a diplomatic career held no interest for him."

"What did interest him?" Dinah asked.

"That's not an easy question to answer briefly. When he came down from university he plunged into the pursuit of pleasure, as do many idle young men who have no need to earn their living and no leaning toward a specific intellectual or scientific area. They spend a great deal of money, tend to live beyond their means, and commit every folly that offers to alleviate the boredom of having no purpose in life. A period of rustification after he outran the constable soon taught Charles that everything in this life must be paid for one way or another. Besides, he had too much pride to come begging to me to get him out of dun territory, so this stage was fortunately not too prolonged.

"You might describe the period that followed as one of artistic dilettantism. His interest in the decorative arts was genuine enough, but it was clear to me that in acquiring a reputation as an arbiter of fashion and taste *à la* Brummell, it was the competitive aspect, the desire to be considered above others, that dominated his actions, despite his pose of caring for nothing. I am persuaded the years of being bested by his cousin in every undertaking played a major part in all this."

"Were . . . were you very disappointed in him, sir?"

Sir Humphrey smiled into the anxious little face peering up at him. "Some men would have been well pleased to see their sons attain this sort of distinction. For your ears only I shall confess that I am not among their number. I was convinced that Charles had too keen a brain and too much energy and will to be satisfied with this . . . trivial kind of life indefinitely, but I have learned from my many mistakes during his adolescence. There were times when I had to bite my tongue to keep back some criticism, but I have never attempted to interfere in my son's life. I have won back his affection slowly—"

"Oh, I am persuaded you never lost that, sir!" Dinah protested, distressed.

"Not entirely, no, but Charles's aloofness extended to me, and no wonder when I failed him so often during his childhood. As I've said, for Cam's sake I tried to treat both boys alike, and in so doing, convinced my son that he must be less to me than his cousin, who could best him in all boyish endeavors. It has taken a long time to regain his trust. Cam was away in the army for years, but his return three years ago and subsequent entrance into the diplomatic service probably delayed Charles's realization that he wanted to do something more with his own life. On his side the youthful competition never ended, in the sense that he still needed to demonstrate to his cousin that he scorned such attainments as Cam sought and achieved. He rededicated himself to frivolity for a period."

"Cutting off his nose to spite his face?" Dinah suggested diffidently.

"Exactly. Matters improved after Cam married Natasha. She is a dear girl and she and Charles are very good friends. She has kept him in the family circle, for which I am exceedingly grateful. He and I have gradually achieved a genuine closeness that gladdens my heart. And just lately he has pleased me very much by deciding to stand for Parliament." Sir Humphrey paused and beamed a smile at Dinah, who responded in kind.

"So that is what he meant when he hinted to me that he was nearly ready to do something productive with his life!" she cried.

"He said that to you? Then you are honored indeed, my dear, for no one else knows that we have been investigating the possibility, not even Cam and Natasha as yet."

Sir Humphrey's glance at her had become speculative, and Dinah promised hastily, as someone sought to capture his attention, "I shan't say a word to anyone."

After Sir Humphrey excused himself, Dinah sat quietly in her corner mulling over the things she had learned about Charles. It seemed he and she had both lost a loving mother at a young age and felt themselves bereft of all love and comfort thereafter. Charles had suffered the additional hardship of being forced into competition for his father's affection—or so he thought—with a cousin who was his superior in the physical prowess boys coveted most. An image of a young boy with intensely blue eyes trying to conceal his pain behind a determinedly uncaring exterior rose up before Dinah's eyes and a sense of fellow feeling overtook her. Charles's impregnable exterior had been achieved at great cost. His superb self-confidence was an armor that might possibly have hidden cracks in it.

"You are looking very pensive," said a soft voice above her ears.

Dinah turned her head and lifted startled eyes of liquid silver, her pupils contracting to mere pinpoints.

"What were you and my revered parent discussing so seriously?" Charles asked, admiring the porcelain clarity of her pale skin and the sweetly curved mouth.

Her mind had been so full of him that Dinah blurted, "You," no thoughts of coyness or concealment intervening.

A tiny flame kindled in Charles's eyes and the drawl was more pronounced than ever. "Should I be flattered or alarmed, I wonder?"

"Neither," she said with her usual candor. "Your father told me that you are going to stand for Parliament."

"And what was your reaction to such presumption?"

"I don't think it presumptuous at all. I can picture you making stirring, cleverly reasoned arguments in the House of Commons."

"But not impassioned arguments?"

Unable to sustain his piercing regard, Dinah lowered her eyes, but she answered bravely, "If passion is called for, I can envision it perfectly well."

Someone spoke Charles's name at that moment, so he made no reply, but the little flame burned even more brightly in his eyes before he turned away, and he gave her a smile of singular sweetness.

In the days that followed Sir Humphrey's revelations, Dinah's thoughts returned to the Talbot men more often than she cared to acknowledge. The polite world would no doubt think it ludicrous that she should pity three such popular and well-placed men, but pity them she did for the strains, past and present, that marred their family relations. There were no villains in the affair, only three victims of an unhappy combination of events that had cast ordinary human fallibilities into sharp relief. Sir Humphrey, in a praiseworthy desire to render comfort to his orphaned nephew, had unwittingly failed his own son, who desperately needed his approval in the face of constant assaults on his self-esteem made by his cousin's physical superiority. Cam, having lost his own father, would naturally reach out to his uncle, grateful for his affection and not overly concerned for the young cousin who resented his presence. It was Charles's plight that tugged most insistently at her heartstrings, however, because she comprehended in some measure the sense of abandonment he must have felt as he watched his cousin assume the role of a second—and perhaps favored—son to his father.

For the first time since their acrimonious introduction in Natasha's saloon, Dinah felt she had gained some understanding of Charles's complex character. She had judged him early on the basis of his acerbic tongue and found him wanting in humanity. When he had patiently carted her all over London to see the places of historical interest, she had attributed his attentions to a desire to please Natasha and taken shameless advantage of his time and knowledge of the city without feeling any real appreciation of the sacrifice entailed. It was Charles whose keen eye had devised the look that would make the most of her meager physical assets, and it was Charles who had arranged for her acceptance as a pupil by Mr. Crossman. He had brought her books to enlighten her ignorance and rescued her from awkward social situations uncounted times. Why had she never recognized that these were not the actions of a cold, unfeeling man?

Dinah's conscience pricked her savagely as she recalled a hundred small kindnesses on Charles's part that had gone unremarked or had been grudgingly acknowledged by her. She had been so self-absorbed, first with her artistic endeavors and then with that foolish infatuation with Godfrey Bellingham, that she had never once considered Charles's feelings or even wondered what they might be. It was true that his mocking attitude while performing small services tended to preclude anything warmer than a cursory expression of gratitude. He deliberately gave the impression he did not wish to be thanked for what was not done out of real affection or consideration for the recipient. The more she thought about the course of their acquaintance, however, the more Dinah questioned whether this might be a defensive posture against being wounded by a lack of appreciation on the part of those persons for whom he bore an affection. This line of reasoning led inevitably to the more basic question of whether *she* was included among this select group.

Dinah was oddly reluctant to confront this possibility, at first dismissing it out of hand. She was far too ordinary to appeal to Charles Talbot on a personal level, unless perhaps he thought of her as a child ill-equipped to deal with the world and therefore in need of guidance and protection. She recoiled from this explanation, instinctively disliking such a version of herself in Charles's eyes, though the reason for her dissatisfaction did not become clear to her until the evening she accompanied Cam and Natasha to a private ball in Bedford Square.

Dinah and Charles had not met in the two days since his father's dinner party. When he sought her out early in the evening she experienced an unaccountable shyness that rendered her tongue-tied at first, to her chagrin. Fortunately, Charles was not in a teasing humor; in fact, he seemed unusually disinclined for conversation. He held her rather more closely than was quite proper during their waltz, a solecism she would have protested a fortnight ago, and smiled at her with an intimacy that quickened her breathing and clouded her intellect. She was adrift on a sea of contentment for an idyllic dance and her entire being screamed a loud internal protest as the music wound down to a stop. Charles too was reluctant to end the dance, if she did not mistake the length of time that elapsed before he removed his hand from her waist. His words as he glanced around the ballroom were prosaic, however.

"I have the next dance with Natasha. She and Cam are over there to our left. Shall we walk that way?"

Dinah placed her fingers on his extended arm and moved in the direction he indicated. "Who is that lovely-looking woman they are talking to, Charles? I don't believe I have seen her before. It's unthinkable that one would fail to recall such beauty."

"That is Lady Frobisher, my cousin's lost love."

"*What?*" Dinah stopped short, her astonished gaze swinging to her escort's face. "Are you bamming me?" she demanded inelegantly, noting the dancing devils in his eyes.

"Not at all. Cam became betrothed to the fair Priscilla before he was sent to the Peninsula War years ago. He had the great good luck to be jilted by the lady, who married a title almost before his troop ship reached Portugal. Then to prove he is indeed fortune's favorite, out of all the soldiers serving in that campaign, he became an intimate of Natasha's brother. When Phillips found he was being sent on to America after the end of fighting in 1814, he commandeered his returning comrade's services as watchdog for his sister, who was making her come-out that spring. Cam presented himself on Natasha's cousin's doorstep in a dutiful spirit and subsequently secured the prize, proving once again that it is far better to be lucky than deserving in this life."

Charles flashed his mocking smile at a sober-faced Dinah and took her elbow to steer her toward the trio under discussion. "So you have escaped the honor of meeting the elegant Lady Frobisher up to now? It will be my pleasurable duty to repair that omission, I see."

Charles's narration had been lightly, even humorously

given, but a slight shudder ran through Dinah as the delicious sense of well-being engendered by their waltz drained away, leaving her chilled.

Greetings were exchanged and introductions made in due course. Natasha and Charles, with an occasional assist from a languid Lady Frobisher, shared the brunt of the conversation embarked on by the quintet in the few moments before the music struck up again. Cam wore the politely attentive expression of someone concealing boredom, and Dinah had been struck speechless by the cool perfection of the woman Charles had referred to in disparaging accents as "the fair Priscilla."

A tall, willowy blonde with a graceful figure and exquisitely modeled features, Lady Frobisher possessed a classic beauty that could not be denied by anyone with two eyes and a modicum of respect for the truth. After a few moments of fascinated, almost clinical observation, Dinah concluded that the woman would make an easy but rather uninteresting subject to paint. There was nothing beyond the lovely coloring to challenge the artist. Even when she smiled or spoke, Lady Frobisher exhibited no animation or expressiveness. After listening to her measured utterances for a time, Dinah could see that she was not stupid like the handsome redheaded Miss Dunstan. Rather, Lady Frobisher seemed to lack that inner spark of personality or humor that could lend character to lifeless physical perfection.

Presently the music commenced and Charles led Natasha onto the floor. Two men had edged Cam aside and engaged him in a serous discussion, leaving Dinah at a standstill beside the inanimate beauty. Not wishing to be thought unsocial, she searched her mind for some innocuous topic. Her eyes on Charles and Natasha whirling by in a fast waltz turn, she gave voice to spontaneous admiration. "Natasha and Charles are the most accomplished dancers on the floor, and so beautifully matched and stylish in appearance."

"Yes," Lady Frobisher agreed. "He makes the most of the crumbs that fall from his cousin's table."

This cryptic remark cast Dinah into confusion. "I beg your pardon, ma'am?" she said, glancing into calm blue eyes.

"It was common knowledge that Natasha Phillips favored Charles Talbot above her other suitors and that she married

Cam after some sort of scandal that was hushed up. Charles has been her chief cicisbeo since they returned from Brussels two years ago. At least in public, Cam raises no objections to the arrangement. It's all very civilized," Lady Frobisher finished with a delicate shrug of shapely shoulders.

Dinah, staring into that flawless face and listening to appalling charges made in clear tones of perfect indifference, had to fight a wave of nausea that rose in her throat, threatening to suffocate her, before she could murmur an inarticulate excuse and flee to the ladies' retiring room.

16

A period of desperate reflection served to restore enough of the tenor of Dinah's mind that she was able to get through the rest of the evening without betraying the distress Lady Frobisher's callous gossip had caused her. There had been a series of shocks, starting with Charles's announcement that Cam had once been betrothed to the blond beauty. She had scarcely digested this information when Lady Frobisher had stated as established fact things that if true wholly destroyed the foundation upon which Dinah had based her understanding of the people closest to her these past months. The icily beautiful woman, who appeared devoid of human emotion, had alleged that Natasha would have preferred Charles to Cam except for some unknown scandal that compelled her to marry Cam. If one accepted that premise, then the friendship between Charles and Natasha could be construed as a discreet liaison being conducted with the knowledge and tacit consent of an uncaring husband.

The sordidness of the suggestion had caught Dinah by the throat and she had been too sickened to attempt a rebuttal of Lady Frobisher's claims at the time. A few private moments spent recalling the very real devotion Cam and Natasha displayed for each other had served to convince her that whatever conditions had prevailed at the beginning of their marriage— and she remembered Natasha's hints that all had not been propitious—theirs was now a true love match. Dwelling under their roof, she was in a unique position to declare at least one of the blond woman's allegations false. The sick, hollow sensation that she strove to conceal had been caused by the much more creditable implication that Charles had been in love with Natasha for years, coming as it did on the heels of Dinah's si-

multaneous realization that she herself was in love with
Charles.

There was no unrestrained weeping on Natasha's shoulder
in the carriage that night or in the days that followed. Nor did
Dinah seek the relief of indulging in a hearty bout of tears in
private, for it would have been totally unavailing in the present
situation. This was not the acute bitter wound of betrayal
which is in part healed by the therapeutic process of thinking
ill of the betrayer. How could Dinah think ill of Charles for
loving Natasha, who was so eminently lovable?

Despite Lady Frobisher's unkind insinuations, there was
nothing in the least dishonorable about Charles's friendship
with Natasha. He was scrupulous in avoiding any public attentions to her that could legitimately make her the object of gossip. It was true that Dinah had upon occasion noted the perfect
rapport between the two with a twinge of wistfulness that bor-
dered on envy, but Charles was more to be pitied than blamed
if he could not return Natasha's pure friendship with equally
platonic feelings.

By the same token, she could not fault him for not loving
herself. One didn't give one's heart to order; hearts were noto-
riously capricious in their choice of objects upon which to
pour out their warmth. She and Charles had become quite
good friends. If of late she had sometimes fancied she detected
something more intimate than friendship in his eyes, then the
fault lay with herself. Certainly she had an unfortunate history
of seeking affection from people who were unable to gratify
her wishes.

Understanding the way matters stood did nothing to lift the
pall of depression that had enveloped Dinah from the moment
of accepting that her feelings of respect and friendship for
Charles had deepened into love. Though she treasured their
friendship, she knew from her own mother's experience that
marriage does not prosper where all the affection is on one
side. She could envision the insistent though unspoken demands for reciprocity inherent in that unfortunate situation and
the eventual guilty resentment of the person unable to return in
full measure the feelings being lavished upon him or her. The
picture struck chill in the marrow of her bones and she vowed
to remain unwed forever rather than voluntarily subject herself

to such a constant source of humiliation. She would not become the beggar at the gate.

It seemed she had developed some stiff-necked pride after all, she acknowledged with mordant humor as she set about concealing her unhappiness from Natasha while she worked on the final stages of the portrait. Whether this pride would survive and sustain her willpower under the persuasiveness of Charles's frequent assumption that he knew what was best for her was something she did not wish to put to the test, however. Now that he was contemplating a career in government, he might also decide it was time to settle down and take a wife. Apart from his odd protective streak, he liked her well enough and they enjoyed a similarity of interests that made conversation flourish between them. Since he could not have the woman he really loved, he might well decide she would do better than some emptyheaded beauty who expected constant tribute as her due. If she did not wish to be put in the invidious position of having to refuse what she desired most, it was time to bring her London stay to an end.

When Dinah broached the subject of returning to Devon, she could not help but be warmed by Natasha's distress at the idea of parting from her friend so soon.

"Oh, but Dinah," Natasha protested, "the Season is not over yet. Have you forgotten that there is to be the opening of the new Waterloo Bridge in less than a fortnight? This is your chance to see the Duke himself, who is to participate in the dedication ceremonies with the Regent. Besides, I received a letter from Peter this morning written from France. He and Serena will be passing through London early next week. You cannot possibly leave without meeting them."

The young women were in the studio working on the portrait when Dinah made the tentative announcement of her intentions. In her consternation Natasha had moved out of her pose, giving the other girl a little time in which to bolster her argument as she directed the repositioning of her subject's hands.

"The portrait will be finished before then, Natasha. That would seem to be an excellent time to take my leave so that you and Cam may enjoy a real family visit with Lord and Lady Phillips without having extraneous persons around."

"You are not an 'extraneous person,' Dinah Elcott; you are my dear friend," Natasha said reproachfully, "and I wish you to know and like my brother and his wife, who is a delightful person also. Unfortunately, they can only remain in town for a day or two as they are on their way to Serena's family home for her sister's wedding. Come, promise you won't even think of leaving until after their visit," she said coaxingly.

Against her better judgment Dinah allowed herself to be persuaded to give her friend this promise, part of her perversely pleased that she would not have to say a final goodbye to Charles for at least another sennight.

The sensible side of her sought to prepare for this unhappy inevitability by curtailing the amount of time she spent in Charles's company after her talk with Natasha. This was an excellent plan in the abstract, but the smooth execution of it demanded rather more cleverness at manipulating others than one of Dinah's forthright nature possessed. She knew she had been clumsy when Charles turned a look of bafflement on her one night at a private ball after she had just refused him a waltz on the transparent excuse of fatigue.

"If I have offended you in some way, Dinah, I wish you will tell me so that I may try to make amends," he said with a simple sincerity that was almost her undoing.

"Of course you haven't offended me, Charles. Why should you think such a thing?" she returned with an attempt at insouciance, though her smile was a wobbly effort.

"When a lady's attention is firmly fixed elsewhere whenever a gentleman approaches and she declines his invitations more often than not, it is clearly incumbent upon him to examine his conscience or change his dentifrice," Charles replied with a ghost of his mocking smile.

"Now you are being quite nonsensical," Dinah said primly, meeting his searching glance only briefly before hers skittered away.

"Am I? I can see I have embarrassed you and shall take myself off before I add to my crimes." He swept her a graceful bow and retired, leaving Dinah staring after him unhappily until Cam, who had been an unnoticed spectator of the scene, stepped up to her and launched into an amusing monologue until she had recovered her composure. He asked her no questions and kept his own counsel, refraining from mentioning the incident even to his wife.

Not surprisingly, the atmosphere between Charles and Dinah deteriorated to a state of strained civility after this awkward encounter. To Dinah each meeting was like dying a little as the easy friendship they had forged receded even further. Had it not been for the creative excitement of finishing Natasha's portrait, Dinah would have been sorely tempted to sneak away while she still had some memories left to treasure in her exile in Devon.

Lord and Lady Phillips arrived in Portman Square on the day Dinah completed the painting. Natasha, who had declared herself heartily sick of her white gown and threatened to burn it the instant the portrait was done, was yawning at her desk when the sounds of bustling about downstairs reached them through the half-open door to the studio. She was out of the chair in a flash and heading for the door, her face alight with joyful anticipation.

"They're here, Dinah—Peter and Serena. Let's hurry down to greet them," she said over her shoulder.

"I'll be down presently, Natasha. I'm covered in paint as usual. You go now," Dinah said, making shooing motions with her brush as Natasha hesitated, then flung a smile at her friend as she tore out of the room.

It was actually closer to twenty minutes before Dinah approached the saloon on lagging feet. She still found it something of an ordeal to go among strangers, but in this case she had purposely dawdled over changing into a clean dress to allow Natasha and her brother to enjoy a private reunion. She heard Natasha's excited tones mingling with a feminine voice speaking in a slower cadence, then both broke off at the sound of masculine laughter just as Dinah crossed over the threshold and paused, blinking in surprise.

The man who got to his feet at her quiet entrance was a fair-skinned giant who bore no resemblance to his dainty sister in coloring or features. His light brown locks were faultlessly arranged and his eyes were the calm blue of a lake on a summer's day. His slow movements and air of indolent grace must be deceptive when it came to his mental processes, however, for Natasha had told Dinah that after one look at the woman who became his wife, Peter had made up his mind to marry her. Dinah had no difficulty in believing this when her eyes shifted to Lady Phillips. The tall statuesque redhead with a look of faint amusement on her lovely face was her husband's equal in every respect. Both were dressed in the newest French fashions.

They were an impressive pair indeed and fully warranted the pride in Natasha's voice as she cried, "There you are at last, Dinah. This is Peter."

"I am delighted to meet you, Miss Elcott," Lord Phillips said with a twinkle in his eyes as he bowed over Dinah's hand. "I hope you will make allowances for my sister's partiality and accept the impossibility of ever producing enough encomiums to satisfy her."

"Quiet, you wretch," said his loving sister.

The smile that flashed across Lord Phillips's face suddenly was so like Natasha's that Dinah smiled in recognition, her feeling of strangeness vanishing as she murmured a greeting.

"May I present my wife, Serena," Lord Phillips went on, slipping an arm about the waist of the smiling woman who had come up to them by now.

Dinah's eyes widened at the betraying bulge that had not been apparent at first glance. "How do you do, Lady Phillips. Natasha did not tell me you are increasing. May I offer my warmest felicitations."

"Thank you, Dinah, and please call me Serena. Natasha didn't know. We wished to surprise her, but she has been scolding like a fishwife for the past ten minutes." Lady Phillips shot a mischievous look at her sister-in-law.

"Mostly because you have been traipsing all over the world in your delicate condition," Natasha retorted.

"This from the woman who traveled across Europe in the winter in the same condition, unbeknownst to her husband!" Lord Phillips expostulated. "Have done, my dear. Serena is going along magnificently as you can plainly see, and we are safely back on English soil almost three months before the baby is due."

Dinah noted the tenderness in the smile he gave his wife as he assisted her into a chair and decided she liked Natasha's brother very much indeed.

"Natasha tells us you have been painting her portrait," Lady Phillips said with an interested look at Dinah. "I hope we may see it before we leave London?"

"Even I haven't seen it yet," Natasha explained. "Dinah felt that since it was Cam's idea that she paint me, the portrait belongs to him and he should see it first."

"It is completed except for a very little work on the draperies," Dinah said when Lady Phillips looked disappointed. "If Cam approves, you may certainly see it. I . . . I hope you are not expecting to compare it with really professional work," she added anxiously. "I have not been painting in oils for very long. This is the first real portrait I have attempted."

Everyone hastened to reassure her on that point, but Dinah's nerves were definitely on the stretch when they all entered the saloon after dinner that evening to see the covered canvas reposing on an easel. She gnawed on her lips compulsively as she accepted Cam's invitation to unveil the work and stepped back, clutching her hands together in front of her to control a tendency to shake.

The young woman staring out of the canvas was obviously on the verge of smiling. Though her lips were only slightly parted, the beautiful dark eyes already contained the beginnings of a smile. Her demeanor was eager, open, and incredibly alive. Though seated, she appeared on the point of rising to greet the viewer with a warm welcome.

The portrait's reception was all any artist could wish for.

Lady Phillips drew in her breath sharply. "My word, I almost expect her to walk away from the canvas!"

"Only someone who knows and loves Natasha could capture her essential nature so well," Lord Phillips agreed, walking closer to examine the canvas.

Dinah's eyes were riveted on Cam, who stood motionless staring at the painted reproduction of his wife's vivid face for what seemed like an eternity to the anxious artist. At last he took a deep breath and sought her glance, his own softened to near-reverence. "You have exceeded my wildest hopes, Dinah." He took her chin in his fingers and kissed her. "Thank you, my dear."

Natasha glanced from one smiling face to another, her expression puzzled, before saying hesitantly, "It is a perfectly lovely painting, Dinah, but surely you have flattered me beyond my desserts."

Dinah laughed in sheer relief. "We don't really see ourselves as others do, Natasha. The face that stares back from the mirror is generally devoid of expression, and it is expression that renders each person unique."

Cam walked over to a tray sitting on the tea table and proceeded to pour out five glasses of champagne. As he handed them around, he said with a small smile, "We need my cousin Charles for a learned critique of the brushwork and finer points of the painting, but I would like to propose a toast to the artist, Dinah Elcott, a talented and charming young lady whom Natasha and I are pleased and proud to call our friend."

Dinah's cheeks pinkened and her eyes glowed with pleasure as three voices echoed, "To Dinah."

When Charles came to pay his respects to Lord and Lady Phillips the next morning, he showed no disposition to deliver any educated criticism of the portrait. He walked into a room bustling with humanity, thanks in large part to the antics of young Justin, who was entertaining his newly arrived relatives with his bag of tricks under the indulgent eyes of both parents. On spotting the man in the doorway, the toddler broke off the song he was singing and dashed forward to grab his cousin's hand.

"Come see, Chars! Dinah paint Mama's picture!"

Charles, who had opened his mouth to return the greetings of the adults, glanced down at the cherub and followed his pointing finger. He let himself be towed over to the easel, where he stood gazing at the painting with the same complete stillness Cam had exhibited the previous evening. The room was silent except for Justin's excited prattle, which did not penetrate Charles's total concentration on the portrait.

At last he turned to a tensely expectant Dinah. "It is magnificent, Dinah. I am at your feet in admiration," he said simply, the timbre of his voice slightly roughened.

Serena Phillips, from her position in the corner of the long sofa nearest to the easel, eyed him with quickened interest. Her elegant brows arched slightly as she glanced past Natasha, who was scooping up her vociferous child, and met the alert gaze of Cameron Talbot, who had stationed himself beyond the easel where he had a clear view of his cousin's face. A wordless question was posed and answered in the affirmative, judging by Serena's satisfied expression as she settled back into the cushions again.

An hour later when the men left for Tattersall's where Peter wished to look over some horseflesh, Serena's expression was more speculative than satisfied. The conversation had been lively and wide-ranging, with everyone interested in the travelers' impressions of Egypt, Greece, and Italy, but she had been surprised to find Charles Talbot much less inclined to take an active part than in the past. As for the young artist, she was even more reticent than on the previous evening. She and Charles seemed to have nothing at all to say to each other, causing Lady Phillips to question her earlier hunch that romance was in the air.

Dinah excused herself to finish some task in her studio a few minutes later, and Serena pounced on Natasha the second the door clicked shut behind her.

"What is going on between Charles and Dinah? Have they quarreled?"

"Not lately that I have heard. Why do you ask?"

Serena looked disappointed. "There was something in Charles's voice when he praised the portrait that made me wonder if there was a romantic attachment developing between them, but they barely spoke to each other afterward."

"They have become good friends this spring, but Dinah is recovering from an earlier disappointment in that area. My impression is that she is disinclined to venture in that direction at present. As for Charles, who knows how Charles really feels about anything? He guards his inner self so determinedly."

"Well, it was only a hunch, except that I thought Cam agreed with me. He was observing Charles so closely earlier."

"I would love to think it might be true, but Dinah is talking of going home in the very near future," Natasha said doubtfully.

"Obviously all is not well between them; they don't act like comfortable friends. I think they would make a good pair. Dinah's talent is something Charles can really respect, and yet socially and personally she is unsure of herself and would probably welcome his protection and guidance. At lease she would be less inclined than many women to resent his bossiness. It's unfortunate that Peter and I must be off tomorrow or I might have tried to give matters a push in the right direction, but I promised Verity that I would stand between her and my mother when it comes to wedding plans."

Natasha's gurgle of laughter ended in a fit of coughing. "I never thought I'd see the day you turned into a matchmaker, Serena," she gasped when she could speak again. "The vice of all happily married women."

Serena remained unruffled by her friend's teasing. Her eyes glowed as she said softly, "I am happy, Natasha, happier than I ever envisioned. Peter is so . . . wonderful," she concluded after searching for the telling adjective.

"I could have told you that last spring had you been willing to listen," Natasha retorted. "Isn't it odd that Peter should have been responsible for my meeting Cam and it was I who introduced him to you, though I cannot take equal credit, of course, because he would have found some way to meet you properly after that incident in the hills when you two saved the boy." She coughed again and put a hand to her throat.

"You know, we don't have to go to the theater tonight if you are coming down with a cold, Natasha," Serena said, looking concerned.

"It is your only night in town. I'll be fine. This is just a tickle in my throat. Don't mention it to Cam; he tends to be overly protective about Justin and me and would dose us with half the pharmacy at the first sniffle if not checked by wiser heads."

"Such as yours?" Serena's mischievous smile appeared. "I shall deny on the rack that I ever said it, but I find it not entirely disagreeable to be cosseted a bit these days, as long as it is Peter who is doing the cosseting."

The women exchanged a smile of perfect understanding as they set off for the nursery to play with Justin.

The Talbot box was easily the most popular in the theater that night as people flocked to greet the returning travelers. In the midst of so much genteel jollity Dinah's silence went unnoticed except by Charles, and Cam was the only person who suspected that Natasha was not feeling quite the thing. She was looking flushed and her voice was a trifle hoarsened, though she declared she felt fine when he suggested they might leave before the farce came on. It was raining when they came outside and they had to wait longer than usual for the line of carriages to collect those ahead of them. Natasha was shivering so violently by the time they all piled into the carriage that Cam took off his coat and wrapped it around her, keeping her within the circle of his arm until the shivering subsided.

"It is bed for you, my love, the moment we get home," he said with tender concern. "I hope you are not sickening for something."

"It is just a head cold, Cam. I'll be better in the morning."

Natasha's optimistic prediction was not fulfilled, however. She dragged herself out of bed against Cam's advice to wish her brother and sister-in-law Godspeed, but she was so heavy-eyed and hoarse that the household united in sending her straight back to her bed after the briefest of farewells. Cam sent the footman to Newbury's in St. Paul's to purchase some essence of colt's foot to ease her cough, but it did not answer. By midafternoon it was clear to Dinah that Natasha was suffering from more than a simple cold. She was feverish and racked by painful fits of coughing. Cam, coming home early from the Foreign Office, sent immediately for the doctor.

Dinah was waiting with Cam in his study when the doctor pronounced the dreaded diagnosis of pneumonia. She saw the fear that stared out of his eyes for a moment before his countenance settled into hard controlled lines as he listened intently to the doctor's plan of treatment and his confident prognostication that careful nursing combined with Mrs. Talbot's strong constitution would see her safely through the illness.

"You must not expect rapid improvement, Mr. Talbot," the physician warned the anxious husband as he prepared to depart. "Pneumonia is a serious illness that must run its course."

The doctor's words became almost a silent prayer during the next three days as Natasha's condition seemed only to worsen. There were brief intervals when she was rational but longer

spells of delirium when she recognized no one and seemed to
be wrestling unseen demons. The nurse who arrived to take
charge of the sickroom upon the doctor's recommendation remained there for less than a day. Dinah took it upon herself to
send her packing when she discovered the woman snoring in a
chair by the fireplace while her patient writhed on her bed begging for a drink of water. She persuaded Cam that she, Mallory, and Mrs. Evans could handle the nursing chores among
them, since it was mainly a case of constant sponging to try to
bring the fever down, and keeping Natasha as comfortable as
possible during the bouts of delirium when she would attempt
to throw off the covers and rise from her bed to go to her crying child. During the worst times Cam's was the only voice
that seemed to have a quieting effect on her. He stayed away
from his office entirely, keeping within call in case his presence should be required, or taking Justin into the gardens for
fresh air.

Natasha was held in great affection by all the servants, who
pitched in willingly to support the sickroom efforts. Even the
martinet who ruled the kitchen bestirred herself to concoct
tasty broths and cool drinks that would slide down a raw
throat. Coaxing Natasha to take nourishment was no easy task,
and here again Cam was most successful at getting her to
swallow anything.

Despite their efforts they could not deceive themselves that
Natasha's condition was improving. The doctor, calling on his
patient daily, expressed his satisfaction that she was holding
her own but warned that the crisis was yet to come.

Needless to say, all visitors had been turned away by Dawson during this period, but he was kept busy answering the
door to inform anxious callers of Natasha's condition, or to accept gifts of flowers and fruits sent by concerned friends.

On the fourth day of Natasha's illness, Dawson opened the
door to a smiling Charles Talbot.

"Good afternoon, Dawson. Are the ladies in?" On noting
Dawson's hesitation, Charles asked, "Is something wrong?"

"Can it be that you have not heard of Mrs. Talbot's illness,
sir?"

"I've been down at Seven Oaks for a couple of days. What
illness?" Charles demanded. Some of the healthy color drained

from his skin as Dawson gave him the bare facts. "Where is my cousin?"

"In his study, but he left strict orders not to admit anyone, sir."

Charles thrust his gloves and hat into the butler's reluctant hands. "I'll tell him you did your best to keep me out," he promised over his shoulder as he headed for the study, where he knocked briefly before going in.

"Dawson told me about Natasha—" Charles broke off as the man staring out the window turned around. The naked suffering on his cousin's face stopped his breath for a second; then he blurted, "Good Lord, she's not—?"

"No!" Cam passed a hand over his face and took a step away from the window. "The doctor insists that she is doing as well as can be expected, but she seems to be getting weaker, and the fever persists despite all our efforts. She is rarely rational for more than a few moments—"

"Natasha is strong, Cam. Years of exercises and dancing have made her very fit."

"That is what I keep telling myself, but when I speak to her and she doesn't know me I can't help feeling that she is slipping away from me."

"Not Natasha. She knows how to hold on to what she loves."

A light came into Cam's somber eyes for a moment. "She does, doesn't she? Thank you, Charles. I have been allowing myself to grow morbid." He raked his fingers through his already disordered hair and summoned up a half-smile. "Will you take a glass of Madeira?"

"Thank you, yes; then I'll take myself out from under your feet, but I am yours to command if you need any errands run, or anything else I can do."

"Don't rush off, Charles. I've brought work home with me, but I can't seem to concentrate on anything."

"It's not surprising. Natasha's danger is too all-consuming to spare the mental energy for mundane work." Charles accepted the glass his cousin offered and raised it. "To Natasha's quick recovery."

"Amen." Cam swallowed a gulp of the wine and waved Charles to a chair.

Conversation was sporadic between the cousins over the next couple of hours, interspersed with quiet periods when each gave reign to his own private thoughts until one or the other made an observation that produced some additional comments or discussion. At one point Cam mentioned that his uncle had told him of Charles's plan to stand for Parliament. He was strongly in favor of the idea and they discussed strategies until Charles noticed that his cousin's eyes kept straying to the closed door.

"The waiting is hellish, isn't it?"

Cam nodded. "Even worse is the feeling of utter helplessness. I would fight the entire world to keep Natasha safe, but there is not one single thing I can do to change the present situation." He groaned harshly and got up to refill their glasses, restlessness apparent in his barely controlled movements.

"It must be terrible to love someone so much," Charles mused.

Cam shrugged. "It's the other side of the coin. There's no escaping the vulnerability that goes with loving." He held out the glass to his cousin.

"I'm not sure I am capable of traveling that particular road—or willing to, for that matter," Charles said with an attempt at lightness that did not fool his cousin.

"It is strange, but just lately I have wondered if you might not be farther down that road already than you quite realize. And willingness has nothing to do with the matter, I fear."

Charles squirmed under Cam's penetrating green gaze and he glanced away, saying with a touch of bitterness, "Since that is a two-way street, the whole question is irrelevant at present."

"Is it? Don't you think it is time you stopped playing the coward, Charles? Nothing ventured, nothing gained."

Charles did not pretend to misunderstand the sense of his cousin's words, but he argued, "I could queer everything by acting too hastily. She is still getting over her infatuation with Bellingham. She'd probably think I am after her fortune like all the others if I approached her now. Besides, she has been giving me the cold shoulder lately."

"Are you aware that Dinah was talking about returning to Devon just before Natasha took ill?" Cam asked, brushing away his cousin's craven arguments and cutting to the heart of the matter.

"No!" Shock held Charles motionless for a second, and before he could question his cousin further the study door was flung open and Dinah came hurrying into the room.

"Cam, the fever has broken! She is quite lucid and she is asking for you."

"Thank God! And thank you too, Dinah, for all the devoted care you have given Natasha these past terrible days." Cam swooped and kissed her cheek on his way out of the room, pausing at the door to command his cousin, "Give Dinah a glass of Madeira, Charles. She needs it. I'll give Natasha your love."

Like his cousin, Charles had jumped to his feet when Dinah burst into the room, and he'd had sufficient time to assess her appearance, which was haggard to say the least. She hadn't stopped to remove the stained apron that covered her crumpled housedress, her hair was ruffled, and her arms hung limply at her sides while two tears of relief slid down her pale cheeks unchecked. In Charles's eyes she looked beautiful.

"My poor darling, Cam is quite right; you stand greatly in need of a restorative," he said gently, putting his own glass into her hand and guiding it to her lips. "Drink it," he commanded, and she took an obedient sip. "All of it," he urged, at which point her lips twisted into a travesty of a smile.

"B . . . bossy Charles," she said gamely, then disgraced herself by dissolving into tears.

Down through the ages men have been paralyzed by the spectacle of a weeping woman, but Charles was equal to the situation. He deposited the wineglass on a nearby table and scooped Dinah into his arms. Ignoring her muffled protests, he settled into a capacious wing chair with the crying girl comfortably cradled in his lap, her head nestled against his chest while he waited for the storm to subside. He was ready with his handkerchief at the precise moment when it was required and did not attempt to interrupt Dinah's incoherent apologies as she mopped up her face. It was only when the embarrassed young woman tried to extricate herself from her compromising position that Charles again exercised a masculine initiative. His arms tightened about her and one hand pressed her head back against his shoulder. "Don't move," he said. "This is nice, if slightly damp."

"I have ruined your coat," Dinah said, but she ceased her struggles.

"A little salt never hurt anything."

Dinah chuckled, then sighed and reluctantly raised her head a few inches to look at him with pink-rimmed, candid eyes. "Thank you, Charles, for coming to my rescue once again, but I promise I am perfectly recovered. You can let me go now."

"But I don't wish to let you go." The reasonable tone of this objection served to alarm rather than reassure Dinah, and she wriggled unsuccessfully against his tightening embrace.

"Charles, someone could come into this room at any moment."

"Let 'em come."

"But what would they *think*?"

"If they come in in the next sixty seconds, they'll think— quite rightly—that I am kissing my intended bride."

"But I can't marry you, Charles. You love Natasha."

"Yes, certainly, but I am *in love* with you, you little slow top." He administered a gentle shake for emphasis.

"Oh, Charles, are you really?"

Correctly interpreting the hopeful light in his beloved's lustrous eyes, Charles abandoned argument in favor of demonstration. His mouth fastened onto her soft lips in a kiss that began as a gentle reassurance, then escalated by rapid stages into a passionate demand that Dinah met unflinchingly. Both were trembling when they finally drew back to stare at each other in mutual wonder.

Dinah blinked her long lashes and drew in a shaky breath. "May I take that as an affirmative reply?" she asked in the interests of establishing a perfect understanding between them.

The blue flame was back in Charles's eyes. "If you didn't quite hear me the first time, I'll be happy to repeat my answer," he said, bending down to do just that.